**What readers say about other books by**
**Glyn Smith-Wild**

### 'Sanctuary'
### A story of Mystery and Romance

*"I can safely say that from the first to the very last page, I had no idea where the story was going, which is great testimony to the writer and the writing."*

*"This book had everything. Romance, suspense, travel, buying a house in a unique place and fixing it up, interesting people, action, conflict, even a little sex. You name it, it was there."*

### 'Repercussions'
### A story of Drama, Deception and Duplicity.

*"The story is not just of intrigue. There is a sweet story of friendships, romance and the fine living in France that is so pleasantly described."*

*"Another hit in my book!"*

# The Reckoning

**Glyn Smith-Wild**

**OBS**
*Supporting New Writers*

Published in the United Kingdom 2014

OBS, 25 Tweed Close, Honiton, Devon EX14 2YU

Copyright © Glyn Smith-Wild

*All characters and events in this publication, other than those clearly in the public domain, are fictitious and any resemblance to real persons, living or dead, is purely coincidental.*

A catalogue record for this book is available from the British Library.

ISBN-13: 978 0957389335

## Chapter 1

With a mug of coffee in his hand, his laptop under his arm and a headful of dilemmas Ben made his way across the driveway. Turning left, he passed the two old barns and picked his way down the gravelled pathway which ran through the vegetable garden, to his favourite spot. He had crept out of the cottage, carefully closing the front door behind him. This was where he came to work, meditate, or just lose himself in his thoughts.

From the patio area down by the stream he could look down over the undulating valley below, dotted with small areas of woodland but mainly of open pastures. In the distance he could see cattle grazing and closer, a tractor was plodding its way back and forth across the width of the fields. Whatever time of day he came here, the position of the sun projected a different picture. From pastel pinks of early morning to the rich colours of spectacular evening sunsets, the ever-moving shadows changed the panorama minute by minute.

Opening his laptop, he emailed Maurice, the accountant at SRX Solutions, his old employers in Bracknell. He knew he had had dealings with Donald in the past.

*Maurice. I need to pick your brains. I'm still having problems with Donald O'Hanlon. I'm convinced he was*

1

*responsible for an attack on Mary that very nearly killed her. Now he's disappeared and I desperately need to find him before he tries again. It's just a long shot, but do you still have mobile telephone numbers, email address, website details? I can't imagine he would still be using any of them, but you never know. I've no idea where he is, but I think he maybe in the UK. Is there anybody you know who might be interested in working with me to find him? Regards, Ben.*

A click on the 'Send' button saw the message depart into cyberspace.

*****

Here at his cottage, *La Sanctuaire,* in the Loire Valley, the morning air would normally be fresh and crisp as if the heat and grime of the previous day had been rinsed away. Not so today. This morning the air was stuffy, heavy, even before the day had begun. The sun was lazily trying to show its face through the high cloud cover but was barely succeeding.

It would probably be an hour or more before anyone else would stir, and he had a lot of thinking to do.

Ben smiled inwardly as he recalled that the original idea of moving to France had been to get away from the emotional disasters that had beset his life in England; to escape from the veracity of losing Mary, the girl of his dreams.

Mary, now thirty-five, was stunningly beautiful. Her shoulder length dark brown hair, deepest brown eyes and her hourglass figure still turned many a man's head. Previously she had lived with him in England, happily he thought, for five years. Then one day she had simply announced that she was leaving him for Donald, a man many years her senior.

From his very first visit, Ben had always dreamed of living in France, and, when Mary left, he took the opportunity to move here and start a new chapter in his life.

A year later, Mary had reappeared along with four months old Alex Benjamin. Until that day he wasn't aware that he had a son.

Here he was today, then, living in one of the most beautiful parts of the world with Mary, Alex Benjamin and Katie.

It was almost a year since Ben had brought Katie to *La Sanctuaire* to recover from her ordeal of being abducted by a gang intent on finding her husband, Dave. With the discovery of Dave's body in Albania, she had no plans to return to England soon.

The course of friendship between Mary and Katie had not been an easy one. Katie's presence at *La Sanctuaire* had reignited a long held jealousy by Mary who knew that Katie had once held affections for Ben. Calming the water had been down to Ben. It took a while, but he had succeeded and life had settled down for them all.

Until, three weeks ago, that is, when a young man, now known to be Tommy Williams, had brutally attacked Mary. He had driven into the front garden on a motorbike and stabbed Mary in her abdomen. The wounds were critical and resulted in her having to spend ten days in hospital, much of it in intensive care.

It had been touch and go at first, but she pulled through remarkably well and made a quicker than expected recovery. She had returned home last weekend and only last night, they had been celebrating her recuperation.

He was the only one who could not relax. He was convinced that the attack was an attempt to murder her, set up by Donald. The fact that she was alive and well was wonderful, but he was sure that as far as Donald was concerned, the same fact was a catastrophe.

Ben was convinced that he might well try again.

The French police had not taken seriously his theory that this was a contract killing organised by Donald, that had gone wrong. They had rightly pointed out that there was no tangible corroboration to uphold his allegations. They were perfectly happy that they had arrested and charged Tommy Williams with grievous bodily harm, and that he was locked up awaiting trial.

Ben had to agree that everything he had discovered about Donald was based on hearsay. He had no concrete evidence at all. Nevertheless, he was convinced that Donald had also murdered a young girl in South Africa, and more recently had been travelling with another man who was found dead on a ferry when it arrived at Harwich. Once again, the police in England were saying that there were no suspicious circumstances and that the man in question had died of natural causes.

He had to track down Donald.

## Chapter 2

Five days had passed since Donald returned from his exhausting trip to South Africa. He was holed up in a Travelodge on London's Waterloo Road, but this morning he was excited. Today, he would be able to tap into the funds that he had realised from his expedition to retrieve the diamonds that he had previously hidden at Kimberley.

Since the first night of his arrival at the hotel, he had scrutinised every news channel on the television in his room. On the first night, BBC carried the story of a prominent businessman who had been found dead on the Stena Line Ferry. He relaxed when sometime later there had been a statement from the police that they didn't consider there were any suspicious circumstances. They were of the opinion that the man had simply died in his sleep and were not looking for any other person in connection with the death. Since then, other than articles that were carried in a couple of Sunday newspapers, the story had dematerialised. He had got away with it.

Donald, however, was taking no chances. He stayed in his room whenever he could, venturing out occasionally to eat, even then, making sure that he didn't visit any store or café more than once. He spoke only to order a meal or to pay at the supermarket, always using cash.

This morning, however, was going to be the start of yet another chapter in his life, one of many. The financial restraints of the past few months would very soon be history.

Opening his laptop, he connected to his account with a private bank in Algeria. No questions would be asked there about a deposit of almost two and a half million pounds. Donald would be able to launder small amounts into his many bank accounts in the UK as and when he wanted.

His friend Lucas – the man found dead on the ferry – had demanded a 75% share of the deal, but from the start, Donald had decided that he was being much too greedy. In fact, he had determined that Lucas would get nothing. He had watched as Niels, the buyer of the diamonds in Amsterdam, had transferred the whole of the proceeds to Donald's Algerian bank.

He watched, now, as the website page appeared on the screen, prompting Donald for his ID and password. Donald keyed them in carefully.

His account details sprang up, showing that he had a total of 5450 US dollars in his account.

Donald stared at the screen. There must be a mistake. The money should be there by now. An icy shiver went down his spine. He desperately needed the funds.

He decided to leave it until later in the day, but there was a nagging fear in his head that something had gone terribly wrong.

It could be simply that there was a delay in the transfer of the funds, but the more he thought about it the more he began to realise that Lucas could well have double-crossed him. Had his friend realised that he might not get his seventy-five per cent, and paid the proceeds into his own bank account instead? Yet Donald knew he had seen the details on Niels' computer screen. He had confirmed his bank account details, and he had watched as Niels pressed the 'Send' key.

Could it be that Niels had fooled them both?

Donald suddenly realised that he had no idea who this Niels person was. Lucas had told him that he had used Niels' services many times in the past. They were, supposedly, good friends.

His mind in a whirl, he left the confines of his basic room to enable the staff to clean it. He wandered up Waterloo Road towards the river, trying to become as incognito as he could amongst the throng of city workers on their way to work.

He stopped for an All Day Breakfast at a kiosk and, took a seat on a nearby bench, struggling to eat the food with a plastic fork from a paper plate. As he sipped his coffee from the polystyrene cup, he couldn't get the state of play out of his mind.

If he *had* been duped, what was he to do? He had spent most of his available funds on the trip to South Africa. He had successfully managed to bring out over two million pounds worth of good quality diamonds and Lucas had helped him to sell them in Amsterdam.

Donald desperately needed the money as his existing operations had been severely hit by his poor investments and the deteriorating state of the European economy. He was in a crisis.

An hour or more exploring the many shops along The Cut did nothing to relieve his tension; if anything it made matters worse. He bought himself two pairs of Jeans, a selection of casual tops, a pair of trainers, a black woollen hat and a grey hooded fleece.

Making his way through the tunnels into Waterloo station, he had to walk past the appalling sight of the "cardboard box" dwellers. He cringed as he saw the more sensible ones still curled up in their sleeping bags. Others had abandoned their pitches but were obviously planning on returning. Dry, protected pitches, he presumed, were at a premium.

At half past eleven, he bought a couple of sausage rolls and a Chelsea bun and trudged his way back to the Travelodge.

He hadn't shaved for five days and he knew he was hirsute enough to be able to sport a respectable beard in just a few days more. He did his best to shave his head using his electric razor, carefully collecting the thick mop of hair and putting it in a plastic bag for disposal. It was not a perfect job, but it would do for now. Each time he ventured out, he wanted to look different. If the media were to link him to the demise of the man on the ferry he didn't want anybody to recognise him. He doubted anybody would, but he couldn't take the risk.

**Chapter 3**

Georgina was the next person to stir at *La Sanctuaire*. She had slept none too well on a sofa in the living room and had been pleased when it was time to get up and stretch her legs. Like Ben, she grabbed a coffee, made her way into the garden, and spotted Ben sitting, as he often did, on his own down by the stream.

An old work colleague of Mary's, Georgina had seen that Mary and Ben belonged together and had orchestrated their reunion. However, more recently her own feelings for Ben had changed and she now struggled with an unrequited love.

Ben heard her walking down the path and looked round to see this pint-sized figure coming towards him. Georgina was petite, just topping five foot six and with pixie-like features that she hated, but to onlookers were extremely attractive. She had freckles, like stardust sprinkled over her cheekbones and her almost black eyes, whilst small, were intoxicating. She didn't have to smile; her face always conveyed her character - ebullient, funny and happy.

During the dark days after Mary had left him, Georgina, or 'Grunge' as she was known at the time, was a breath of fresh air to Ben. She managed to pull him out from his despair without trying. It was just the way she was, the things she said. She introduced him to a wild, crazy lifestyle he didn't know existed. There was never any suggestion of romance, they were just good together and enjoyed each other's company.

'Hi, sleepy head. Come and join me. I've not been here all that long myself,' he said patting an adjoining chair.

Georgina didn't look her best on this morning. As well as being very dishevelled, she had an uncharacteristically melancholy look on her face.

'What's up?' Ben said, taking in her expression.

'I didn't sleep too well last night. I'm just a bit tired,' she lied.

'Don't worry, you'll be able to sleep on the train, won't you?' Ben said, at which point he thought she was going to burst into tears. He saw her bite her lip hard to stifle her emotions.

'That's the other thing. I've got to go home today,' she said with tears welling in her eyes.

'That's true,' Ben said, 'but at least you'll have your own comfortable bed to sleep in. I always think ---'

'Sod the bed, Ben. I just love it here. I just don't want to go home. Each time I come to visit, it gets harder to leave.'

What she wanted to say – to scream – was that it was leaving *him* that was the problem. It was him that she came to see. Yes, the Loire Valley was beautiful. Yes, the weather was so much better than in the UK, but it was *him*. The fact that he was totally unaware of her feelings made it so much worse. She was afraid to tell him how she felt in case he wouldn't invite her to visit any more. It was getting worse. She spent most of her days thinking about him. Sooner or later she was going to blurt out how she felt about him.

'I tell you what, then,' Ben said. 'Why don't you come over for a proper holiday during the winter? You'd have a comfortable bed then. You could have the Dairy Cottage all to yourself. Or you could bring someone with you. How would that be?'

'I'll think about it,' she replied.

'Think about it? I thought you'd jump at the chance. It would be free, of course.'

An uncomfortable silence arose between them. Georgina thought he was going to say how special she was again but, fortunately, he didn't.

'Ben ...' she said eventually.

Ben looked at her.

'Yes?'

'Oh, nothing,' Georgina said as she saw Mary walking down towards them with Alex toddling along beside her.

'Hi, you two. What are you up to?'

Georgina felt herself begin to flush.

'Just sharing a coffee. Georgina's going home today. She feels a bit sad,' Ben explained.

Mary said nothing, but offered a half-hearted smile to Georgina.

Oh, shit! She knows, Georgina said to herself.

'I'd better start packing, I guess,' Georgina said. 'I'll see you later.'

When she was out of earshot, Mary turned to Ben.

'You do know that she's crazy about you, don't you?'

'Who? Georgina?'

'Who else could I be talking about? Yes, quaint little Georgina. Don't tell me you haven't noticed. She can't take her eyes off you.'

'No. I think you've got that wrong, Mary. There's never been anything between us.'

'But you do like her, don't you?'

11

'Yes. That's true, but there's never been anything more than that. She's been a good friend. After all, it was she who brought you here with Alex all those months ago.'

'I know. But this visit has been different, hasn't it? She invited herself. Previously, she's always waited for an invitation.'

'Hang on, Mary. She came over to help out when she learned that you were in hospital. She didn't come to see me. She came to help.'

'Ben, I think that was just an excuse. She came because of you.'

'Well, I just can't agree with you. I think you've got it all wrong. You used to feel that way about Katie and me. Now it's Georgina. I know you're not the only woman in my life, Mary, but it's you I love – only you. Let's drop the subject can we?'

'OK, but I don't think it would be wise to invite her back until she's got over it, which I'm sure she will. Anyway, I came down here to tell you that your *petit déjeuner* is on *la table*,' Mary said in her Franglais.

Ben took hold of Alex's hand and walked back to the cottage with Mary. He found it difficult to take in what she had said. He liked Georgina. She had been of enormous support to him when Mary had left him eighteen months previously. She had managed to bring him out of his shell, bring him back to life in a way that nobody else could. They had gone to places that he would never have dreamt of going – crazy clubs and pubs, live music gigs – and they really enjoyed each other's company right up to the time when he moved to France. But there was never any suggestion of passion between them.

If Mary was right, how did he miss the change in Georgina's feelings for him? What's more, how was he going to deal with it? He could hardly tell her not to come again. That would be so rude, so cruel. He would keep a careful eye on her, and see if he recognised the symptoms for himself.

When they entered the cottage, Georgina was in the living room, but she didn't look up. Ben looked at her and saw once again how unhappy she seemed. He told himself that it could just be the fact that she was going home and nothing to do with anything else.

'When do you want to leave?' he asked her.

'I don't want to leave at all.'

'I know, but what time train are you catching?'

'Just after two o'clock, I think. That gets me home at a reasonable time.'

'OK. I'll take you to the station after lunch.'

'There's no need for you to do that, Ben. I want to go into Angers, anyway, so I'll drop Georgina at the station. You can stay here and look after Alex,' Mary announced.

Ben could do nothing more than nod his approval, but he couldn't help but notice the tone in Mary's voice. Georgina looked up at him, and her face said a thousand words.

Mary was right, then. This lovely, funny, if sometimes eccentric girl had apparently fallen for him. He never imagined in a month of Sundays that this could happen and he felt overwhelmingly sorry for her. If the opportunity were to arise, should he talk to her? Would it make things better if she knew that he knew, or could it make things a lot worse?

Katie sauntered into the room, sleepy eyed and they all sat in the kitchen to enjoy their croissants and coffee. Ben tried but wasn't able to catch Georgina's eyes. She was doing everything she could to avoid eye contact with him, mainly by helping Alex with his breakfast.

Ben left the table before he had finished his drink, and wandered out into the garden. He wanted her to follow him, but he doubted she would. Mary would find some reason to deter her.

Georgina got up to go upstairs.

'Is Ben OK?' Katie asked when she was alone with Mary. 'He seems a bit distant this morning.'

'Yes, he's alright. He's had a bit of a shock this morning. I had to enlighten him that Georgina rather fancied him.'

'He didn't know that?'

'Apparently not.'

'What is it with blokes? Sometimes they can be so bloody thick. I thought he must have been aware of her affections for him.'

'Well, he says not.'

'Oh, the poor girl, I know what she's going through. It's a soul destroying feeling.'

'What? You and Ben you mean?'

'Well, no. I wasn't referring to Ben. I have to admit, and you already know, that I had my eye on Ben for quite a while a few years back, but at least he was single then.'

'He's still single now. That's what worries me, I think. You know how a man's ego works.'

'Does Ben *have* an ego? That's one of his charms, I always thought. He's so unassuming.'

'I guess you're right, but I'm always nervous in circumstances like this.'

'Then you're more of a fool than I thought,' Katie said. 'After everything he's done for you, you can't trust him? I thought true love was all about trust. Am I wrong?'

'Of course not. You're absolutely right.'

'But you've never trusted him with other women have you? What about your outburst when you first arrived here and saw me! I've never seen anything like that.'

'The least said about that the better, I think.'

'But this is the same thing, isn't it? Except that he isn't – or wasn't – aware of the situation this time.'

The conversation came to an abrupt halt when Georgina reappeared. She looked around the rooms.

'Where's Ben?' she enquired.

'Out in the garden, I think,' Katie answered.

Georgina went toward the front door.

'Oh, Georgina,' Mary said before she could leave. 'There's something I'd like you to do for me.'

'OK, I won't be a minute. There's just something I want to ask Ben.'

'I meant ---' But Georgina had already gone. 'Oh, shit,' Mary said.

'Relax, Mary. Whatever she wants to see him about, there's nothing you can do to stop it. Trust. You remember?'


Ben was in the larger of the two barns when he heard Georgina calling him. Whatever was about to happen, he was sure it wouldn't be good.

'Oh, there you are. Are you trying to hide from me?'

'Not exactly,' Ben replied nervously.

'Ben, I've got to talk to you before I leave. I can't leave it any longer.'

'Sounds serious,' Ben said, hardly daring to look at her.

'I just wanted to tell you that I won't be coming back.'

Ben went to speak, but Georgina continued.

'You might not know this, but I've fallen in love with you.'

'I thought we were just mates, buddies, friends.'

'We were Ben but it all changed the first time I came over here with Mary and Alex. I saw a new, a different side to you. I saw you with Mary, I watched you with little Alex, and I fell in love with this other, this new Ben. I saw a kind, gentle man who would do anything for the people he loved. And now I've seen you looking after Mary in and out of hospital.'

Again, Ben went to interrupt.

'No, don't stop me now, Ben. I've been bottling this up for ages and I don't want to stop now.'

Ben nodded.

'Mary knows how I feel. I've seen her watching me, and there's no way I want to spoil your lives together. So I think that it's best if I don't come here again. I will tell her the same before I go. It will make things much easier for you both.'

'I don't know what to say. You are right about Mary knowing, though. She's just told me! I had no idea that you felt that way about me. I'm flattered and honoured. But it's so sad to think that you won't visit us again – very sad.'

'Tell me about it. I'll probably cry all the way home, but I'll get over it sooner or later. I am behaving a bit like a silly schoolgirl, and I ought to start growing up, I guess.'

Ben said nothing, but took Georgina into his arms and hugged her, planting a kiss on the top of her head.

'I'm so sorry, Georgina, I really am. I know what you're going through. Something like I went through when Mary left me for Donald. It was terrible. I discovered then that it's probably more painful to mourn the living than grieve for the dead. But I was lucky. You came along and helped me through it.'

'And I enjoyed every minute. It was fun – well, most of the time. I know it's awful of me, but I sometimes wish I had never brought Mary back into your life. But at the time I hadn't fallen for you. As I said, it's only since I saw you in real life – the real you – that I've been like this. I can't tell you how jealous I am of Mary.'

'What can I say?' Ben said.

'Best say nothing, Ben. I'll go back to the cottage now and have a word with Mary. Thanks for hearing me out. And if you ever need me ...' the sentence was left unfinished. She doubted that he ever would, anyway.

She turned away and made her way out of the barn, holding back her tears and trying to plan how she would approach Mary.

Ben stood in the middle of the barn, bewildered and confused. If only he had realised how things were developing he could have treated her differently. He had frequently given her hugs, once or twice held her hand as they walked up the lane back to the cottage. These things almost certainly would have given her the wrong impression.

He would be sad to lose her from his life. She had been so good to him, so good for him when he needed help.

He sat on a bale of straw, which brought him rather suddenly back to reality. It was less than two weeks ago that he sat here facing the man who had tried to kill Mary. He recalled his fury that day. With the help of Jean-Pierre, the old man who owned the farm further up the lane, he had put a noose around the man's neck and left him strung up to a roof joist while he went to the hospital to be with Mary.

The police were now holding the young man, Tommy Williams, awaiting trial.

Tommy was too scared to admit to the police that he had been paid to carry out the attack for fear of reprisals, but he had confirmed, privately, to Ben that this was the case. However, the name of the man who had instructed him was no more than a nickname – 'Bear'. Ben had no idea who this person was, but he did know *where* he was.

He intended to make contact, somehow, with 'Bear' once everything had settled down at *La Sanctuaire*.

He was also determined to find Donald, who seemed to have disappeared into thin air, but that, too, would have to wait.

## Chapter 4

When Georgina entered the cottage, Mary and Katie were deep in conversation which stopped abruptly as she walked into the living room. It was so obvious that Georgina stopped in her tracks. She was a Yorkshire girl and was renowned for speaking her mind and this was not going to be an exception.

'Sorry,' she said. 'I've clearly interrupted something. I wonder if, by any chance, I was the subject of your little chat?'

'Why would that be?' Mary asked awkwardly.

'I just thought ---'

'You thought right, Georgina,' Katie said. 'We *were* talking about you.'

'And Ben, perhaps?'

'Right again,' Katie said. 'We're concerned about you.'

'Now why is it that I have my doubts about that, Katie?'

'Think what you like, Georgina, but that is a fact. I've known about your feelings for Ben for quite a while. It was you who told me that day at Clapham Junction.'

'So you passed on this information to Mary! Thanks a bunch.'

'She didn't have to,' Mary said. 'It is so obvious how you feel about him, I couldn't have missed it. What surprises me is that Ben hadn't seen it, or so he says.'

'It's quite true, he hadn't. I've just been to talk with him, and told him to his face that I've fallen in love with him. If you could have seen his face, you'd find it easy to believe that he didn't know. Anyway ---'

'You actually told him?' Mary said.

'Yes, and if you'd just let me finish, I also told him that I would not be coming to visit again. That was what I was coming here to tell you as well. So you see, you won't be troubled by me any more. I just hope that makes you happy, because it doesn't me.'

Mary and Katie looked at each other, not knowing what to say. Katie broke the silence.

'Well I think you are doing the right thing. I think you're very brave and I quite understand how you feel about Ben. What is there about this bloke that acts like a magnet?'

'Yes, just look at the three of us, at one time or another we all found ourselves under his spell,' Mary added.

'And you are the lucky one,' Georgina said, staring with unfriendly eyes at Mary. 'You did everything wrong. You did more to hurt him than either of us, and yet here you are in this beautiful place with your lovely little boy who you didn't even tell Ben about for four months, and Ben adores you! It's very unlike me to say things like this but I really despise you. I'm so madly jealous that ...' she couldn't finish the sentence and ran from the room in floods of angry tears.

As she ran out into the garden, she collided with Ben who had noticed dark, thundery rain clouds building and decided to return to the cottage.

Instinctively, he put his arms out and found himself in a passionate embrace. He knew he ought to push her away from him, but he couldn't. The girl was distraught, tears streaming down her face. Neither of them said anything, neither of them moved.

'I think we should go back inside,' Ben said eventually.

'I don't think so, Ben. I've just said some awful things to Mary. I think the best thing I can do is to go straight to the station and go home. I've never acted like this before, and I don't like myself very much at the moment.'

Ben released his grip on her, looked her in the eye and said so softly that she could hardly hear him: 'But you've never been in love before, have you?' Georgina shook her head.

'No,' she said, 'and I so wish I wasn't now. I used to know who I was and what I was doing. Now I don't know anything other than that I love you so much that I could burst.'

'So what was the terrible thing that you said to Mary?'

'I told her that I despised her for the way she had treated you in the past, and that I was thoroughly jealous of her.'

Ben smiled. 'Oh dear, I don't suppose that went down too well, did it?'

'I've no idea. I just ran out as soon as I'd said it. I can't see anything funny about it.'

'No, I don't suppose you can. It's just that it must have come as such a surprise to hear something like that from you! Hardly Georgina-esque is it? Come on let's get back in there and try to calm things down. It's going to pour with rain in a minute.'

Georgina tried desperately to hide the signs of her tears, and they walked back into the cottage with Ben's arm firmly around her waist.

Mary and Katie looked up as they entered but before either of them had time to say anything Ben announced that

Georgina was going to start packing straight away and that she was going to the station earlier than was planned.

'And I will be taking her,' he concluded. 'We'll talk about it when I get back.' With that, he followed Georgina to the bedroom where she had kept her belongings.

As he watched her throw things randomly into her bag, he considered that nobody had ever loved him like this. Yes, Katie had lusted for him, but that was just Katie, that was just sex. What about Mary? Did she ever love him like this? For the first couple of years that they had lived together, their relationship was totally platonic. They had only lived together so that they could buy a decent property between them. Over time it had changed, they had become lovers and everything was perfect. Then, at a whim, she had gone to live with Donald who was almost old enough to be her father. Just like that!

Months after Alex had been born, she decided she wanted to come back. And who was it that arranged that? Georgina. He couldn't take his eyes off her as she prepared herself to leave. He felt totally responsible for her despair, utterly wretched to see her like this. Yet, there was nothing he could do to help her.

As soon as she had packed everything, they walked downstairs together.

'What time is the next train?' Mary asked.

'I've no idea,' Ben replied. 'I just think it is better for everybody if Georgina leaves here now. I'll see her on to the next train, whenever that is.'

He bent to kiss Mary, but was offered a cheek.

**Chapter 5**

Sunday mornings were always the same in Alupa Street on the outskirts of Kimberley. Seventeen-year-old Dingane would be found on the street in the hot, dusty South African heat playing football with his younger brother, Baruti, and some of the kids from the street.

Everybody looked up to Dingane. The kids respected him because he always had time for them, and he was fair. The older generation admired him for his achievements at school. He wanted to be an English teacher and had studied hard to attain the necessary grades. If he got the right results, he could go to college in Johannesburg next year. His father, who had worked in the mines all his life, died just over a year ago and for a while Dingane thought his dreams of college had died with him. However, his father had been a shop steward in the Miners' Union and Dingane had been awarded a bursary, in memory of his father, to continue his education.

There were the familiar noises in the street. In addition to the shouts and yells emanating from the young footballers, there was the cacophony of sounds of African music coming from parked cars and through the thin walls of the shacks and houses lining the road. Two dogs came running at full speed down the road, the front-runner carrying a large bone, and the chaser barking at full volume, obviously claiming the bone to be his. Parents and children could be heard arguing. Fathers were taking the opportunity of working on their old cars, trying to make sure they would last for another week.

Mixed with the wafts of petrol and diesel emissions were the spicy promises of Sunday lunches soon to be served to hungry recipients.

When the game came to its half-time, the boys grabbed their now luke warm water bottles that they had brought from their homes, and sat on the kerb to drink.

'Have you told them about the other night?' Baruti asked his brother.

'No,' his brother replied sternly.

'Told us what?'

'It's nothing.'

'Come on, you've got to tell us now. What happened?' a mix of voices said.

'No. It's between me and Baruti. It's nobody else's business.'

'I'll tell them, then,' Baruti said, not waiting for his brother's permission. 'Dingane and I had gone down into town and we met up with these two truly cool girls. My one let me feel her tits. Man, she was hot. I reckon next time she might let me ---'

'Oh, shut up, Baruti,' his brother retorted.

'You're only saying that because yours didn't let you do anything. Anyway, it didn't look like she had any tits. She was so skinny.' Baruti had to duck to avoid his brother's fist. Dingane continued the story.

'Anyway, we were very late getting back. It was early hours of the morning and we were going to have to break into our house to get in. Mum thought we were both tucked up in bed. We were just walking along St. Pauls Road when

24

we saw this big 4x4 driving towards us. Dead slow it was going, and just before it reached the crossroads, the driver turned off the car's lights and it slowly came to a halt.'

'Wow! What happened next?'

'If you shut up, I'll tell you.' Dingane said sharply.

'Baruti and me both backed into a hedge out of sight and watched as the passenger got out of the car with a shovel in one hand and some kind of bag in the other. He crossed the road and went into the rough ground by the crossroads.'

Baruti took over the story.

'The car drove away, almost silently still without any lights until it got further down the road, then the lights were turned on again.'

'What about the man who got out?'

'He just carried on walking until he was completely out of sight. All we could see was the light from his torch.'

'Then we heard him digging,' Dingane added.

'Yes. We could hear him using his spade for a while, and then it all went quiet.'

'Is that it?'

'Not quite,' Dingane told his friends. 'It must have been about ten or twenty minutes, then we saw the man coming back, and then the car returned and the man clambered back inside, and they drove off the way they had come.'

'What do you reckon that was all about?' one of the boys asked.

'Not a clue,' Baruti said.

'Why don't we go and have a look at where he went? We might find some clues.'

Baruti agreed that it might be a good idea, like playing detectives or something.

'Yeah, like Charlie Jade!' someone added.

Dingane, always the more cautious of the two brothers wasn't so sure that it was a sensible thing to do, but was entirely overruled by his fellow footballers.

Throwing their water bottles onto the road, they ran most of the way up Alupa Street to the crossroads and crossed St Pauls Road onto the parched, dusty landscape that was so dry that it hardly managed to support any life other than scrub and the odd extremely hardy tree.

Barudi led the way as they climbed over the stony terrain, repeatedly slipping on the loose shingles under their feet.

'It must have been around here, somewhere,' he said. Then, taking a few more steps, he found himself looking down into a huge hole that had been dug under the roots of one of the trees.

'I've found it!' he shouted to his friends, who all came running to where he was standing.

Dingane pushed his way to the front next to his brother.

'That's some hole!' he said. 'What's that under the tree?'

Barudi stepped down into the hole and poked his hands further into the hole.

'It's some kind of cage,' he said. 'I'll see if I can get it out.'

He struggled for a few minutes but found it impossible to move the metal object.

'See if there's anything we could use as a lever,' he said to his friends, but was stopped from saying any more by his brother.

'No, hold on,' Dingane said. 'Don't move anything. Don't touch anything.'

'Why?' Barudi asked.

Dingane bent down and picked up what at first appeared to be a piece of gravel. Then another, and another.

'Diamonds!' he said. 'That's what they were doing. They were collecting diamonds. The man must have spilled some when he was getting them out of the cage.'

Suddenly there was a deathly silence amongst the boys. They all knew the consequences of being found with diamonds. Regardless of age or gender, the penalty for possessing even the tiniest stones was imprisonment of one kind or another.

'Put them down,' he ordered his friends. 'It's not worth it. It's just not worth the risk.'

'So what are you going to do, Dingane?' Baruti asked. 'Just leave them here? That's nuts. We could get rid of them on the black market, couldn't we? We might not get much – they're not very big, but we'd get something for them. You can't just walk away and leave them here.'

'No,' Dingane said in the most authoritative voice he could muster. 'I can't let any of you take the risk. I am the oldest one here and I am saying no. We leave the stones here. I will report the findings to the mine bosses, and they can do what they want. Now let's get out of here.'

Despondency showed on every face, but they listened to Dingane. They knew that he was right. Slowly, they made their way back to Alupa Street, but the football match was cancelled.

'Don't say a word about this to anyone,' Dingane warned them. 'Not even your mums and dads. This must remain our secret. OK? Promise me?'

The young footballers nodded their agreement and made their ways home to the shacks that they called home.

## Chapter 6

By the time Ben and Georgina left *La Sanctuaire*, the rain had set in. Swirling in torrents in the strong south-westerly wind, it made driving difficult. There was little conversation during the short journey to the railway station at Angers. Neither knew what to say. It was an awkward silence, each of them wanting to speak, but neither of them able to find the words.

Ben manoeuvred the car into the station car park, opened the passenger door for Georgina, and reached in to take her two bags. Wordlessly, they made their way toward the impressive glass and steel entrance and over to the departures board.

'We've got about fifty minutes to wait,' Ben said. 'Shall we have a drink in the station cafe?'

'There's not much else to do is there?' Georgina replied.

Together, they walked over to the cafe, chose a table and ordered coffees and croissants. It seemed that the uncomfortable silence was going to continue until, just as Ben was taking his first sip of coffee, Georgina found the courage to speak.

'Ben, we can't sit here for fifty minutes not talking to each other. We'll look like a married couple!' she said, trying her hardest to raise a smile.

'Agreed,' Ben said. 'What shall we talk about?'

'How about we talk about you?'

'I can think of more interesting subjects. What had you in mind?'

'I've been kind of planning this on the way here. I don't expect you'll like what I'm going to say, but since I might never see you again, what the hell? I'll just say it.'

Ben's eyes widened, but said nothing, allowing Georgina to continue.

'I just want to ask you first of all, how much you love Mary.'

'I love her very much, you know that.'

'And how much do you think she loves you?'

'I guess she would say the same. What is this?'

'This is telling the truth time, Ben. Because, whatever you think, however much you think Mary loves you, I have my doubts. I don't doubt your love for her but ---'

'This is silly, Georgina. This stinks of childish jealousy. I don't think I want to hear any more.'

'OK. Consider this,' Georgina continued. 'She leaves you without any warning to go and live with Donald. Then a few weeks later, she discovers she's pregnant. It couldn't be Donald's child, so it must be yours.'

'Yes?'

'But she didn't tell you.'

'She didn't know where I was.'

'That's crap. If she had wanted to, she could easily have tracked you down. So if you don't agree with that, consider this. If things had worked out with Donald, do you think she would ever have told you that you had a son?'

'I don't know. The situation didn't arise.'

'Ben,' Georgina said with more intensity in her voice, 'when she got in contact with me, things were beginning to turn nasty between her and Donald. It was only then – only when she was in trouble – that she considered telling you about Alex. Even then, she thought she could do it by texting or emailing you. I told her that was not on, and that is why I brought her here to tell you about Alex face-to-face.'

'That was probably the best day of my life. I can never thank you enough for doing that.'

'Sure. Let me say straight away that I didn't do it for her. I did it for you. I thought you had the right to know about your son.'

'All the more reason I should thank you, then.'

Georgina was deep in thought before she continued, leaning across the table and lowering her voice.

'But she didn't really intend staying here, did she? Having introduced you to your son, she was planning to go back to Reading. Am I right?'

'Not quite. She had some reservations. She said ---'

'Reservations? She tried every excuse not to stay, Ben. She didn't want to live here. So what do you think changed her mind?'

'I think I managed to persuade her that her fears were unfounded and that we could have a good life here with Alex.'

'What if I were to tell you a different version? When Katie, Mary and I were working together in the kitchen preparing for Madame Delphine's party, she was going on about all the reasons she couldn't stay here. It was Katie who told her – and I'm sure she meant it at the time – that if Mary decided to leave you again, she would step in.'

'Did she indeed!' Ben said.

'She did. You can ask her. But I said exactly the same thing, although I had to add that I doubted you would even look twice at me.'

'Really?'

'Really what? That I said it or that I didn't think you would even look at me?'

'Both, really.'

'Clever answer, Ben. Anyway, where was I? Oh, yes. So was it your convincing her of the benefits of staying here, or could it possibly have been the threats – especially from Katie? You know how desperately jealous Mary was of Katie. I just wonder if it was that threat that changed her mind.'

Ben reached over the table, and pressed his hands into Georgina's, his fingers warm on her palms. He had very conflicting emotions. He felt angry that anyone could presume to invade his private life, yet he felt sorry for the girl across the table from him.

'Have you finished now?' he asked quietly. Georgina nodded.

'Obviously, I can't argue with most of what you've said. You were there. I wasn't. All I remember – I can hardly forget it, can I? – was the moment she told me that Alex was my son. It was such an emotional reunion. I never doubted for one moment that our love for each other was as strong as ever, and when she agreed to stay here, I felt my life was complete again.'

'I know. I saw all of that for myself, Ben, and there's no way that I want to disturb that love. I merely wanted to say that for the most part, everything was done for her benefit rather than yours.' Georgina pulled her hands away from Ben's hold, and looked at her watch.

'My train leaves in ten minutes. I'd better get a move on. Thanks for the coffee, and for listening to my ranting on. All I'm saying, I guess, is that if she loved you half as much as I do at the moment, she would have handled things very differently. I hope everything works out for you. I want to know that you're happy. I'm going to miss you terribly, but I'm a big girl and I'm sure I'll get over you sooner or later.'

They both moved away from the table, and Ben tried to grab her for a final good-bye, but she simply walked away from him toward the platform where her train was waiting.

The last he saw of her was when she climbed up into the train.

'I'm sorry,' he mouthed silently.

She did not look back.

He didn't wave.

# Chapter 7

Dingane helped his mother with the washing up after the Sunday lunch of roasted chicken and vegetables.

'I'm going to see Mr Smith this afternoon,' he announced.

'What do you want to talk to him about?' his mother asked.

'Things to do with my studies,'

'Well, can't that wait until tomorrow? Why do you need to see him today? It's the weekend. It's his day off, you know?'

'It's something important. I'm sure he won't mind if I go to see him.'

'It had better be something very important to disturb him on a Sunday afternoon. But if you have to ...'

'I'll just put these things away,' he said. 'Thanks Mum.'

Before his mother could find more objections, Dingane sped to his bedroom, put on some smarter clothes and ran out of the house. Grabbing his worn out bicycle, he peddled for all he was worth the couple of miles to Mr Smith's house.

'Oh, how I would like a new bike' he said as he rode along the dust covered roads. 'I've had this old thing since I was about ten years old.'

Mr Smith was his mentor. He was a senior member of the Union of Miners, and he monitored Dingane's work and progress. He felt that Dingane was, in part, his responsibility since his father's death. He really liked this young man, and was dedicated to his future education. He considered Dingane as his own son in the same way that the boy regarded him as a father figure.

The house was small and somewhat dilapidated. There was only Mr Smith and his wife, a frail lady who looked a lot older than her years, living in the house.

Dingane threw his bicycle onto the road outside the house, and ran to the door, knocking loudly. Mr Smith saw him arrive.

'Come on in, Dingane,' he called out.

Pushing hard on the door, Dingane made his way into the single room, which acted as dining and living area as well as a small kitchen.

'That's right. Come in. Sit down,' he said, then called up the stairs, 'Martha, Dingane's here. I'm sure he'd like to see you.'

Mrs Smith replied from somewhere upstairs.

'So what can I do for you, young man?' he said returning to Dingane.

'I don't know where to start,' Dingane said. 'It's nothing to do with my studies, but I think it's important.'

Dingane recounted the story of what he and his brother had seen a few nights before, and the discovery they had made this morning.

'So I've come to see you because I don't know what I should do or who I should tell,' he concluded.

'Well, now, Dingane, I'm not too sure myself. But one thing is for certain, you should not tell anyone else about this. The first thing the mine bosses will think is that

34

someone in our community is involved, and we all know what will happen if they think that.'

'I've made all the kids that were there this morning swear that they will not say a word to anyone – their friends, their families – nobody. And they have promised me they won't.'

'That's good. We will have to handle this very carefully. How many stones do you think there were?'

'I'm not sure. They were pretty small, but I didn't hang around to count them.'

'Yes, but were there just a few, dozens, hundreds?'

'Dozens, maybe. No more than that.'

'OK. Tell me exactly where you found them.'

Dingane drew a small map on the back of an envelope that was on the table.

'They were in a big hole under a tree – the only tree in the area – a deep hole. You can't mistake it.'

'Good boy. Now, you can leave it all with me. I'll find a way that I can tell the right people – someone who will believe me. But you are right to let me know about this. I will sort it out somehow. You are sure that none of your friends kept any of the diamonds?'

'Of course. I didn't let anybody touch anything once I'd seen the stones'

'Good. Now you just forget all about it. I'll sort it out for you.'

'I knew you would,' Dingane said.

'Now. Will you stay for a drink with us? You can tell us how your studies are going. Have you heard anything from Johannesburg?'

'No, but I wasn't expecting to hear yet. I have to get some grades first.'

'Right. And how are things going at school? Are you still doing well.'

'I'm not top of my class at everything, but I'm doing well at the subjects that matter.'

He stayed with Mr and Mrs Smith for over an hour before he cycled home. He felt relieved that he had handed over the worry of what had happened to somebody who he knew would deal with it the right way.

Arriving back home, he went to his room intent on completing the English essay he had been set on Friday.

## Chapter 8

Ben decided not to go back home immediately, but to visit his friend, Madame Delphine.

He drove into the city centre, parked his car in the underground car park, and walked over to his favourite restaurant. No sooner had he entered the bistro than Madame Delphine came over to him.

'Ben. How nice to see you. You don't often visit during the day. But welcome, anyway!' she effused, planting the obligatory kisses on both cheeks. 'Oh, but something is wrong, Ben. I can tell.'

'You are so observant,' Ben replied. 'It's my lack of such powers that are making me feel so bad today.'

'And am I allowed to guess?' she teased.

'You can try.'

'Has Georgina got anything to do with it?'

Ben looked up at her with wide eyes.

'Er, yes, it has. How did you know?'

'Dear boy,' she said, 'it was obvious for all to see that she is in love with you. Did you not realise that?'

'No. That's the whole problem. I didn't. It seems that everyone else was aware of it, but not me. Not stupid old me.'

'Come with me,' she said. 'It's not busy here today. I'll get you a glass of wine. We can go into the back office and have a little chat.'

There was no arguing with the lady. She took Ben by the arm and led him through the kitchen to a small office behind it. There, she pulled a chair round to the side of her desk and gestured for Ben to sit down. In less than a minute, she returned with a carafe of red wine and two glasses.

'Tell me exactly what has happened.'

Ben felt the relief flowing through him as he recounted everything that had happened in the last twenty-four hours, finally telling his friend the things Georgina had said about Mary, and how she had just walked away without so much as a backwards glance.

'So you're upset.'

'Of course. I feel terrible.'

'And what do you think she is feeling right now?'

Ben was not expecting this less-than-friendly response.

'If you are feeling terrible, Ben, consider what she must be going through. The poor girl. Just try to consider how you would be feeling if things were the other way round. Suppose that you were desperately in love with her and she had walked out of your life. That would be more than "feeling terrible" wouldn't it? That would be indescribable.'

'But what if the things she said about Mary were true? What if I've misread all of those signs as well?'

'Do you think they are true?'

'I don't know what to think. I don't think I believe all of what she said, but it's just made me a bit unsure. There could be an element of truth in it. Georgina is known for being blunt and saying things that people don't want to hear.'

'So she has sown doubts in your mind, is that what you're saying?'

'Yes, she has.'

'And how are you going to deal with that?'

'God knows, Madame Delphine. I just don't know. It's going to be hard not to be wondering all the time.'

'Let me ask you this, Ben. Let's just say that some or all of what Georgina has said today is true, will you still feel the same about Mary? Is your love for her strong enough to take this? I doubt whether you will ever be able to find out how much of what Georgina has told you is true, so are you going to be able to love Mary in the same way as before?'

'I thought you might be able to help me. You're just making things worse.'

'I'm a bit like Georgina. I tell things as they are, Ben. You didn't really think I was going to pat you on the back and say "There, there" did you?'

'No, but ---'

'So what are you going to do about it?'

'What *can* I do?'

'As I see it, Ben, you have two choices. Either you let these doubts eat away at you until you find that you don't love her at all.'

'Or?'

'Or you can take the much more difficult route and face her with some of the things Georgina has said about her.'

'There's no way she will admit to any of that!'

'Depends how you handle it, Ben. Georgina is certainly going to come up in conversation when you get home. It'll probably be the first thing you talk about, especially as you left the house in a hurry the way you did.'

'I don't know whether I can do that. I hate confrontations of any kind. I'm useless at these truth games.'

Madame Delphine went on to say that everyone involved in this had been affected in one way or another.

'It's not just you, Ben. It's not just Georgina. It's Mary too. She's a very insecure lady, you must know that. She sees everything as a threat. Katie, Georgina, possibly even me! Anything that might come between you and her is a potential danger.'

The chef poked his head through the door.

'When you've got a minute ...'

'I'll be with you in just a second,' Madame Delphine replied. 'Ben, I'll have to go. We're designing a new autumn menu. Just be bold, be honest. I'm sure it will all turn out right.'

'Thanks,' Ben said as they both rose from their chairs and made their way out through the kitchen.

As he was leaving the restaurant, Ben noticed two men sitting at a table, deep in conversation. One of the men glanced up as he walked past and acknowledged Ben as if he recognised him. Ben nodded to him but didn't consider that he knew the man and walked out into the rain.

As he was about to enter the car park he realised he *did* know the man at the table. His name was Claude Boulet, a Commissaire de police, whom he had first met when Mary was taken to hospital following her attack. He turned on his heels, back to the restaurant.

As he entered, the two men appeared to be preparing to leave. Ben stood back and waited until the men bade their farewells and the Commissaire went to the bar to pay the bill.

'I'm sorry I didn't recognise you just now,' Ben said.

'No need to apologise and certainly no need to come back.'

'To be honest, I was just wondering if you had a few minutes to spare. I'd like to talk with you.'

'OK, but I can't be long.'

They sat back down at the table that Claude Boulet had recently vacated.

'Right – er, Mr Coverdale, isn't it? How can I help you?'

'First of all, can you assure me that our conversation will be off the record?'

'Yes, provided that you are not going to admit to a felony.'

'No felony on my part. It's to do with the attack on Mary.'

'But I've already told you that I do not have jurisdiction over that.'

'Yes, I know. But you did say that if I didn't get satisfaction from the local police, I could come back to you.'

'That's true. So what do you want to tell me?'

'As you know, Monsieur Boulet, I have always thought that this was a contract killing that went wrong. The problem is that I have no physical proof – that is until now.'

The police officer didn't react, letting Ben continue.

'This is where the confidentiality bit comes in. I spoke with the attacker while he was in custody, and he told me that I was right in my assumption. He was being paid. But not by Donald. He didn't know anything about Donald. He said he was being paid by his dealer in Paris who goes by the name of Bear.'

'Bear?'

41

'So he says. I have no reason not to believe him, but – and this is a big but – he dare not admit this to the police because he's terrified of what the consequences might be.'

'But he definitely named Bear as his instructor?'

'Absolutely. He told me where he operates from and everything. Do I get the impression that you know of this guy?'

'Not personally, but I recognise the name. It's not one you would forget, is it? If I remember correctly, he has been under observation on several occasions but there has never been enough evidence to bring him to trial.'

'Until now, perhaps?'

'Look, Ben. I tell you what I'll do. I have a colleague, a friend really, who works with the narcotics section in Paris. If your man, what's his name?'

'Tommy Williams.'

'Yes. If Mr Williams is willing to give evidence against this Bear person, we may be able to bring him in for questioning. They'd like that.'

'The problem is, though, that he's denying this to the police. He's telling them that he heard voices in his head, and they seem to believe him. He's scared of what Bear might do to him.'

'This is the best I can do, Ben. I'm not officially involved in this case. Let me talk to my friend, and we'll take it from there. I've got to go now, so you'll have to leave it with me. Have I got your number?'

Ben gave the Commissaire his mobile number and, with a handshake, they parted company, and Ben once more crossed the road to the car park and made his way home.

## Chapter 9

Tommy Williams felt safe whilst he was in custody. He was being well treated and fed and considered that this was by far his best option for the time being.

He was maintaining his testimony that it was the voices in his head that had led him to carry out the attack on the girl. The authorities, whilst finding it hard to believe, could not see any other motive for his actions. They had suggested to him what Ben believed, that he had been contracted to carry out the attack but Tommy said that was rubbish. He told them that he had found the knife and stolen the motorbike. He said it was the combination of the voices and his drug habit that had made him carry out the attack. He had stuck stolidly to this story from day one of his arrest.

His case had been handed over by the local police to a man called the *procureur* who was, as far as Tommy could make out, some kind of lawyer. Until now, this man had been responsible for taking the matter forward. Every piece of information by him, the victim, and any witnesses was recorded in his file.

He had become the perfect prisoner. He had done everything he could to persuade the authorities that he was to be trusted. Slowly, he was being offered certain privileges. Nothing major, but extra drinks and food if he wanted, lights were left on in his cell late into the evening enabling him to read. He was no trouble to anyone, and his guardians were beginning to like him.

Doctors had examined him on several occasions and, most recently, a psychiatrist had tried to discover more about the "voices". Tommy had enjoyed the challenge and he felt he had managed to convince the doctors quite adequately. He had been offered the services of a defence lawyer, but had refused the suggestion for the time being.

This morning he had been told that, because of its severity, his case was being passed over to a *juge d'instruction* who would make the final preparations for the trial. It would be his decision whether the case went to trial or if there were alternative punishments that would fit the crime. The *procureur* had explained that his responsibility for the case had now finished.

'Under the *juge d'instruction* you will have more rights. For instance, if you wish, you may insist on attending – with or without your lawyer – any meetings with witnesses or prosecution lawyers,' he told Tommy.

'How soon will the trial take place?'

'That again is up to the judge. There are alternative ways of handling cases like this, some take less time than others.'

'But surely if I'm pleading guilty, it will not take long.'

'It doesn't work like that in France. There is no such thing as "pleading guilty" as there is in England. Here, every case has to be heard. It might be by just a single judge or by a jury. The trial is built around the evidence in your file. You have no choice.'

'I see,' Tommy said. 'Maybe I should be thinking about getting a lawyer.'

'It might well be wise. But as from now the matter is not in my hands.'

Tommy said goodbye to the *procureur*. It seemed as if his tenacity about the "voices" might be paying off. He presumed that somewhere in his file would be the psychiatrist's report, throwing some doubt on his mental state. He must continue to act the part. If he took on legal advice, he may be able to learn what sentence he could expect.

He was trying his best to keep fit. Press-ups, bunny-hops and squats were part of his daily routine. He was eating well and had almost recovered from the withdrawal symptoms of the heroin. He had put on some weight and he could see for himself that his complexion was changing from the pallid look caused by his drug abuse to a more normal, healthy tone. There was only one thing he craved now and that was fresh air. He dreamed of wandering off, taking in the sights, sounds and smells of the countryside.

He wondered whether, if he were to ask ... then decided that was probably a step too far. He must bide his time and do everything he could to ensure that his punishment was as lenient as possible. A long prison sentence was something he wanted to avoid at all costs. The only benefit it held, as far as he could see, was that he would be out of the reach of Bear and his drug-dealing cronies.

The judge who had been assigned to Tommy's case was a woman. She was in her late fifties and was highly respected by her colleagues. She seldom showed any emotion whether dealing with defendants, lawyers or victims. Her face was as stern as her eyes were steely blue. She wore her straw-coloured hair coiffured in a style that was popular some twenty years earlier. Piled up on her head and held with hairpins, it was always perfect, never a single hair out of place.

She spent two hours or more studying Tommy's file, puzzling over certain aspects of the case. She decided not to discuss this with her colleagues, but to meet with the parties as soon as she could. That way she would be able to form her own opinions and, whilst that would have little effect on the trial, she would be satisfied in her own mind as to exactly what took place.

If she had a weakness, it was her illogical dislike of the English, but she made a note in her electronic diary to make contact with Mr Coverdale the next day.

Tommy Williams' record was neatly filed away with the other cases with which she was currently dealing and she made her way home to her immaculate apartment in Angers where she lived alone with her two cats.

## Chapter 10

Donald's emotions fluctuated between fury at what had happened to him, and disbelief of how stupidly ingenuous he had been to put his trust in the one person he thought he could. He still could not determine who had carried out the double-cross, his friend Lucas or this previously unknown character, Niels. Today, he vowed to take the first steps to finding out. Prior to his trip he had abandoned his car in an underground car park near Clipstone Street in London's West End. The first thing he must do is to retrieve it. He had to be mobile again.

Taking the underground to Great Portland Street, he walked into the car park and found that his car had been clamped.

The man at reception, not the most appealing person in the world, told him that it would cost eighty-five pounds to have it released and there would be a further one hundred and fifty pounds in parking fees. The total amount must be paid before the car could be un-clamped.

'We will take a debit card,' he said.

'I don't have a debit card with me,' Donald replied.

'Cash, then?'

'I don't have that kind of cash on me.'

'Then, I'm afraid I can't do anything for you, sir.'

Donald was livid. Had the man not been protected by the window, he undoubtedly would have taken a swing at him. As it was, he walked away shouting over his shoulder that he would be back later.

Within ten minutes he found a branch of his bank where he withdrew enough cash to cover the present problem and put a few pounds in his pocket.

He retraced his steps, and handed over the two hundred and five pounds to the man at reception.

'Just one minute. I'll get you a receipt for the cash.'

'Sod the receipt,' Donald said angrily. 'Just get the clamps off my car.'

'It doesn't quite work like that, sir. I'll now have to inform the clamping people that your car is ready to be released, and they'll send one of their mechanics over.'

'When?'

'When what, sir?'

'How soon will the clampers be here?'

'I can't say, sir. It depends where they are. Could be an hour, could be a lot longer, maybe three or four hours. I just can't say.'

'Three or four hours?'

'It could be, sir. It might be even longer. I just don't know. If you leave me your mobile number, I'll call you when your car is free.'

Donald knew he was fighting a losing battle. He was still feeling paranoid about being traced and refused the offer. He swore at the receptionist and made his way out of the car park into the centre of a fume-laden London.

He bought himself a cheap pay-as-you go phone and registered it for use while having a cup of coffee.

It was on the third hourly check-in at the car park that his car was unclamped and he was finally able to drive back to the Travelodge on Waterloo Road.

This was not how he had planned things. Originally, he had intended to ditch the car at the car park. He would be able to buy a decent car for himself from the diamond bounty. But there was no bounty. He was in a far worse financial state now than before his trip to Kimberley. Everything had to be sorted out again, and resurrecting his old leased car was just a part of the new plan.

Arriving at the hotel, he copied some contact names and telephone numbers from his Blackberry to the new phone.

The first person he called was his second-in-command, Chas.

'Hi, Chas. It's Donald,' he said.

He couldn't see the reaction that his call had upon Chas but the man, normally of healthy complexion, became pallid, and his whole body tensed as he replied to 'The Boss'.

'Hi,' he replied. 'How are things? Did your trip go well?'

'No it fucking didn't. I think I've been ripped off, double crossed, whatever. I've come back with nothing. Abso-bloody-lutely nothing.'

'Anything I can do?'

'Not at the moment, but if I need you I'll call you. How did the business in France go? All sorted?'

'I don't know, boss.'

'Don't know? How can you not know?'

'All I know is that Bear found a bloke to do the job. Since then I've heard nothing. Bear hasn't asked for the second payment and he's gone off line, if you know what I mean.'

'So is the girl dead or still alive? You must know that.'

'No, I *don't* know. I guess something might have gone wrong and that's why he's not answering his calls.'

'You're a bleeding idiot, Chas. You haven't heard anything? What about the bloke who was supposed to be doing the job? Where's he?'

'I don't know boss. It's all gone quiet.'

'Right. Tomorrow you get yourself over Frogland and find this Bear person. He knows the rules. If you think he's playing silly buggers with me, then do what has to be done. And don't come back with any stupid excuses. Just get some results or ...'

'Yes, boss. I know what you're saying. I'll get over there tomorrow.'

'Too bloody right you will. This is your last chance, Chas. Don't blow it. Don't let me down this time or else ...'

The call was cancelled before Chas could reply. He knew he could be in deep trouble but wasn't keen either to meet Bear or to carry out the alternative mission. He had no alternative. He dreaded to think what would happen to him if he failed this time.

## Chapter 11

As Ben got out of his car when he arrived home, the rain had stopped but there were ominously dark clouds away to the west, and he could hear faint rumbles of thunder. It looked as if they were in for a stormy night.

Mary and Alex had heard him arrive, and opened the tiny front door of the cottage before he reached it. His son reached up his arms for his Dad to pick him up.

Ben received a sloppy wet kiss, and snuggled him in his arms tightly, then he turned to Mary, not knowing what to expect.

'Did she get off OK?' Mary said lightly.

'Yes, she caught her train. I doubt we'll be seeing her again. She seemed almost angry when she left.'

'Who with? Me? You?'

'Who knows? Probably with both of us, with everybody, with the whole world. I don't know.'

'And you. Are you alright? I sense some tension. You're not angry with me are you?'

'Why should I be?'

'I just wondered.'

Ben didn't know where to go from here. He could hear Madame Delphine's voice: *You can take the much more difficult route and face her with some of the things Georgina has said about her.*

51

They went into the living room and Mary watched him, waiting for him to speak again.

'Do you remember the day of Madame Delphine's party?' he asked.

'I could hardly forget it. Why?'

'Do you remember both Katie and Georgina saying that if you left me again and went back to England they would be happy enough to take your place?'

Mary was obviously not expecting that.

'Yes, I remember them saying something like that.'

Ben gathered all the courage he could.

'And is that the reason you decided to stay here?'

'Is that what you think?'

'That's not what I'm asking.'

'But that's what Georgina thinks, is it?'

Ben didn't answer. He was now waiting for Mary to say something. For the first time, she looked away from him and he was beginning to regret having started this conversation.

'Alex is looking tired. I'll get him up to bed.' She said.

'You haven't answered my question,' Ben said, holding on to his son. 'I've always thought that the only reason you agreed to stay here was because I had done a good job at persuading you. Perhaps it wasn't like that.'

'OK, Ben. That wasn't the only thing that was said that day. Katie, especially, told me how good you had been to her, how you spent time teaching her French and so on. They both told me things that I didn't know – how they had seen you outside with Alex in the dark, showing him the stars, for instance – and they made me appreciate how important he was to you. It was very moving, and it made me realise that I was being very selfish. That's why I changed my mind and decided to stay.'

They both looked up as Katie came into the room from the kitchen.

'I'm sorry,' she said. 'I couldn't help overhearing what you were saying. I have vivid memories of that day, too and, at the time, I meant every word of what I said. I also remember that when Georgina said the same thing, that she added something about her doubting Ben had similar feelings for her. In fact, Mary, it was Georgina that did the persuading more than me.'

'I think you're probably right, Katie. She told me straight out that I would break Ben's heart if I left him again. It really made me think.'

'It must have been so hard for her. Not so much then, but more recently when she really started to fall in love with Ben,' Katie said. 'I'm not surprised that she blew her top today. She must have known that this was the last time she would see you, Ben.'

The discussion was beginning to embarrass Ben and he merely nodded. Mary, however, had not finished.

'So what else did she say about me before she left?' she asked Ben.

'Roughly the same as she said to your face, as I understand it,' he said.

'What? That she's jealous of me? That she thinks I hurt you? That I did everything wrong but still won the prize?'

'Is that what she said to you?' Ben said with surprise.

Katie decided she did not want to hear any more, and went up to her bedroom.

'Yes. That's exactly what she said to me,' Mary continued. 'It was hurtful, but I've got to admit that she wasn't altogether wrong. There are things that I've done that I'm not exactly proud of.'

53

'I suppose we can all say that. I'm sorry all this has happened. I had no idea how she felt. If I had, perhaps I would have handled things a bit differently. But it's over now. I just hope we can put it behind us.'

Ben was still holding Alex against him and, when he looked down at his son, he realised that he was fast asleep.

'Would you just look at that!' Ben said. 'You can put him to bed now.'

Mary gently took the sleeping boy from Ben and carried him up to their bedroom. The house was quiet now and for a while she sat on the bed just watching Alex breathe and had to agree that she was a very lucky lady.

At the same time, she was shaken by today's events. She wondered what else Georgina had said to Ben. She couldn't help recalling how outspoken and forceful her friend had been when they had met before she had come to France with Alex. She could remember word for word her fiery response when asked if she had Ben's telephone number. *'Yes, I have, but I'm not going to give it to you. I've got a much better idea. I'll take you to see him. I think this has got to be a face to face thing, don't you? You can't tell him on the phone or text him. That would really be awful.'*

This strange girl always spoke her mind. She was renowned for it and Mary had to admit that in most of their altercations, Georgina made sense, however unpleasant it may have seemed at the time.

From the beginning, when she had learned that Mary was leaving Ben, she had warned her that she was making a big mistake. How true that had turned out to be!

Then there had been her outburst when Mary announced that she was pregnant with Ben's child. Georgina had told her that she was lucky to be carrying his child. When she asked her why she thought that, Georgina had said: *'Cos you've got a little bit of Ben growing inside you, that's what! I tell you something, I wouldn't mind carrying his child. He's probably one of the nicest guys I've ever known.'*

And today, how bold she had been to admit to both her and Ben that she was in love with him and how sad it must be for her to know that Ben did not have any reciprocal feelings for her.

For all that, Mary knew that her romantic apple cart had been well and truly upset.

## Chapter 12

Chas toyed with the idea of phoning Bear before he made the journey to Paris. He had three separate numbers for the dealer, each of them to be used for different types of contact. Chas wanted to keep this call private, untraceable, and called the appropriate number.

'Number not recognised,' a voice said.

Chas re-dialled.

'Number not recognised'.

The second number was for known callers only. All other calls were barred. Chas heard the call trying to connect and then the phone went dead. There was no voice, no explanation. The phone was lifeless.

Left with only the third number, Chas delayed dialling. This was Bear's social number. He kept this one for his friends and family. If ever the police wanted to trace his calls, this is the number they would find, and there would be nothing sinister or suspicious about any of the incoming or outgoing calls. If Chas were to use this number, he would be breaking the rules. Not only that, he could be traced as making the call.

Bear was a necessarily secretive man. He did not use social media. There were no Facebook, Twitter or any other social media sites connected to him.

Chas, it seemed, had no alternative but to go to Paris, turn up on the man's doorstep and face up to him.

He packed an overnight case, and made the journey to St. Pancras station where he caught the next Eurostar train to Paris.

During the journey, Chas had time to contemplate on his life, and particularly on his involvement with the Boss.

Donald O'Hanlon had recruited him five years previously, purely on his track record. He had spent more years than he liked to admit in prison of one kind or another. His accomplishments started with petty crimes such as shoplifting and minor burglaries while he was still at school, but had progressed quite rapidly into larceny and street theft. His first stretch was as a result of aggravated burglary when he was twenty and his criminal education was much enhanced during his stay in Wormwood Scrubs.

Within days of his release, he was contacted by a ring who were into more organised robberies with much higher rewards and Chas was incorporated into the group. There were a few close encounters with the law, a few arrests and more than one charge was made against Chas and his friends. In each case, their lawyers managed to find a way out for them.

Finally, however, their luck ran out when the raid they had planned on a security company's offices went badly wrong. There was a violent fight and Chas was charged with actual bodily harm, found guilty and sentenced to seven years behind bars.

Once again, the lawyers worked hard on his behalf and eventually upon appeal, the trial was found to be unsafe and Chas was acquitted. That was when he heard from Donald O'Hanlon.

'I'm looking for someone with some bottle,' Donald had said. 'You look like the kind of bloke I need. Interested?'

At their initial meeting Donald had warned him that some of his duties would be distasteful, but his anonymity would be assured provided he always followed the rules. Chas had no hesitation in accepting. Soon afterwards, he impressed Donald enough for him to become the Boss's second-in-command, and as of today, still held that position.

He was extremely well rewarded, but he wondered how much longer he could hang on to his job.

Things were not looking good. This trip to Paris could herald the end of a very remunerative way of life.

The train pulled into Paris Gare du Nord, the brakes issuing what sounded like a satisfied sigh. Chas alighted and wandered through the huge concourse toward where Bear's operations were housed.

From outside, the four-storey building was a normal second-hand shop selling everything from footwear to furniture, tricycles to televisions. It was an ideal set-up. Bear's punters needed what he had to offer, but frequently could not afford to buy it. How simple, then, for them to be able to sell their belongings, whether legally acquired or not, to satisfy their cravings and at the same time offering their dealer a legitimate front.

Chas wandered over the road to the store, surprised to see a handful of unsavoury characters gathered by the entrance. The conversation appeared to be heated, but Chas neither spoke nor understood French.

'Problem?' he asked casually, and was immediately bombarded by loud voices and garlic breath.

He held up his hands, as much to protect himself as to stop the noise.

'I no understand,' he said. 'Bear not here?'

When they realised he was British, one young woman came forward.

'Bear is not here,' she said. 'He has not been here for over a week. Nobody knows where he is. The people in the shop don't know where he has gone or when, if ever, he is coming back.'

'I see,' Chas said, looking at the sad, worn out faces of the people surrounding him.

'Do you know anything of his whereabouts?'

'Me? No. I've been trying to get hold of him myself, but he's not answering any of my calls.'

'You need coke?'

'No. I just needed to talk to him.'

'Are you his supplier then?' the girl persisted.

'No, nothing like that. It's just business.'

The girl fixed her eyes on his, showing her disbelief.

The next thing he knew was his overnight bag being ripped from his grasp, the contents being tipped onto the pavement in front of his eyes.

'What the fuck?' he started to say before his arms were seized by two of the men, and one by one, the contents of his pockets were pulled from him, most joining the contents of his bag.

One of the men, a big fellow with arms like telegraph poles, held up his passport in one hand and a handful of credit cards in the other.

'Hang on,' Chas tried to say before one of the telegraph poles swung at him, knocking him to the floor.

The group of addicts scampered off down the road. It was probably the first time they had laughed in days.

Chas tried to collect up his remaining belongings from the pavement, stuffing them frantically into his travel bag. He was aware of blood running down his face and into his right eye, but didn't know where it was coming from.

A small crowd had gathered round him as he raised himself from the ground and found a tissue in his pocket, which he used to mop up some of the blood. He didn't know what to do.

As he turned, intending to walk over the road to the station, he saw the girl who had been in the group running back toward him.

'Are you OK?' she asked.

'That's a bloody stupid question,' Chas snapped back at her. 'No, I'm not OK. Your friends have walked away with my passport, my credit cards and most of my cash. I don't think that's OK, do you?'

'Sorry. Yes, it was a stupid question. What I mean is, is there any way I can help you?'

'You can get your friends to let me have my stuff back. That would be helpful, but it looks like they're long gone.'

'Yes, they are. Maybe I can help you get cleaned up? I have an apartment – well not exactly an apartment, more a room – not far from here. You can use my bathroom, such as it is, to clean up your cut. I was a nurse once, so I might be able to help you.'

'OK, I'll take you up on your offer. I don't have much choice. But it'll have to be quick. I must get to a bank before your friends get busy with my credit cards.'

The girl took his arm and walked with him the two blocks up Rue de Maubeuge, turning left into a narrow street. They stopped at a dust-covered black door, and she punched in a number to enter. It was dark inside, but they made their way up two flights of stairs and entered her apartment.

'Sit down,' she said, pushing some magazines from an armchair. 'I'll get some water to bathe your cuts.'

Chas was surprised by what he saw. Considering the dilapidated condition of the entrance and the stairs, this little apartment was bright, clean and tidy. Whilst the room was small, it was well looked after. The living area had a sofa and an arm chair at one end and a kitchenette with a small table and chairs at the other. Bright coloured abstract paintings adorned the walls and a few photographs and ornaments were scattered over some shelves. It was remarkably cheerful for such a small area.

There was a room divider, behind which he could see an open door into a bathroom, and he presumed her bedroom was hidden there as well.

'You still nursing?' Chas called to her.

'No. I was sacked for stealing drugs from the hospital. Biggest mistake I ever made. I serve burgers now.'

'So you're still an addict ?'

'I don't think I am. I still use stuff, but I'm not desperate like the others there this afternoon. I use Bear – that's the dealer's name – because his stuff is safe. He never cuts it with any other shit.'

'But that must mean it's pricey. I can't see how some of your thuggy friends afford it.'

'Oh, they do some cutting themselves. They can get their hands on stuff like Benzocaine, and mix it themselves, silly sods. Then they sell it on. Real shit.'

She came back from the bathroom with a bowl of warm water and some paper towels.

'Sorry,' she said, 'I don't know your name. I'm Lizzie.'

Chas was not going to tell her his name but said 'Hello, Lizzie.'

'This will sting a bit,' she said.

'I promise to be brave,' Chas replied with a grin.

Within a few minutes, the wound on his forehead was cleaned up and the bleeding had almost stopped.

'It needs a plaster on it,' Lizzie said, 'but I haven't got any.'

'No problem,' Chas said. 'I'll get some from the station. In the meantime, can you tell me where the nearest HSBC is?'

Lizzie gave him detailed instructions to Boulevard du Temple, which she thought, was the nearest Branch and Chas left her tiny apartment, grateful for her help.

## Chapter 13

Ben saw the bright yellow *La Poste* van pull up outside *La Sanctuaire* and sauntered over to the post box by the gate. He waved to the postman and retrieved his post from the box, glancing at the envelopes as he went back indoors.

Other than junk mail, there were two addressed to him personally. Throwing them onto the kitchen table, he made himself a pot of coffee and while it was brewing, he opened the first of the letters.

It was from the hospital in Angers. He had been expecting this. It was the bill for Mary's treatment. Because she was not registered with a doctor in France at the time, Ben had to accept responsibility for the cost of the treatment.

When he saw the bottom line he could hardly believe his eyes. He knew it would be a sizeable amount, but this was unbelievable and he wondered where he was going to find this kind of money. He folded it and put it in his pocket.

The second letter was from the office of the *Juge d'Instruction* in Angers.

If the first letter had shaken him to the core, this one simply made him nervous.

The letter was requesting that he, Mary and Katie attend the offices in Angers to meet with the judge to discuss the attack on Mary. Further, they were advised that Tommy Williams and possibly his counsel could be at the meeting.

The letter also stated that there were certain elements of the case that needed to be clarified before it could be taken to trial. There was no indication what these 'elements' were. It was signed on behalf of Mme E. Bervois.

Ben poured his first coffee of the morning. This was not how he liked to start a day. Hopefully, he thought, it would get better.

No sooner had he sat down than Alex came toddling into the kitchen, followed closely by his Mum. When the little boy saw his Dad, he gathered pace, rushing over to Ben with arms raised in the air. Ben lifted him onto his lap and gave him a hug, receiving in return a soggy kiss.

Mary came over, put her arms round his shoulder and bent down to kiss him.

'Is everything OK?' she asked, sensing something wasn't.

'I've just got this,' he said, showing her the letter from the Judge.

'What's all this about?' Mary said. 'I thought everything was sorted.'

'Apparently not,' Ben replied. 'I'll phone her later and make an appointment. She might give me a better idea of what she needs to discuss.'

Mary poured herself a coffee and came to sit next to Ben who was trying to find something in his pocket.

'And there's this!' he said handing the hospital's bill to Mary. 'I knew it would be expensive, but I never expected anything like this,' he said.

Mary casually looked at the document in her hand.

'It's OK,' she said calmly. 'I've got my Health Insurance card with me. We shouldn't have to pay anything, or not much, anyway. I'll pop into the hospital next time in Angers and sort it out with them. I'm sure it will be OK.

Ben recalled his unpleasant confrontation with a woman he nick-named "White Coat" when Mary was taken into hospital. He hoped Mary would have a better experience.

'My God,' he said. 'That is such a relief! I don't know where I would have found that kind of money. I'd have to put you on the streets, I think!'

'Not much business in *Sainte-Justine*,' she joked.

'Oh, I don't know, I've seen you turning a few heads when we've walked through the village.'

By this time, Alex's breakfast was ready, and Ben transferred him into his high chair and, much against the boy's wishes, helped him with his breakfast.

It was mid-morning before Ben opened his laptop, scrolling through the regular amount of unwanted mail until he reached one that caught his attention.

*Jan Kruger back in Kimberley?* The subject line read.

Ben opened the file. It was from his contact in South Africa.

*Thought I should let you know that there are rumours going around the mining community that Jan Kruger has been seen in Kimberley. It's not confirmed, but the media are onto it and there's quite a bit of excitement going round. I'll keep you posted if I hear any more. Regards.*

Ben kept the page up on the screen and stared at it. This all made sense to him. Firstly, Jan Kruger, or Donald as he was known over here, was spotted by Georgina in

65

Paris boarding a flight to Luanda. Then a few days later he arrived back in England on a Stena Line ferry – the ferry that had a dead man on board when it docked.

Georgina had seen the report on the television news, and called the police to tell them that the dead man was not travelling alone, but was accompanied by Donald. They didn't seem to be interested. They had made up their minds that this was death by natural causes. They did, however, follow up the address that she gave them for Donald when they saw on the boat's CCTV that there *was* another man seen with Lucas Berber on several occasions during the crossing.

When the police arrived at Donald's opulent house in Wallingford, it was deserted. There was no sign of anybody living there, no furniture to be seen through the windows, no car in the garage.

As far as Ben was aware, no further effort had been made to find him. Donald had disappeared and Ben was determined to locate him, but didn't know where to start.

He decided to reply to the email.

*This fits in with what we know of his recent movements. He was seen with another man, who we now know to be Lucas Berber, boarding a plane to Luanda from Paris. We don't know what they did after that, but we can presume that they were on their way to South Africa. The next we heard was that they returned to England on a Stena Line Ferry, which probably means they travelled back through Europe and sailed from Hook of Holland to Harwich. We only know this because when the ferry arrived at Harwich, a passenger was found dead in his cabin. And that person was Lucas Berber. Feel free to pass on this information to the Police Department over there. Thanks for keeping us informed. Best Regards.*

Ben was about to call the Judge when his mobile phone informed him of the receipt of a text message. It was from Claude Boulet, and was concise.

*We need to talk. I have contacted my colleague in Paris and they are willing to be involved, but need more concrete information. Call me.*

Ben would have liked to discuss this with Mary, but he remembered that last time he tried it turned into a heated argument, and he didn't want to risk a replay. He did, however, need to find out when the three of them were available to visit the judge.

He found Mary and Katie in the living room, playing on the floor with Alex. They were all in fits of laughter.

'You coming to join in?' Mary asked.

'Not at the moment,' Ben said. I've got a few things to sort out. We've got to go to Angers to meet with the Judge for one thing. When's the best time for you two?'

'What, me as well?' Katie said.

'Yes, she wants to see all three of us. Obviously Mary hasn't told you yet.'

'Why does she want to see me?'

'Because you were the first person on the scene, I suppose. She says there are a few things she needs clarifying. I don't think it's serious; nothing to be worried about.'

'Things like this always make me nervous,' Katie said.

'Me too,' Mary echoed. 'I say we get it over with as soon as possible.'

'OK. Are there any times that don't suit either of you?'

'Not really as far as I'm concerned.' Mary said. 'What about you, Katie? You've got a more active social life than me.'

'I wish!' Katie said. 'I haven't seen Antoine for almost two weeks now. I think he's gone off me, or something. So I'm free anytime really. I agree with Mary. Let's get it over with.'

'Right. I'll call her and get the earliest appointment I can. Is that OK?'

The girls nodded their approval and returned to their game with Alex.

Ben went out to the garden to make his call. He was not able to talk with the judge but an efficient secretary made the appointment in two days' time for them and asked them to bring with them anything that could be relative to the case.

Claude Boulet wasn't available to take his call either, so Ben left a message on his voice mail to say that he could make himself available at any time.

## Chapter 14

Lizzie's directions were good and Chas attempted to make himself understood by the surly looking teller. While he was trying to explain his dilemma, he had to feel sorry for the poor sod who had to go home to this every night. She wasn't necessarily unattractive. It was that the whole of her miserable little life was printed in the wrinkles and furrows that made up most of her face.

Chas got the impression that she could have understood him had she wanted to, but she steadfastly refused to do so.

'Credit Cards,' he repeated, each time more slowly and louder than the previous time

'*Oui,*' she replied curtly. '*Cartes de crédit. Qu'en est-il de vos cartes de crédit?*'

Chas looked blank. He had no idea what she was saying but was saved any further embarrassment by a smartly dressed, Arab-looking man who offered his help. Chas told him briefly of his predicament.

'So you want to cancel the cards? Do you know the card numbers?'

'No. Neither of them are with HSBC, but I thought they would be able to trace them through my account.'

'Difficult, I think. Do you have any proof of identity with you? Your passport, maybe?'

Chas told him that his passport had been stolen at the same time.'

'Of course. British passports are quite valuable these days. Which credit card company do you use?'

Chas gave him what information he could and the man took over the conversation with the teller with the furrowed brow. Chas didn't understand a word of what was being said. He had to trust that his temporary saviour was not transferring the cards into his own name or something similar. There were certain looks between the two suggesting the stupidity of the English. How could they get themselves into such a mess?

After a few minutes the man turned to Chas and said that he needed to contact the number on the back of his cards in order to report them stolen.

'But the cards have been stolen! So I must now chase after the thieves and ask them if I can just get the telephone numbers on the back of the cards?'

At that moment the teller called the man back and spoke more gobbledegook to him, and the man waited while the woman disappeared, returning a few seconds later with a credit card in her hand. The man wrote down something on a compliment slip and returned to Chas.

'She remembered that one of her colleagues had cards with the same company. This is the telephone number that is printed on the back.'

'*Merci*,' Chas mouthed to the woman who tried her best to smile back at him. 'And thank you, too,' he added to the man who was already moving away towards the exit.

All I have to do now is find a telephone.

He made his way back to the counter, gave the woman sufficient security to enter his account and withdrew some Euros. He then left the bank and walked back toward Gare du Nord. He must find a telephone. When he started to search for a public phone he realised that they all worked with telephone cards or credit cards. He couldn't find one that accepted cash.

He decided that he had no alternative than to check into a cheap hotel for the night. There he might be able to use a phone to make his calls. The local hotels all looked shabby, so he walked back toward the bank, remembering that he had seen one or two that looked OK.

It was as he was walking along the road that he spotted Lizzie. She was walking toward him on the opposite side of the road. She glanced over, suddenly recognising him, and waved. She crossed the road.

'Hello again,' she said. 'How did you get on at the bank?'

Chas recounted his confusion and the help that he got from the Arab-looking man.

'All I need now is a telephone that accepts cash,' he said.

'You can use mine,' Lizzie told him. 'I'm just going home now to get ready for work this evening. Come with me. I can help you with the French if you need it.'

'Are you sure? I'm quite happy to pay for the calls.'

They walked briskly back to her apartment block, up the dingy stairs once more and into her room.

Lizzie was an attractive girl. Chas guessed she was in her early thirties. She had very dark hair – almost black – with a few streaks of auburn weaving through it. She had a long face with sharp features. Her eyes were deep hazel brown, her pale complexion exaggerating their drama, and whilst she was far from skinny, she could not be said to be overweight.

'There you are,' she said pointing to a pretty blue telephone tucked away neatly in the corner of the room.

Eagerly, Chas picked up the phone and cradled it in his shoulder whilst he dialled the number. He waited for several minutes before his call was answered. Once again, he thought he was going to face a problem with identification, but eventually he managed to recall the answers to the questions stored on his account and was able to impart the information to ensure that his cards would be stopped within a matter of minutes.

'How are you going to get home to England without your passport?' Lizzie asked when he had finished the call.

'Oh, bugger. I hadn't even thought of that. I guess I'll have to get to the Consulate.'

'They'll be closed by now,' Lizzie said. 'You'll have to go in the morning.'

'You're right. I was just looking for somewhere to stay the night when I saw you. So I'll get out there and carry on the search.'

'No need,' she said. 'You can sleep here if you like. I'll put a mattress on the floor. I'll be out till late, so you'll be on your own.'

'You trust me to stay here on my own?'

'Look around you. There's not much to steal from here, is there?'

'Yes, but ---'

'It's entirely up to you. You don't have to. I just thought...' She didn't finish the sentence.

'How soon do you start work?' Chas enquired.

'Eight o'clock.' She informed him.

'That leaves us plenty of time then. Will you let me buy you dinner somewhere?'

She looked at Chas. There was no expression on her face and he expected her to dismiss his offer.

'That would be very nice,' she said. 'There's nowhere round here, but I do know a good bistro not far away.'

She changed out of her jeans, sweater and trainers into a long tangerine top worn over dark brown leggings and high heels. The overall effect was striking.

They walked from her apartment to a bistro by the name of *Le Tire-Bouchon*, which, he was told, translated into English as The Corkscrew. It was a pleasant evening, and they grabbed a table on the terrace outside, overlooking the huge and imposing church of Saint-Vincent de Paul.

Hardly had they sat down before the proprietor greeted Lizzie enthusiastically.

'Lizzie,' he said in broken English. 'It's good to see you again.'

'And you, Jean-Philippe. Are you well?'

Chas watched the animated conversation between the two, until Jean-Philippe went back into the restaurant.

'I hope you don't mind, but I've ordered a rather special wine. They have different guest wines every week, and, apparently, this week's is one of the best.'

'That's fine by me. You obviously come here often.'

'Well I used to come more often than I do now. I used to be able to afford it.'

They made small talk while deciding what to eat, and Chas was surprised how easy it was to talk to this young woman. It was some time since he had entertained in this way, and once he had relaxed, he began to enjoy it even more. As time went on and the wine took effect, he found himself unwinding, something he had almost forgotten how to do.

Lizzie was a perfect companion, and as they talked, Chas realised that her eyes were really beautiful. What he had seen at first glance as being simply brown, were in reality multi-coloured, the centre of the iris being black surrounded by a circle of rich hazel. Whether it was the comfortable ambience or the effect of the wine, he didn't know, but he found her eyes almost hypnotic.

He returned to earth suddenly when she said 'Why were you looking for Bear?'

Chas thought quickly.

'Oh, just a bit of business. Nothing exciting.'

'So you were surprised when he wasn't there.'

'Not really. I didn't have an appointment or anything. It was an 'off the cuff' thing, you know?'

'Long way to come on speculation isn't it?'

'Just bad timing. He does have a habit of going away for a few days. He's got property all over the place.'

'Lucky old him! Who says crime doesn't pay?'

Chas was desperate to change the subject and suggested they order another bottle of wine, but Lizzie said it was time they got back to the apartment.

'Have you decided to stay?' she asked.

'I can hardly refuse,' he said, 'after such a·nice evening can I? Thanks very much.'

They ambled their way through narrow streets back to Lizzie's bijou apartment where she brought out an inflatable mattress, an electric pump and some bed linen.

'You'll have to do it yourself, I'm afraid. I'm going to be late for work.'

'No problem' Chas said. 'I've got all evening.'

She changed quickly into her working attire, comprising black trousers, red tee-shirt and matching red baseball cap emblazoned with the "Super Burgers" logo.

'Very smart,' Chas said when she reappeared.

'Don't knock it,' she said. 'It's an income. I'll see you later.'

'Later,' Chas replied as she let herself out.

Just before she disappeared she turned her head and called back 'I still don't know your name!'

Chas busied himself with the bed and pretended he hadn't heard.

**Chapter 15**

Donald had never visited Lucas's home before but he knew the address. Today he was looking smart but casual. His beard was trimmed and what hair he had was tidy. He had never met any of Lucas's family so was satisfied that he would not be recognised. He would merely call to offer his condolences to whoever was there in much the same insidious way that King Herod had suggested visiting the infant Jesus in order to worship him.

The object of the visit was to attempt to find out anything he could about his missing millions.

Lucas did not share personal details with anyone, and especially not with Donald, so he knew very little of Lucas's family. He knew he was married, and he believed that he once mentioned a daughter. Other than that, he was walking into the unknown.

The drive out of London on the M4 was the usual headache. It took him more than two hours to reach Reading on his way to Kintbury, a few miles further west.

Driving through Reading brought back memories of Mary. This was where she had once lived. This was where she had shared a flat with her bastard boyfriend, Ben. This was where he took her home after their secretive nights out together. The recollections were bitter-sweet. His time with Mary was the ultimate in love-hate relationships. His feelings for her and, indeed, for her boyfriend, Ben, were now entirely murderous.

By the time he had driven through the town, his heartbeat was far higher than it should have been, and his eyes held an evil stare. Even his plans to have her 'dealt with' had failed. Both she and the boyfriend were still out there. Just how much did they know? What, if anything, were they intending to do? And when?

He felt unnerved by his lack of information, apprehensive of being found and destroyed by what they knew. He would, he must, find a way of dealing with them both.

But today, he was making his first efforts to find out where his money was.

His SatNav guided him from Reading to the village of Kintbury. He drove through the quaint village centre with its corner shop which sold just about everything and on toward the Kennet and Avon Canal. If Donald had not had such urgency in his visit, he would undoubtedly have stopped to have a drink and discover more about the village but he was on a mission.

Following the computer voice, he traced his way to Lucas's house. Built of red brick, with dark grey shingles and a roof of black slates it was unpretentious, yet luxurious. It was exactly as Donald had imagined it, standing back from the road behind a black-painted wooden fence.

The side of the garden faced onto the canal with steps down to a landing platform, framed by two weeping willow trees.

Donald parked his car a little further up the road, and walked back toward the house.

And stopped in his tracks.

Parked in the driveway, alongside the house was a police car. He hadn't anticipated this. Why were the police there? They had said there were no suspicious circumstances to Lucas's demise. So why...?

He retraced his steps up the road, and sat in his car. This was not good. Once again, he was being forced to reconsider his tactics. For someone who was used to being in control, this was fast becoming a nightmare.

Inside the house, a detective inspector and his young woman sergeant were following up the lead that suggested that Lucas Berber had a travelling companion when he journeyed back to England.

Lucas's daughter, Angela, had invited them into the house.

'We would like to speak to Mrs Berber,' they told her.

'You can talk to her by all means,' she replied, 'but I must warn you that she suffers from dementia so I can't guarantee that you will get many answers – not that make any sense, anyway.'

She led the officers into a comfortably furnished lounge where Mrs Berber was sitting in an armchair, looking out over the garden, seemingly dozing.

'Mummy. These are police officers. They would like to talk to you about Daddy.'

'What about Daddy?'

'Hello, Mrs Berber. It's about Mr Berber's death, I'm afraid. I'd like to ask you a few questions.'

'Who's she?' Mrs Berber said, swinging round in her chair and pointing at the sergeant. 'What's she doing here?'

'She's a police woman, Mummy.'

'Mrs Berber,' the officer continued. 'Do you know anybody called Donald O'Hanlon?'

'Yes. I did once know a Donald. Nice man he was. We used to go swimming together and sometimes to the pictures. They were such happy times.'

'I'm sure they were, Mrs Berber, but the Donald we're taking about is possibly a friend of Lucas. Do you know him?'

'Of course I know him. He's my husband!' the old lady said, and then turning to her daughter said 'What *is* he talking about?'

The officer turned to look at Angela, who shrugged her shoulders.

'You see what I mean?' she said.

'Can I ask *you*, then?' he said to Angela. 'Do you remember your father mentioning a Donald O'Hanlon?'

'I'm afraid not, officer. I've been living in The States for the last couple of years. I've come home now to help with Mummy, now that Daddy's dead. I don't know what I'm going to do with her yet. I guess it will have to be a home. She won't want to come home with me, and I'm the only one left in the family.'

'I'm sorry,' the detective said, realising that this interview was leading nowhere. 'I hope it all works out for you. We'll leave you in peace now.'

'Peace?' Angela said. 'I wish!'

Donald sat for some minutes considering his next move when he saw the police car reverse out of the drive, swing round and drive right past him up the road. He didn't move. For all he knew, it was possible that there could still be a police officer in the house. There were two people in the car that had just driven past him, but he had to be as certain as he could that there were no officers remaining there.

After ten minutes, he had made up his mind what to do and had devised two scenarios depending on who would greet him at the house. He left his car, walking casually back to the house and up the short drive. The front door was flanked on either side by white marble statuettes of naked girls holding urns.

He reached forward, rang the doorbell, and was greeted by a smartly dressed young woman with recently coiffured ash-blonde hair and flawless make-up.

'How can I help you?' she said in slightly American English.

Donald's second scenario came into play.

'Hello,' he said. 'I'm a freelance journalist, and Universal Press has asked me to put together a piece about Lucas Berber. I don't want to intrude, but one thing we don't have is a recent photograph of Mr Berber. I wonder if you have something I can use? Do I presume you are his daughter?'

'Yes, I'm Angela, and I'm getting a bit fed up already with all the callers. First it's the police, and now the press.'

'The police?' Donald said innocently. 'No problems, I hope.'

'No just routine, they said. They were asking about a man called Donald something-or-other. They tried to ask Mummy, but she's too far gone to know what time of day it is. Anyway, just wait a minute, and I'll see if I can find a recent picture for you.'

Donald remained composed regardless of his heart thumping away. He peered inside the house, trying to make a note of the layout. It was not easy; the house was probably older than it looked and the rooms off the hallway seemed to be random. He could just see into one room and saw an elderly woman sitting in her armchair. That must be Mrs

80

Berber, and she's of no use to the police. Some good news at last, he thought.

'I'm sorry, Mr ...'

'Holden-Smith,' he replied to the query. 'Martin Holden-Smith.'

'Well, I'm sorry, Martin. I should have invited you in. Come in, anyway. I've found a few photos that look quite recent. See what you think. Are any of them suitable?'

Donald was led into the big room where the old woman was still sitting, staring vacantly out of the window into the garden.

'This is Mummy.'

'Pleased to meet you, Mrs Berber,' Donald said rather loudly. There was no reaction.

Angela handed him half a dozen photographs. 'Here, take a look through these.'

Donald took a cursory glance through the photographs, and picked out three at random.

'These will do fine,' he said.

He was beginning to wallow in the fact that the man who was responsible for the death of their husband and father was standing here in their house. The audacity of it amused him. Any minute now, they'll offer me a cup of tea, he thought.

'One other thing,' he said. 'Do you have a date for the funeral? I know there are many local people who would like to be there.'

'As it happens, we have only had that confirmed today. The post mortem was completed yesterday and showed nothing unusual. It seemed that Daddy died in his sleep after a bit of a boozy ferry crossing. He had signs of angina but he did like his drink, so this time it looks like he went a bit too far.'

Donald could see that although she was putting a brave face on things, her eyes were beginning to moisten. It was time to make his exit, he thought.

'The funeral is next Friday at the local church,' she said.

'Thank you so much,' Donald said solemnly. 'I'm so sorry to have disturbed you. I hope everything goes as well as it can. I'll make sure you have a copy of the article before it's published.'

'Thank you. Goodbye,' she said as she closed the door behind him.

Still trying to subdue a smile, he sauntered back to his car and flung the photographs onto the back seat.

'Mmm, not a bad morning's work, I suppose, but I still don't know where my money has gone.'

Back inside the house, when her daughter returned to the lounge, the old woman said: 'Who was that, then? Was that Donald?'

'No, Mummy. That was a man from the press. He just wanted a photograph of Daddy.'

'Why does Donald want a photo of Lucas?'

'No, Mummy. It wasn't Donald. It was a reporter – Martin something.'

'Sounded like Donald to me.'

'I'll get you a cup of tea, Mummy. I think you're getting a bit confused again.'

## Chapter 16

Nobody knew how the story got out, but The Diamond Fields Advertiser ran a story on page three with the headline "Jan Kruger Back In Town?".

The report stated that a man meeting Mr Kruger's description had been seen late the previous Wednesday night. CCTV confirmed the sighting at the petrol station where he filled up a car with diesel, for which he paid in South African Rands.

*Mr Kruger,* the article said, *a middle manager with a major mining company in Kimberley, disappeared seven years ago without any explanation at the same time as a coloured girl, Laila Pienaar, went missing. There was no conclusive evidence that the two incidents were connected.*

*According to another source, Mr Kruger was accompanied by Lucas Berber. Ten years ago Mr Berber was suspected, but never convicted, of being involved in the illegal selling of diamonds to buy arms for rebel groups in neighbouring countries.*

*The Police Department in Kimberley and the Border Agency are working closely together to trace his arrival and departure but at the time of going to press have no comment to make. They are asking anyone who saw either Mr Kruger or Mr Berber to contact them immediately.*

Mr Smith, Dengani's mentor, had reported everything that he had been told by the boy to the mining company and was told not to mention it to anyone else, and that the company would handle it from now on. Mr Smith was only too happy to leave it in their hands, as it had all the marks of a time bomb waiting to explode.

The wasteland where the diamonds were discovered by the kids from Alupa Street was swarming with people from the mine and local police. The forensic team were there, dusting everything in sight hoping to find something that would help in the investigation.

'Whoever did this made sure that no clues were left here,' one of the forensic team said, 'and if we are to believe that it was Kruger who buried them here, that was at least six years ago, so even if there were traces left, they would have been washed or blown away by the weather long since.'

The police left the scene, leaving the people from the mine to clear the site, picking up every stone that had been left behind. They stored them safely in a hessian bag to be taken back to the company.

By now, the grapevine had started working overtime and word spread quickly through the township. It fast became the talking point wherever there were people eager to find out more.

Mr Smith was relieved that there was no suspicion of the workers being involved. The authorities were happy to accept the account with which he had presented them. It would have been all too easy for them to suspect the black workers and divert their investigations onto them.

The description of the vehicle involved corresponded perfectly with CCTV coverage at the garage. Unfortunately, the registration of the vehicle was unreadable, but it was clearly hired from one of the many tour operators in the area. Which one, they were yet to ascertain.

It was mid-morning when Ben received an email from his friend in South Africa, with a copy of the article from the Diamond Fields Advertiser.

*I sent on your remarks about Lucas Berber travelling with Mr Kruger to the police, and they took that on board very readily. Maybe now they will be able to make some headway. I do hope so. Thank you for your support. If I hear any more, I'll let you know straight away. Kind Regards.*

Ben printed out the email and the attachment from the newspaper and added them to the file that he was compiling for his visit to the judge. He was hoping that he could use the forthcoming meeting to augment his belief that Donald O'Hanlon or Jan Kruger – whichever name they chose – was not only involved in the Kimberley girl's death, but the demise of his colleague, Lucas and, more importantly, the near-fatal attack on Mary.

He became aware of his mobile buzzing somewhere and went about trying to locate it, eventually finding it under a pile of magazines on the sofa.

The call was from Claude Boulet.

'Ben, can we get together this afternoon? I understand that you are meeting with the *juge d'instruction* later this week, and I want to talk with you before the meeting. Would it be easier if I came to your house?'

'You'd be very welcome, if that's convenient for you. Do you know where we are?'

'I've got a pretty good idea.'

'Just drive straight through the village and as you are about to leave it, take a very steep left turn, and *La Sanctuaire* is a few hundred metres on the right.'

'Got it. I'll be there about three o'clock, is that OK?'

'That's fine. Look forward to seeing you again.'

Ben looked up to see Mary behind him.

'Who was that?'

'Claude Boulet,' he replied.

'Do I know him?'

'No. He was the Commissaire who was at the hospital the night you were rushed into intensive care. He was very kind, very understanding, and we've kept in touch. I met him again the other day at Madame Delphine's place.'

'And?'

'And I updated him as to what is happening with Tommy Williams, and the case generally. He's just phoned to say that he wants to talk to me before our meeting with the judge.'

'What about? I thought everything was going to plan.'

'Well, not quite. You don't know this, but when I had a brief chat with Tommy, he admitted to me that he was, indeed, being paid to attack you.'

'Don't tell me. By Donald?'

'No. That's the thing. Not by Donald but by somebody called 'Bear' in Paris.'

'So why hasn't he told the police that? Surely it would be helpful to his case, wouldn't it?'

'He's too scared of what Bear might do to him, so he's sticking to his original story of hearing voices in his head.'

'So how is this Claude involved with all of this?'

'I told him what I've just told you and he has heard of this Bear person before, so I guess that's what he wants to talk to us about this afternoon.'

'D'you mind if I sit in on this?'

'Of course not. I expected you to. It's all about you after all!'

'I'll see if Katie can look after Alex while he's here. I'm sure she will.'

'Is Katie OK? She seems very subdued recently. Do you know why?'

'No I don't, but I agree with you. She's certainly not her usual self. I don't think she's seen Antoine for a while, so it's probably something to do with that.'

'Probably.'

Claude Boulet arrived nearly half an hour later than he had said and apologised profusely, kissing Mary on both cheeks and shaking Ben's hand.

Mary brought a pot of tea and some muffins that she had cooked the previous day into the living room.

'How nice,' Claude Boulet said. 'A real English afternoon tea!'

'Yes,' Mary said. 'I'm not totally French yet.'

'Do you want Katie to be in on this?' Ben asked the Commissaire.

'Not at the moment, but we might want to include her later. Let me tell you why I'm here. I passed on what you told me about this man, Bear. I was right in thinking that he had been of interest to the police in Paris for a long time. He has been questioned about his involvement in the drug scene on many occasions, but each time his lawyers found some way of getting him released without charge. Usually it was minor technicalities, but, nevertheless, he never got to trial.'

'Do you think we might be more successful this time?' Mary asked.

'Well, to be honest, I don't think so. If Mr Williams is refusing to tell the truth about Bear, then once again, we have no proof. So we must find a way to convince Mr Williams to change his story.'

87

'How can we do that?' Ben asked. 'He's stuck with his story of 'voices telling him what to do' from the very beginning. He's not likely to change his story now. As I understand it, he's been through psychiatric sessions and even they accept his version of events.'

'OK. This is what I propose. I intend to come with you to meet Mme Bervois and I will put pressure on Mr Williams that he is likely to serve a much longer sentence if he is found to have lied to the police than he is by sticking to his story.'

'But he's terrified of Bear. He knows what will happen to him if he tells the truth.'

'I know. That's what's happened so many times. Witnesses refuse to come forward because of their fear. So as well as the threat, I'm hoping I can persuade Mme Bervois to promise Mr Williams that if he will stand as a witness against Bear, and we are able to convict him, his sentence would be dramatically reduced.'

'That sounds good to me,' Ben said.

More tea was poured before Claude Boulet continued.

'The other thing that you ought to know, Ben, is that we have an undercover police woman already working on this case. She's very experienced in this kind of work, and she's going to keep a watch on Bear's place, looking for anything or anybody that might lead to information, evidence and so on. She's had some good results in the past and we're hoping she can help us a lot with this. She goes by the name of Lizzie.'

## Chapter 17

For the first two days after she returned home from France, Georgina felt totally depressed. She so wanted to phone Ben and apologise for her outbursts but forced herself not to. She told herself that she had nothing to apologise for. Everything she had said was true. She had only pointed out a few things about Mary that Ben might not have realised. If she were to show regret for what she had said, it would almost be an admission that she didn't really mean what she had said, and that in itself would be a lie.

She had expected to cry all the way home, but she didn't. There was still an element of ire within her. She was able to act as if nothing of importance had happened that day.

When she arrived home, that was another matter. She had never wept like this in her life before. She considered that not only had she seen the last of Ben, but she had made absolutely sure that he would never, ever want to see her again. *Quel imbécile!*

When she woke from her sporadic sleep, her pillows were cold and wet from her tears. When she looked in the bathroom mirror, a tired, drawn, lifeless girl faced her. This was a side of herself that she had never seen before. She always felt deflated when she came home after seeing Ben but this was new. This was serious.

She wasn't expected at work today so she did her best at patching up her face and tried her hardest to behave as she would normally. But it wasn't normal. It was far from normal. She had thrown away the only slim chance that she had of somehow, sometime, somewhere getting together with Ben.

Perhaps a strong black coffee might help, she thought. Out of habit, she turned on Capital Radio only to hear Katie Melua singing "The Closest Thing to Crazy".

'Damn you, Dave Berry,' she screamed at her digital radio. 'That's all I need.' She should have turned it off. Instead, she found herself singing along with it, tears cascading down her cheeks. Every word of the lyrics must surely have been written just for her. She was in deep, so deep she might drown any second.

Her misery lasted for two whole days. She had never imagined that such unhappiness could exist. She felt alone, dejected, rejected and stupid.

'I don't suppose he's feeling anything like this,' she said to her reflection in the mirror that hung over her fireplace. 'I doubt he's even noticed that I've gone. I'm probably just a joke to him.'

That was the moment that she vowed she would put it all behind her. No man, not even Ben, was worth this amount of pain.

'Enough,' she told her reflection. 'Tomorrow things are going to change, girl. Tomorrow is the first day... Oh, forget the bloody clichés, woman. Just get on with it!'

Next day, her first port of call was going to be the hair salon where she used to work – with Mary.

The girls that she recognised welcomed her, and even her old boss, Ray, came out to say hello.

'What can we do for you, Grunge?' he said and then corrected himself 'Sorry, it's Georgina now, isn't it.'

'You know bloody well it is,' Georgina replied. 'I grew up when I stopped working for you!'

'Wow. That hurt.' Ray said, and one of the girls told him that it served him right.

'Is Penny free?' Georgina asked.

Ray didn't have to answer. Penny was coming over to Georgina and said 'I'm not free, but I am available,' she said.

They spent some time looking at hairstyles on the internet until Georgina saw one she liked.

'That's something quite different for you,' Penny said, 'but it will really suit your features.'

'You mean my pixie face and pointy nose?'

The two girls had worked together at Ray's salon *Hair Today* until about a year ago. There was much catching up to do. The only subject Georgina was not going to discuss was Ben Coverdale. She watched Penny as, bit by bit she created the new look.

When she worked there, Georgina was very popular with the younger clientele, as she created some very modern, often outrageous, styles. Penny had always produced styles more suited to the blue rinse brigade. What she was doing for Georgina was quite unusual for her, but the end result was a triumph both for her and her client.

'What do you think? Is that something like you had in mind?'

Georgina was delighted with Penny's handiwork. It did indeed compliment her attributes. From the front the style was almost boyish, short and with a parting. At the back, the hair was longer and curved into her neck. Penny had highlighted her naturally brown hair with amber, and the overall effect was excitingly new.

'All you've got to do,' Penny said, 'is to put a few more smiles on your face. You owe it to your new hairstyle – and, of course, the stylist.'

'I'll do my very best,' Georgina said.

'Look, I don't know what's troubling you and you obviously don't want to talk about it. But it's evident that you have some kind of problem. I just want to say that if ever you do want to talk to somebody, I'm always ready to listen.'

'No change there, then. You were always the mother figure. Thanks. It's all a bit raw at the moment, but when I feel I can talk about it, you'll be my first choice.'

'Good. We still meet up on Friday nights at The Prospect. You'd always be welcome to join us – a bit like old times. Mind you, you wouldn't recognise the place. It's had a face lift. Most of the old smells have gone, but somehow it's not the same. It was the stale beer and tobacco smells that made it what it was – but, anyway, we still meet up on Fridays.'

'I might take you up on that. I don't have much of a social life at the moment.'

'Good. Look forward to it.'

Georgina left the salon with a new confidence and was determined that her new look was just the beginning.

There *is* life after Ben, she told herself. There *must* be.

## Chapter 18

It was not as warm as usual at *La Sanctuaire*. There was a chill in the air and the wind had a bite to it. Ben was not in his usual place down by the stream. Instead, while Mary had gone shopping with Alex, he was in the kitchen, poring over his laptop when Katie walked in.

Ben looked up to greet her and was pleased to see a smile on her face, something that had been missing for over a week. He conveyed his thoughts to her.

'I've at last heard from Antoine and I'm hoping to see him in a couple of days. Mind you,' she added, 'he's got some explaining to do. How can he just push off like that without saying anything?'

'He's been away, then?'

'I guess so, but I don't know any more than you. As I say, there will be some interrogating to do when I see him!'

'If I see him first, I'll warn him.'

Katie smiled.

'I hope you don't mind me asking, but have you and Mary come to terms with the Georgina episode? It must have been difficult for you both.'

'It was,' Ben said, 'but I think we'll survive. I still feel so sorry for Georgina. I've never seen her like that before. I doubt, I hope I never will again.'

'Perhaps you can be just friends again in the future?'

'I don't think she would settle for that. I think it's all or nothing and that's not on the menu.'

'So where do things stand with you and Mary now? Did what Georgina said make any difference to either of you? I'm sorry, Ben. I'm being awfully nosey.'

'It's OK. To be perfectly honest, it did make me have doubts at the time, but it seems to have passed – almost.'

'Almost?'

'Just a few niggles, you know? Even Mary says there is some truth in what Georgina said. I guess it will all become history sooner or later.'

'Do you think you'll get married?'

'I have thought about it, but never seem to be able to find the right moment.'

'If I remember right, Ben, that's one of the things she wanted when you were together before. That was one of the reasons she went off with Donald, wasn't it?'

Ben nodded thoughtfully. Katie was right. Marriage and a family were the two things Mary spoke of then. Now she had one but not the other.

'You're right again,' Ben said, then changed the subject. 'Are you nervous about the meeting with this judge woman tomorrow?'

'Stupid question! Of course I am. I know there's no need to be, but things like this always make me edgy. You must be as well.'

Ben admitted that he was very anxious, and told Katie of his conversation with Claude Boulet, and what he was hoping to achieve.

'Sounds like it is very important, then. What do you know about this bloke, Bear?'

'Absolutely nothing, except that Tommy Williams confided in me that he was being paid by him to attack Mary. He's already known by the police in Paris.'

'This is going to be very interesting. I wonder what's going through Tommy's mind today. If we're nervous, just think of what he must be feeling!'

When Katie left the kitchen, Ben's focus changed. A few minutes previously he had been using the internet to see if there was any further news of Donald, or the rumours in Kimberley; now he concentrated on the possibilities of getting married in France.

What he discovered was enough to deter any foreign national from contemplating such a thing. The list of required documentation was lengthy. Most items had to be originals and many more had to be produced in triplicate. What he thought would be a simple thing to organise was now becoming a nightmare. He very quickly came across an advisory website that reinforced what he had discovered for himself, but offered a straightforward suggestion that made a lot of sense.

The simplest way around this problem was to have the civil ceremony in the UK, and then, if required, have the marriage blessed at a church in France.

He could now suggest something along those lines once he had summoned up the courage to ask Mary to marry him. It was possible, of course, that she might have changed her mind on that subject – a woman's prerogative, after all.

He also asked himself what his reaction would be if she were to say 'no', but that bridge was there to be crossed when he came to it. For now, he had to find the right moment, and that wasn't always easy these days.

\*\*\*\*\*

Chas was scarcely aware of Lizzie coming home. It was in the early hours of Thursday morning, but he didn't stir enough to check the time.

Several hours later, he woke to see her casually stroll across the room in nothing more than her bra and pants. Her wet hair was straggling down over her shoulders where she had recently been in the shower.

What a great way to start a day, he thought.

'Would you like coffee?' Lizzie asked.

Chas choked on his reply. 'Er, yes. That would be great.' He couldn't take his eyes of this young woman. The beauty of her undressed body far surpassed the clothed one. Her lingerie was undeniably French in its brevity and translucence. He must bring himself under control. He was sure his eyes were out on stalks like some cartoon character.

'Sorry,' she said. 'I'm not embarrassing you, am I?' Chas was sure there was a teasing smile on her lips. He shook his head.

'This isn't something I see every morning,' he said. 'But I'm not complaining.'

'At least I put some underwear on. I usually pad around in the nude, but I thought that would be too much!'

She brought over the coffee, and bent down beside him to put it on a small table. His mouth was dry, not from thirst; more from the difficulty he was having swallowing.

'Thanks,' he stuttered. 'I'd better make a move. I've got to get to the British Consulate. Can you tell me the best way to get there, wherever it is?'

'You need to get to Madeleine on the Metro. It's not an easy journey. You have to change twice, I think. But you've got plenty of time to get lost!'

'I get lost on the London Underground, never mind the Metro. Anyway, I'll do my best.'

'I'm just warming up some croissants. Do you want me to do a couple for you?'

'That would be great.' He was still having trouble concentrating with this semi-naked woman just a few feet from him.

'Are you planning on going back to the UK today?' she enquired.

'Yes. That's the plan. Always providing that I get the paperwork from the Consulate.'

'That's a shame,' she said. 'I really enjoyed last night, and I thought we might be able to do something similar this evening?'

'Well I suppose---'

'Great. I expect you will have to wait a while at the Consulate. I'll see you back here as soon as you can. If I'm not here, I won't be far away. Just hang around.'

That suited Chas. He had a couple of things to do before he returned home, and another overnight stay would sit well with his plans.

Within minutes of Chas leaving her apartment, Lizzie was on the phone to Claude Boulet. She told him that Chas was on his way to the British Consulate to obtain papers that would allow him back into the UK.

'I don't know what it is about this man, but I just have a hunch that he is in some way involved in the Tommy Williams business. He's acting a bit cagy. I still don't know his name. Every time I've asked him, he has managed to change the subject.'

'What do you want me to do?' Claude replied.

'My thinking is that we could find out a lot about him if the Consulate would pass on some details about him.

97

Obviously, I haven't got the authority to ask them, but you have, as a Commissaire. If you were to ask them to forward at least his name and address, we could get the British police to make contact with him if we need them to.'

'Yes, I understand. Good idea, Lizzie. I'll get on to it right away. If you don't know his name, can you give me a description?'

Lizzie offered a very detailed portrayal of Chas and was pleased that her observational powers were once again being of use. This evening she would try to extract more details from him. She was sure she had him hooked.

Later in the morning, she took her place near Bear's emporium. The usual group of no-hopers was there but although there was still no sign of Bear, she sensed that something was happening. She joined the knot of dowdy dropouts and listened to their conversations. It seemed as if the drug trading was being resumed today, but without Bear. They had been told to go away and wait.

Lizzie thought it would be interesting to find out who would be conducting the business, so she decided to hang in there with the group.

# Chapter 19

The meeting with the Judge was scheduled for half past three, but Ben, Mary, Katie and Alex got to the rendezvous a half hour or so earlier in case Claude Boulet needed to speak to them before the meeting.

The only problem they had was what to do with Alex if all three of them were required simultaneously. He had had a good lunch before they left, and when they arrived, he was fast asleep. Chances were that he would sleep for an hour or more, so they hoped everything would work out.

The building was nothing like they expected. Situated in a small side street, it appeared from outside to be a residential house. Inside, they were taken to a waiting room that once would probably have been a dining room or lounge.

There was little conversation, but they did have a glimpse of Claude Boulet walking past the door of the waiting room. Whether he was on his way to or from the Judge it was impossible to say. At least they knew that he was here, and was talking to Mme Bervois.

A short time later they were called into a more formal room where the Judge was seated behind a large mahogany desk which was clear of any clutter. The only thing on her desk was a pink file containing the records of every interview with Tommy Williams and any witnesses.

Sitting to one side of the desk was Claude Boulet.

'I believe you have met Monsieur Boulet?' the Judge asked.

'I and my partner, Mary, have,' Ben replied. 'Our friend Katie has not.'

'But you understand why he is here?'

Ben replied again that they were all aware of that.

'In that case, we may begin. Mr Williams will join us in a few minutes. First of all, I have to say that what Monsieur Boulet has requested is quite unusual, and rather unorthodox. I have weighed up the benefits, and have on this occasion agreed to give his proposal a try.'

'Just one thing,' Ben said, addressing the Judge. 'Can I ask you to speak rather more slowly, otherwise neither Mary nor Katie will understand what is going on.'

'I'm sorry. I didn't realise that. Would it be better if we spoke in English?'

'That would be wonderful,' Katie replied.

'Then we shall.' she said.

The judge showed no suggestion of affability on her face. It was set firm. Her eyes, which Ben noticed switched from one person to another all the time she spoke, showed no emotion or feeling. It was clear that she was in charge. There would be no nonsense.

She used her intercom to ask for Mr Williams to be brought in.

When he walked into the room, he looked terrified. He had a woman with him who was introduced as his representative, and they sat next to each other on the opposite side of the desk to Claude Boulet.

'Let me say right from the start, that I am confused and puzzled by this case, and I want to go through exactly what happened on the day of the attack, detail by detail. That is why I have asked you all to be here. The only person who could not be here today is the old man from the farm.'

'Jean-Pierre,' Ben interjected.

'That's right. Apparently he is rather unwell and would have found it difficult to attend.'

Ben and Mary watched as Tommy Williams squirmed in his seat, nervously rubbing his hands together and trying desperately not to look either of them in the eye.

The judge said that she was going to start at the beginning of what she had read and wanted to be interrupted if anything she said was wrong or inaccurate.

'That way,' she concluded, 'we will be able to tidy things up as we go along.'

Opening the pink file, she commenced the strange story of how Mary was allegedly stabbed in her abdomen by Mr Williams, resulting in wounds that meant her having to be taken to intensive care in Angers.

Katie and Mary were the first to be asked to recollect the events, moment by moment. They were interrupted by the Judge on several occasions to ensure that she fully understood the sequence of events. Then it was Ben's turn to tell what he saw when he arrived at the house.

The judge then turned to the part that Ben and Jean-Pierre played in the detaining of Tommy Williams.

'Will you please try to explain to me what you were thinking of when you put a rope round the defendant's neck and strung him up to a joist?' There was considerable hostility in her voice and Ben took his time to attempt to justify his actions. Whether she was satisfied with his explanation, Ben could not tell.

'At one point, Mr Williams,' she said, 'you made a complaint about this treatment, but later withdrew the grievance. Is that right?' Tommy nodded.

'I would rather you answered the questions I put to you rather than nodding your head.'

'Yes,' Tommy said.

'And why did you withdraw your complaint?'

'It was when I realised what I had done. I could understand Mr Coverdale's reactions. I would probably have done the same.'

'I see. So you still do not want to take any action against him?'

'No.'

'Or against the man who had the shotgun?'

'No.'

As the Judge delved further into the story, the question was raised regarding the motives for the attack. Her attention again turned to the defendant who continued to insist that he heard voices telling him what to do.

Claude Boulet turned to him.

'I am Claude Boulet, a Commissaire of Police in Angers,' he said. 'I am involved in this case because we are investigating a man in Paris who goes by the name of Bear.'

For the first time, Tommy Williams gave himself away by showing his recognition of Bear's name.

'So you know him, then?' the Commissaire asked him. Tommy shook his head.

'Is that a "no"?'

Tommy nodded.

'I would advise you to think very carefully about this. I have reason to believe that in fact you *do* know of Bear. I have reason to believe that it was Bear who put you up for the attack, promising a substantial reward if you carried it out.'

Tommy shook his head.

'Mr Williams. Do you know what perjury is?'

Tommy nodded.

'Good. Then I want you to consider your situation. If you continue with your story of hearing these voices, and you are found to have lied, you will be serving a much longer sentence than you would by telling the truth.'

Tommy spoke with his representative in a whisper that nobody could hear. Then he caught Ben's eye for the first time, and quickly looked away.

The Judge continued. 'As the Commissaire has said, he is exploring the activities of this man, Bear. In fact, he is under surveillance as we speak for a number of illegal activities. So far, the police have not been able to convict him due to lack of evidence.'

'But,' Claude Boulet continued, 'all we need is someone who has enough courage to witness against him to be able to bring him to trial. Now, I believe you, Tommy, are the person to do this for us.'

There was no response from Tommy but he did look over to Ben again. Ben looked straight back at him, and raised his eyebrows, trying to help him make the right decision. Tommy spoke again to the woman sitting at his side and eventually spoke.

'Yes, you are all right. I was asked to carry out the attack by Bear. Actually, it was supposed to be an assassination, but it all went wrong. I lied because I knew what would happen to me when Bear found out what had happened.'

'But this isn't the same as your theory is it, Mr Coverdale? You thought that someone else was responsible. Am I right?'

'Yes,' Ben replied. 'I'm still convinced that the man behind this is Donald O'Hanlon.'

'So do you know this man, Bear?'

'No.'

'Do you know of any connection between him and Bear?'

'No.'

'So we still have no substantiation for your beliefs.'

'No,' Ben said as he watched the Judge making copious notes.

There were some minutes of silence as the Judge read through her notes.

'So, Mr Williams,' she said, turning to face Tommy, 'Your story about stealing the motorbike and finding the knife are also untrue. How did you come by the bike and the weapon?'

'They were given to me by Bear.'

'He gave you a motorbike?'

'Yes, Ma'am.'

'Do you know why Bear wanted Mary Willson killed? Did he know her?'

'I don't think so, but he knew where she was living, and he gave me a photograph of her.'

'Is that all he gave you?'

'No. He also gave me some heroin and a small capsule, which I was to take a few minutes before I made the attack.'

'What was in the capsule?'

'I don't know. I didn't ask questions. You do what Bear tells you. He said that taking the capsule would help me to forget what I had done.'

'And it worked, as far as I can see from the medical reports.'

'Yes. I couldn't remember anything for a few days. Then it all started coming back to me, a bit at a time.'

'And now you can remember everything?'

'I think so, yes.'

The judge spent more time looking at her notes, and then abruptly rose from her chair, thanked everyone for attending, and left the room.

Claude Boulet and Ben both went over to thank and congratulate Tommy Williams for his courage in deciding to change his story.

'You won't regret it,' Ben said. 'You may well have helped us to get nearer the truth. Thanks.'

It was only when people started moving that Alex woke up, and made it clear that for him it was time to eat.

'I think that went quite well, didn't it?' Katie said.

'Except when Ben was questioned about the business in the barn,' Mary added. 'I thought you were going to be in real trouble there.'

'So did I,' Ben agreed. 'Why don't we pick something up for Alex, and then go along to Madame Delphine for something to eat. We haven't seen her for a while, and she'd love to see Alex.'

# Chapter 20

After his visit to Kintbury, Donald realised that his search for his missing money was going to be more difficult than he anticipated. He had to make some adjustments. Staying at the Travelodge was supposed to be a temporary measure until he had the finance with which to move on.

Now he found himself with dwindling funds and nowhere permanent to live. His 'Eureka!' moment came unexpectedly. Why he hadn't thought about it before, he couldn't imagine.

He had realised that he still had the keys to the house in Wallingford, and since the owner, Lucas, was now deceased, he wouldn't have to pay rent. As far as anybody knew, the house was deserted. To all outward appearances, it would remain that way.

The following morning he left the hotel early and drove out of London, onto the M1 to Leicester, where his furniture from the house he used to occupy in Wallingford was stored. He cursed himself now for storing everything so far away. At the time, he was looking for a cheap, no-questions-asked company. The result was his now having to drive one hundred and thirty miles and back again.

The journey took him nearly three hours and then he had to locate the storage depot. He was taken to his lock-up where he walked round, selected the pieces of furniture he needed - just the basics, none of the comforts - and arranged to have them delivered to Wallingford the next day.

He was there to meet the van when it arrived and helped to unload the few bits of furniture at top speed. Within half an hour the van was off on its return journey and Donald was back in his old house.

He had all of the furnishings taken up to one large room at the back of the house on the first floor. There was a single bed, a kitchen table with two chairs, an armchair, a small television and a microwave oven. There was also a box with some crockery, cutlery, a table lamp and some other odds and ends that he thought he might need.

It was getting dark when he left the house and walked to his car which he had parked some way up the road. This would be his last night at the Travelodge and meant he had to stop at a cashpoint to withdraw enough to be able to pay the hotel in cash.

The following morning Donald drove once more to Wallingford. The house was impressive, standing in its own grounds and secluded from other properties. He drove through the wrought iron gates and up the gravelled drive where he parked the car in order to open the doors to the double garage. As he manoeuvred the car into the garage it reminded him of the time he had misjudged the available space and had scraped the paint on the near side of Mary's treasured Mini Cooper. She was so upset that he had to arrange, there and then, for it to be re-sprayed the following day. To this day there remained a red smudge on his front bumper.

Once inside the house, the first thing he did was to activate the alarms, locking every door and window, only then making his way up to the room that he had set aside for his use.

Now he had to make some plans. Lucas's funeral was in two days' time, and he knew he had to be there, not as a guest, just an observer. He wondered if he would have been on the guest list. It was a possibility. After all, he was Lucas's friend, but he had not received an invitation.

What interested him most was who else would be there. Were the police investigations serious enough for them to make an appearance? It was essential therefore, that he played his game carefully, considered all eventualities, prepared for any surprises, whilst remaining unnoticed.

*****

Chas made his way to Madeleine station without any problem. Finding his way from the station to the British Consulate, however, caused him problems. He knew it was only a short walk, but he must have gone round the block several times before he came across the modest building. He came to the conclusion that he must have walked straight past it on at least one occasion not realising it was there.

The people at the Consulate were very helpful and accommodating. He gave them all the information they requested to enable them to be satisfied that he was who he said. They even took a photograph of him to compare with passport records held at Newport.

'This might take some time,' he was told.

He said that he would call back later in the day to see how things were going, and asked where the best supermarket was. A woman standing beside him told him that there was a large *Intermarché* not far away, and that he would be sure to find everything he needed there.

His shopping list was long and varied – nail varnish, car reversing light bulbs, playing cards, analogue watches, fire-lighters - the list went on. He should find some, but not all, of the items at the supermarket. The rest would have to be sourced elsewhere.

The *Intermarché* was vast and it took him well over half an hour to walk through all the aisles, picking up many of the required items.

He now had most of the things he wanted. The only things missing from his list were a battery-operated soldering iron and fine wire, which he found in a tool shop close by.

What was needed now was some peace and quiet.

Plenty of both were to be found at the Église Saint-Roch, a beautiful Roman Catholic Church not far from the supermarket. He sat for a few minutes in the garden surrounding the church before walking into the cool, dark magnificence of the Church's interior.

Positioning himself at the back of the church, he put on the pair of latex gloves, and wiped each item to erase any tell-tale fingerprints. Silently, he sorted out the contents of his shopping bag, laying the items out on the pew beside him and then covering them with the bag.

He could have done this blindfolded, but he had to be able to take his time. First, he took the three watches apart, which was difficult in the darkness. Then the elaborate, meticulous work began.

On the two occasions that people wandered into the church, Chas stopped what he was doing and pretended to be meditating. He was not disturbed.

The intricacy of his work took him over an hour to complete, his eyes straining from the lack of light. Eventually he was able to put all the unused elements of his handiwork back into the bag.

With the three completed items secured within rubber bands and secreted in the hooded fleece he was wearing, he left the church. He left behind a cocktail of aromas of nail varnish, sulphur, paraffin and hot metal. Once away from the church he discarded the plastic bag and its contents into a litter bin and made his way back to the Consulate.

## Chapter 21

Madame Delphine had treated them all to another sumptuous meal. As they expected, Alex was the centre of attention. It was becoming a habit now that Madame Delphine would take him to be shown off to all her customers and kitchen staff. It was as if he was her own grandson, and Alex revelled in the attention.

The relief of having the interview with the judge behind them showed on each of their faces, helped in no small way by the amount of wine they had consumed.

It was dark by the time Ben, Mary, Katie and Alex got back to *La Sanctuaire*. Katie was the first to go to bed, whilst Mary prepared Alex, who really didn't want to wake up, for his night's sleep.

'Are you coming up?' she asked Ben as she took their sleepy son up to his bed.

'Not just yet,' Ben replied. 'I'd like to talk to you.'

'We can do that in bed, can't we? I'm really tired.'

'Yes, you're right. I'll be up in a few minutes then.'

'Don't leave it any longer or I'll be asleep.'

Ben watched her as she made her way up the narrow staircase. She was still as beautiful as the first day he had set eyes on her. Her chestnut hair had grown back to its original shoulder length, having recovered from the short style that Donald had insisted she wore. Once again, she had her hair

111

in the natural ringlets that Ben had always loved. Her naturally olive skin was even darker now from the effect of the summer's sunshine, and Ben thought her figure was more appealing now than it had ever been.

He locked the front door, turned off the lights, and then went up to join Mary.

It was good to feel her in his arms. He remembered the times when she was not with him; firstly when she left him to live with Donald, and more recently while she was in hospital recovering from the knife attack. He had missed her terribly. Now she was back, and life was much more fulfilling.

'What did you want to talk about?' Mary asked.

'It's more a question, really.'

'OK. What did you want to ask me, then?'

Ben thought about what he wanted to ask, and how to ask it.

'Well?' she said.

'Will you marry me?' Ben almost blurted out.

It was Mary's turn to cause a delay, while Ben was nervous about her answer. What if she declined? How would he feel then?

She turned her face toward him, her dark brown eyes reflecting the light from the bedside lights.

'Is that what you want?' she asked.

'I wouldn't have asked if I didn't want it.'

Her face lit up as her smile spread across it.

'Then, Mr Coverdale, I would love to marry you.'

Ben found himself having to check the tears that were forming in his eyes, and their two bodies entwined until they appeared to be one. They did not make love, neither of them had the energy after such a demanding, draining day. Within minutes, Ben was aware of her almost silent snoring.

Chas was relieved to see that the usual gaggle of addicts were not to be seen on Rue de Maubeuge. He walked towards the second-hand furniture shop and briefly perused the window before entering.

The range and quality of the goods on display impressed him. The usual tatty element found in many a similar shop was absent here. He wandered around each of the three floors, looking at a range of items in more detail. He didn't hurry. He had plenty of time, and there was no sign of sales assistants anywhere. He guessed it was some kind of cash and carry arrangement.

By the time he had examined each of the floors, he knew exactly where he would position his little packets. He must not push them down into the soft furnishings. That would result in the fire being put out before it took hold. He had to place each one under a piece of furniture that would ignite easily. How thoughtful of manufacturers to aid his cause by telling him which were fireproofed and which were not!

The three watches had been set as accurately as possible to react within minutes of each other.

As casually as he had walked in, he left the building and walked the short distance to Lizzie's apartment. She answered the door with a smile and invited him in.

'How did it go?' Lizzie enquired.

'Absolutely fine. I had to wait a while as you predicted, but at least I can get back into the UK without any trouble. Is it OK if I take a shower?'

'Of course. No problem.'

'Got to look my best for our evening out.'

'Of course.'

Lizzie smiled. She was sure he was hoping for a lot more than he was going to get.

Chas took his time in the shower. He wanted to ensure that there was no chance of any tiny fragments of incendiary material left on him if anyone were to trace him back to her apartment.

When he emerged from the bathroom, Lizzie had set out two glasses and a bottle of wine.

'Help yourself,' she called from the little kitchen.

Chas did as he was asked.

'Did you get a new passport?'

'No. I just got the appropriate papers to get me through customs. I'll have to apply for a new passport when I get back.'

'Will you be going back tomorrow?'

'Yes. I'll get away early morning. I can't impose on you any longer.'

'You're not imposing. I'm glad to have met you – hey, I still don't know your name!'

Chas had no excuse any more, but played a cautious game.'

'Matthew,' he said, 'but everyone calls me Matt.'

'Right, Matt. I feel I know you a bit more now. Shall we go and eat?'

'Fine by me. Can we try somewhere different this evening?'

'What do you fancy?'

'To be honest, I love Italian food. Is there a ---'

'I know the very place. It's a bit further to walk, but it's worth it.'

The evening went well. Lizzie was intent on finding out more about him, and Chas was inventing a new, fictitious life with which to impress her.

For most of his life he had been in the army, he told her, working his way up through the ranks to sergeant. He had seen a bit of the world and was made redundant when his regiment, the west Midlands was merged with others to form the Mercian Regiment. Since then he had drifted from one job to another, but was now hopeful that something might come from this man called Bear. He needed something more permanent, he said.

His storytelling was very convincing. A little of it was based on truth, the periods of his incarceration were filled with situations he had often imagined combined with things that he had read. Nonetheless, the overall picture of his parallel existence was believable.

He learned a little more of her life, not realising that her account was as fabricated as his.

It was a balmy Parisian evening, and they stayed as long as they could before making their way back to her apartment.

'I shouldn't be as late back tonight,' she said as she left. 'So you might be awake when I get in.'

'May well be, unless I get too bored with French TV.'

'Oh, I'm sure you can find a few channels that will interest you. You won't need to understand French, either!'

'Sounds good to me,' Chas said as she disappeared out of the apartment. He listened to her heels clipping their way down the stairs. He had increasingly expectant feelings for the night to come.

## Chapter 22

Donald set off for the short journey from Wallingford to Kintbury to attend Lucas's funeral, allowing plenty of time. He wanted to find a good vantage point from which he could observe what was going on, without being seen himself. He knew that if he went too close, Angela would be sure to recognise him.

He was interested to see who was attending and, indeed, who was not.

When he arrived in the village, he spent some time deciding exactly where to park his car. If things went wrong, he needed to be able to get away quickly. He had studied a map of Kintbury, and decided that his best option for parking was at the bottom end of Station Road. This gave him a choice of several ways to and from the church and an easy drive out of the village, should that be necessary. There were no parking restrictions and he found a small lay-by in which to leave his car.

He had more than enough time to reconnoitre the area and walked each of the three routes to the church. He decided that no one route was better than another and concentrated on selecting a good viewpoint.

Trees surrounded the church. There was no problem with finding a hiding place. He would be able to see everything whilst being camouflaged by the bushy foliage.

Caution was his catchword today. He returned to his car and drove out of the village. He still had plenty of time to spare and found a pleasant pub some five miles away where he enjoyed a very pleasant steak and a pint of beer from a local brewery.

Still leaving enough time for him to get settled in his hiding place, he drove back to the village and was relieved to find that his space in the lay-by was still available.

Grabbing his binoculars from the glove compartment, he walked to the church, and up the narrow paved pathway that led to the entrance. Glancing into the dark interior, he walked straight on, veering left into the cool cover of the shrubs and trees, and waited.

Back at Lucas's house, Angela was carrying out her duties with outward consummate ease. Inside, her nerves were rattling. As confident as she was, this was something new to her. She didn't know any of the people who came through the front door. The only person she knew was her mother, and little use she was for support.

The morning had started strangely enough when a man who said he was from the press and wanted to know if it was acceptable for him to attend the funeral approached her. She explained that she had already told their reporter the time and date of the funeral and therefore expected them to be present.

'Who did you talk to? I don't remember anything about that.'

'I can't remember. I think his name was Martin something-or-other.'

'That's strange. We don't have a reporter by that name. Not to worry. So I presume it's OK by you if I make an appearance.'

'Of course. Did you manage to use the photographs I gave to the other man?'

'Photographs? I don't think we received any photographs in the newsroom. I'll look into this when I get back to the office.'

She had also received a phone call from the police advising her that a plain-clothes police officer would be at the funeral, which she found unnerving.

'Is that necessary?' she asked, and was told that it was only precautionary, whatever that meant.

By now, the house was full, and the chattering that had been subdued at the start was increasing in volume by the minute. It was a respite when the hearse arrived along with three large black limousines.

The funeral director ushered people to the cars and she and her mother rode in the hearse the short distance to the church.

The guests left their cars and snaked their way up the narrow path and into the church. Then she and her mother, who didn't seem to be taking in what was happening, followed the coffin into the church and sat on their own in a pew at the front.

After that, she was on autopilot and realised afterwards, that she could not remember anything that had been said. It was a cold, unfeeling service. It seemed that nobody was here out of choice, but because they ought to be. Did her father have any real friends? When she thought about it, she realised she knew the answer. No, he didn't. When she lived at home she never saw him with friends of his own; just business colleagues.

She remembered her mother having her own circle of friends. Where were they today? Had she been abandoned as well?

Angela told herself that she had to get back to the States as soon as she could. She would suffocate in this horrible atmosphere.

Suddenly the service was over. The pallbearers took the coffin away, and she and her mother had to follow. She nudged her mother, pulling her out of her pew. She had been asleep! How awful, to be so doolally that you don't even know that they are about to bury your husband! What was she going to do with her?

Painfully slowly, the undertakers brought the coffin out of the church and back down the path to the hearse.

This is what Donald had been waiting for but now he realised that he was in the wrong place after all. As the guests came out from the church, they all turned away from his view.

As carefully as he could he had to move further towards the entrance to the church. Now he had a better view. Binoculars to his eyes, he inspected each person in turn. It wasn't hard to pick out the plain-clothes copper. How did they make themselves so obvious?

What made him stop in his tracks was seeing someone he *did* recognise. Niels was here! He had only met him the once in Amsterdam, but there was no mistaking his scraggy form, his dark skin and his bald head that reflected the hazy sunshine.

Donald continued studying the emerging guests, but he could only centre his thoughts on Niels and of how he could get to him. It seemed an impossible task, but somehow he had to manage it. This man must have the answers to the one question that bugged him day and night. Where was the money?

He followed his target, out of sight, down to the road and saw him get into the second of the limousines. The "incognito" police officer crossed the road and got into his own car.

Donald remained crouched under a large shrub until all the cars had disappeared, only then allowing himself to stand and walk out onto the road and back to his car.

The funeral procession had driven away from where he had parked his car. It was a simple matter for him to follow at a discreet distance. The unmarked police car had disappeared. Either it was ahead of the hearse, or the officer had given up and returned to the local police station. At least he now knew which was the police car, and could keep a lookout for it when he arrived at wherever he was going.

The procession sped up once it had left the village and Donald dropped back further allowing a few other vehicles to position themselves between him and the limousines. He could still see the cortege clearly enough to determine when they turned off. The short journey was mainly through narrow country lanes until he saw the four black vehicles turn off through a five-bar gate into what looked like a large field. There was a notice outside announcing that this was "Barley Ridge", a cemetery for those who wished to be interred with dignity.

Donald drove straight past and stopped a few hundred metres further down the lane, parking his car in a farm gateway, which did not appear to be in use. Once again, he had to find a suitable vantage point from where he could see what was going on. The only person who really interested him was Niels.

There was not as much cover here as there was at the church and he could not see that there would be any opportunity to waylay the man here. The best he could hope for was that Niels would return to the house for the wake.

Returning to his car, he drove back to his previous parking space in Kintbury from where he would be able to see the cortege returning.

# Chapter 23

The atmosphere at *La Sanctuaire* was light and cheerful, matching the early morning sunshine and cooling breeze outside.

Ben was in the kitchen making the first pot of coffee when Mary joined him. She pulled him to her and kissed him languorously on his lips.

'Good morning,' Ben said in mock surprise. 'What have I done to deserve that?'

'Do you not remember last night?'

'Last night? Oh, yes. It was a lovely meal wasn't it? But it hardly deserved a kiss like that.'

'Not the meal, idiot. You do remember what you asked me, last night, don't you?'

'Remind me,' Ben said wanting so much to laugh.

'I seem to recall, Mr Coverdale that you asked me to become Mrs Coverdale.'

Ben tried to look bemused.

'Or was it just the wine?' Mary said.

'Well, I guess that all depends on what your reply to my question was.'

Mary's eyes narrowed as she looked at him, hoping to see him smile or even smirk. There was no sign of either.

'I said yes.' she said.

'Bloody hell. Did you?' Ben replied. 'Mind you, you did have more than your share of the wine as I recall.'

Ben was beginning to think that he was digging a very deep hole for himself and in the end he burst into laughter.

'You should have seen your face,' he said.

'You really are a horrible man. You know that?' Mary retorted before being pulled into his arms.

'Will we be getting married over here, or in England?' she asked.

Ben told her that he had looked into the possibility of having the wedding in France but, while he liked the idea, he had been put off by all the 'red tape'.

'You've no idea,' he told her, 'the amount of paperwork involved, mostly in triplicate, and much of it originals. They won't accept copies. It would take a lot of time and effort.'

'You've obviously been thinking about this a lot,' she said. 'So it's not on, then?'

'If that's what you would really like, then we'll do it.'

'But?'

'But I think the easiest way is to have a civil ceremony in the UK. Then, if you would like a church wedding, we can arrange a kind of 'blessing' service over here.'

'That might be nice. But I'm not a religious person as you well know. As far as I'm concerned, just being married to you will be enough for me.'

As was so often the case, Katie walked in on their conversation.

'Did I hear the magic word?'

'Magic word?' Ben said

'Yes. Are you two getting married?'

'Yep. Mary thinks it's about time she made an honest man of me,'

'Brilliant news,' Katie said, kissing each of them in turn. 'When?'

'We haven't thought about that yet, but there's nothing holding us back, so I guess quite soon. We'll be having the wedding in England, not here. How long notice do we have to give, Ben?'

'I think it's two or three weeks for a special licence. I'll have to check to make sure.'

'That would give us plenty of time to get organised.'

'I'll check everything on the internet today, and see what we have to do.'

There were more hugs all round before Alex let them know that he needed his breakfast.

*****

Lizzie got back to her apartment just before midnight. Chas was still awake. He had spent most of the evening fantasising what the night might bring. The images of her padding around in her flimsy French underwear earlier in the day would not go away. They had spent another relaxed, friendly evening together. He must surely be on a promise tonight.

'I'll just put some coffee on and then I'm going to have a shower. Is that OK? Help yourself to coffee if you want.'

Chas thought that was absolutely OK as he listened to her showering, his mind working overtime.

When she returned, she was wearing a long flowing nightdress. It was only just opaque, and Chas thought he could detect enough of what was underneath the gown to be pretty certain that she was wearing nothing else.

124

She smelled good, too, as she brought in the coffees and sat on a chair facing him.

'I'll say goodnight, then, Matt. See you in the morning.'

Chas looked up at her as she left her chair.

'I – er – just wondered if I could ---'

'If you could what?'

'You know – er – if you're feeling lonely, or anything.'

'What? You want to come to bed with me? You want to screw me?'

'Well, I thought ---'

'Well, you thought wrong. You thought very wrong. I don't know how you have the audacity to think that. What is it with British men? One glimpse of breast or bum and you think you have the right ---'

'I'm sorry. I didn't mean to upset you, Lizzie. I thought the signs were there, but obviously I was mistaken.'

'Too right you were. I want you out of here first thing in the morning. I ought to throw you out right now, but I'll let you stay until the morning. Then it's goodbye. Is that clear?'

She was pleased with her performance. Making him squirm had given her some perverse pleasure. It was not something she made a habit of, but she had read his mind from the moment she had walked, scantily dressed, into the room the previous day.

Chas felt very small and utterly dejected. He was just dozing off when he heard the sounds of a disturbance nearby. He didn't react. He pretended to be asleep.

Lizzie was woken, not by the external noises, but by her mobile phone buzzing. She checked to see who the call was from and sent a text back.

*Can't speak. Please text.*

A few moments later she saw the text arrive on her handset.

*Just heard that the premises you are supposed to be watching have been torched. Get back to me asap.*

Lizzie replied:

*Can't leave flat at the moment. Have my suspect here.*

After a minute she received another text.

*Your suspect? Do you think he had anything to do with the fire?*

Lizzie sent a reply saying that she didn't see how he could be responsible as he had been with her since early evening, and had been busy sorting out his UK entry papers before that.

*Mind you,* she added, *I wouldn't put anything past him.*

She was told to watch him very carefully for any signs of involvement. She wanted to go out to observe what was happening, but she had to put up with listening to the hubbub down the road.

She would find out as much as she could in the morning as soon as Matt had left.


Lizzie got up soon after six o'clock and walked into the room where Matt was beginning to wake. This time she was fully dressed, and she kept up her fierce attitude although, if she was honest, she quite liked this man. She doubted that he had been truthful with her, but she had no way of substantiating that.

'Come on,' she said brusquely. 'I want you out of here.'

'OK,' Matt replied. 'What's that smell? Has somebody burned the toast?'

'Yes, it is a bit smoky. A bit more than toast, I think,' she replied, watching him intensely. She could see no sign of any reaction on his face. He was concentrating on getting dressed.

'Coffee?' she called to him.

'If it's allowed,' he replied.

'Just coffee. Don't let your Englishman's imagination think anything else.'

'I think you've made your point, Lizzie, and I am sorry, I really am. I made a complete fool of myself last night.'

'Well that's true,' she said, bringing his drink over to where he was urgently packing things into his bag.

'You've got your papers?'

He tapped his breast pocket and nodded.

'Yes. I think they'll let me in OK. Thanks for your help.'

He drank his coffee as rapidly as he could, and Lizzie saw him to the door.

'Best of luck,' she said as he walked away, down the dark staircase to the road below.

By the time he rounded the corner on his way to Gare du Nord station, she was out on the street herself, running to catch sight of him.

She saw him cross over the road to the pavement on the opposite side to the burnt out warehouse, but he took just a cursory glance toward the building, keeping up his normal pace.

If he has any responsibility for this, she thought, he most certainly is a pro.

The smoke and the water that had been pumped into the building had left it blackened with few windows remaining in the upper floors. The whole of the road had been cordoned off. Lizzie did not want to break her cover and had to wait for an opportunity to talk to one of the fire crew. She asked what had started the fire, but he was unable to offer much information.

'We won't be able to start investigations until the fire is completely under control. At the moment there are still pockets of fire on the second floor.'

'Have you any idea when it started?'

'Not exactly. Early hours of the morning, we think. We got the call at half past two.'

'And it's still burning now. Must have been quite a blaze.'

'Yes. At one point we thought we might have to evacuate people from the surrounding buildings, but we didn't have to in the end.'

That was enough for Lizzie to be able to report back to her station, but before she managed to do that, she had a call from Claude Boulet in Angers.

**Chapter 24**

Katie was alone at *La Sanctuaire*. Ben and Mary had decided that the only way to get everything moving for the wedding was to take a short break in the UK. She had waved goodbye to them earlier in the morning and was bursting with anticipation at the thought of seeing Antoine again after lunch.

It was a beautiful morning. There wasn't a cloud in the sky and the beginnings of autumn were evident all around. It was so peaceful. The distant mooing of cows and the sounds of birds gave the morning a placid, homely feel.

Following Ben's example, she made herself a strong coffee, grabbed a couple of croissants and made her way down to the patio by the stream. She was happy to do nothing more than listen to the sounds of autumn and try to imagine what the afternoon would bring.

She had the whole day to herself. The visitors from Dairy Cottage had already left to follow a Joan of Arc trail that Ben had put together for the guests.

An hour passed before she knew it, and she made her way back to the cottage where she took her time pampering herself. She luxuriated in a warm scented bath before attending to anything else. It was a treat to be able to spend time on herself like this. It was a while since she had any reason to do such a thing. She had hardly been enjoying a hectic social life since Antoine had gone AWOL.

Climbing out of the bath, she realised that her skin was much more tanned now, after the long hot summer. Some of her makeup simply would not suit her new skin tones. She had to dig deep to find the right eye shadow and liner to make the most of her azure blue eyes. Then there was the foundation. Nothing seemed right and in the end, she decided to go natural.

These days she always wore her hair down, mainly to protect her neck from catching too much sun. Today, she decided to try something different, and with the help of some hairspray and a handful of hairpins, she wore it up.

She applied deep red, almost burgundy, nail varnish to finger and toe nails, and only then got round to choosing what to wear.

It was rare for her to wear a bra, but today she chose a white lacy one and a matching thong. Over that she wore a loose summery, floral top and white shorts that showed off her tanned legs to perfection. She didn't wear anything on her feet.

Before going downstairs to pour herself a chilled Chardonnay, she inspected herself in the full-length mirror in her bedroom. She approved of her handiwork. It was nice to dress up for such a special occasion. She had really missed Antoine and she was now counting the minutes before they could be together again.

She had just over half an hour to wait before she expected Antoine to arrive. She didn't know whether they would be staying in or going out. She hoped the former. She was eager to find out where he had been for the last two weeks. It would be much better then, to be able to unwind at *La Sanctuaire* and catch up on each other's news.

The relative coolness of the lounge with its slate tiles and thick stone walls made relaxing very easy for her, and before she realised the time, there was a knock on the door.

With her heart pounding, she ran to open it.

Antoine pushed his way in and grabbed her into his arms, kissing her passionately. Perhaps a bit too passionately, she thought.

His mouth was pressed to hers so forcefully that she could feel his teeth on her lips. She tried to release herself from the embrace, but could not push him away. Now his tongue was forcing its way into her mouth, and attempting to reach her tonsils.

She built up one last effort and managed to disengage herself from him. He may be pleased to see me, she thought, but I don't think I like this.

'I've just opened a bottle of Chardonnay,' she said, pretending that nothing untoward had happened.

'Forget the wine,' he said. 'It's you I want. Come on.'

Seizing her by the wrist, he hauled her behind him up the narrow staircase to her bedroom.

Katie was becoming nervous. Antoine had always been the perfect gentleman – kind, gentle, loving. What the hell was going on? She was pleased to see him, and she hoped that he reciprocated the feeling, but he had changed and it was not a change for the better. Could this really be the same man?

No sooner were they in the bedroom than he started to undress her. More precisely, he started to rip her clothes from her. First, her flowery top was torn away, her pretty bra was pushed up under her armpits, and his hands were on her perky breasts. She felt that he was trying to pop them like little balloons. On all previous sessions he had been so gentle, almost worshipping her body. Today he was rough.

His hands looked huge, squeezing her tits and pinching her nipples until she screamed.

'For fuck's sake, Antoine,' she shouted. 'You're hurting me!'

He took no notice, but threw her on her back onto the bed so hard that she bounced back off the mattress before he leaned over her and put one hand over her mouth whilst attempting to undo his shorts with the other. His efforts were in vain and he abandoned the task.

Instead, his hands were now on the waistband of her shorts, which he pulled down over her bum with one sharp tug. Her legs were pulled up into the air and the shorts tossed away onto the floor beside the bed.

'Jesus, Antoine!' Katie yelled.

There was no stopping him now. Her pretty, lacy thong was literally torn from her and joined her other discarded clothes on the floor. She was now at his mercy, and she didn't think he was going to show her any.

Before she could move, Antoine positioned himself so that he was sitting on her stomach, facing her, while trying again to relieve himself of his shorts. This time he managed it without any trouble, and held her in a supine position while he removed them completely.

Katie looked up at him and couldn't help but notice that he was sporting an enormous erection.

Antoine had not uttered a word since they had reached the bedroom. He had a weird, stony, expressionless look in his eyes, far from loving.

His onslaught was merciless. She lost all sense of time. She just wanted it to end. He seemed insatiable, acting like a wild animal with no consideration for her at all.

Her repeated requests for him to stop were met with more smacks, more violent reactions.

She wasn't averse to rough sex. She had, on occasions, instigated it and often enjoyed it, but this was fierce and brutal. This was rape and she was determined that one way or another he would live to regret it.

After what seemed an eternity, she could hear his breathing increasing in intensity and speed. He was exhausting himself. She was aware of his sweatiness and could actually feel drops of perspiration dripping onto her back as he continued to abuse her. It must end soon. All she could do was grit her teeth, put up with the pain and wait for him to fulfil his perverted desire.

With a series of grunts and cries that were more suited to the jungle than her bedroom, Katie realised that it was over. She immediately moved away from him, glancing back to see a patchwork of stains on her bedcover which included signs of blood.

She ran from the room, almost tripping down the stairs to the kitchen. She didn't know what to do next, but saw Ben's favourite kitchen knife on the worktop. It wasn't big – about five or six inches in length – but it was the first thing she laid her hands on. She glanced down at her legs and saw that she was bleeding, which only increased her fury.

Back in the bedroom, Antoine was coming round from his extreme exertion and he looked up as she entered the room, smiling again which infuriated her even more.

Katie ran towards him with knife in her hand, but he reached out, caught her by her thigh, and pulled her back onto the bed, flinging her like a rag doll onto her back. The knife landed somewhere on the floor.

'You want some more?' he said.

'I doubt very much whether you'd be able,' Katie replied.

'Well, let's just see, shall we?' he smirked. He was about to position himself over her when she raised both her legs, and, using the little remaining strength she could muster, toppled him off her and onto the floor. Such was the effort that she lost her balance, and tumbled off the bed after him landing full force on top of him, her right knee ending up firmly in his crotch.

Antoine let out the loudest scream that she had ever heard. He was doubled up with pain, grasping his genitals in a vain attempt to stem the agony.

Katie had no feelings other than hatred. She went round to the other side of the bed and picked up the knife.

Shaking with rage, she stood over Antoine with the knife raised like a dagger and she saw horror in his eyes. He was no longer able to protect himself.

'Don't worry, Antoine. I'm not going to kill you. You're not worth it. But if you come anywhere near me ever again you'll be going away minus your manhood and speaking in a very high voice. Do you understand?'

There was no response from Antoine.

'DO YOU UNDERSTAND ME?' she screamed.

Antoine nodded. Was there just a glimmer of remorse or guilt on his face?

'Now, get up and get the fuck out of this house. Now! Before I change my mind and cut your balls off here and now.'

While Antoine was trying to move, Katie set about carving up his shirt, shorts and trainers with the knife and threw the resulting bundle of rags at him. Then she stood back and waited for him to stand upright, still nursing his pride.

Still with the knife in her hand, she watched as he walked past her and down the stairs to the front door.

Katie followed him downstairs and locked the front door behind him.

The shower felt cool on her skin, washing away just some of the shame, the humiliation and the guilt. She was sore, her bum stung from all the slapping as the shower gel reached it. Her scalp was sore from the hair pulling and she was sure there would be bruises all over her body by tomorrow. She soaped her body three times and still felt dirty.

She studied her image as she dried herself. This was a different Katie; not the pampered one she had looked at just a few hours before. Even during the awful time she had when she was kidnapped and incarcerated in Germany she had not felt, nor looked like this. The outward appearance was the same but inside she felt she had been poisoned.

She was beginning to wonder if, in some way, she had deserved this. Maybe she had provoked him, and triggered something within him.

She was still trembling after drying her skin. Returning to her bedroom, she flung the stinking, stained bed covers on the floor and curled up in a foetal position in the corner of her bed against the wall, cuddling a pillow.

And sobbed her heart out.

## Chapter 25

B en, Mary and Alex had left *La Sanctuaire* in glorious sunshine, but the further north they drove the heavier the clouds became and by the time they reached Caen, it was pouring with rain.

'Isn't this just typical,' Mary said. 'As soon as you get near to England, the weather takes a turn for the worse.'

'It just makes you appreciate the Loire Valley all the more,' Ben replied.

They had decided to stay for a few days in the UK to sort out a number of things. The priority was to make sure that they could book the wedding and that there were no complications due to them residing in France.

Mary wanted to talk to her ex-colleagues at *Hair Today*, the salon where she used to work. She would like Penny to do something special with her hair for the big day. She would also like to find a dress for the occasion. She had looked in a number of shops in Angers, and had seen some beautiful gowns, but nothing had really caught her imagination.

Ben needed to talk with his business partners. Things had not been going well recently for their IT business. He had been warned by Maurice, his ex-boss that their little back-door scheme into the search engines was about to backfire on them, and it certainly looked as if his prediction had been right.

He also wanted to talk with Maurice about tracing Donald. There were so many whizz kids working at SRX Solutions that he was sure somebody could conjure up a way to track him down.

The ferry crossing was better than they were expecting. The only disappointment was that the driving rain prevented them from spending time on deck. Ben always felt that travelling to the UK was a lacklustre journey. He much preferred the journey to France. There was so much more to look forward to.

Keeping Alex amused for the duration of the crossing was far from easy. On the whole, he was a good little boy. He looked angelic with his sun-bleached curls and wicked smiles, but he was a typical boy and wanted to be doing things all the time now. Ben and Mary took turns in walking him round the boat, visiting the shops and cafes.

Disembarkation could not come soon enough.

No sooner had they driven onto British tarmac than Alex was asleep in his comfortable car seat.

The journey to Katie's house in Reading was, thankfully, uneventful as Alex remained asleep for the entire journey.

Katie had given them the keys and told them to make themselves at home there for as long as they wanted.

'It seems an age since we lived in Reading,' Ben said as they settled in.

'Certainly brings back a lot of memories,' Mary replied. 'Good as well as bad.'

'Yeah. Those years together were good weren't they?'

Mary looked at Ben's face, and gave him a hug.

'They certainly were,' she said. 'Just a pity I ruined everything.'

Over coffee, later in the evening, when Alex had been settled into a carrycot, Ben and Mary sat and reminisced.

'D'you think Katie will come back here to live?' Mary asked Ben.

'I very much doubt it,' Ben replied. 'I think there's something quite serious going on between her and Antoine. I think they'll end up together eventually. I can't imagine Katie wanting to come back here after what happened to her before. She seems very happy in *Sainte-Justine* these days.'

'And in love,' Mary added

'Exactly. It is pretty obvious, isn't it?'

'Good for her then,' Mary said. 'Mind you, I find it hard to believe that she'll ever be a one-man girl. I think she'll find it difficult to behave herself.'

'You may well be right. Antoine will have to keep a careful eye on her. It won't be easy to tame our Katie! She'll get a good price for this house,' Ben said in order to change the subject. 'I know it needs a bit doing to it, but it's a nice house. Just imagine what she could get in France with the proceeds from this.'

They had decided to keep the visit to Reading as short as possible. They had left Katie on her own at *La Sanctuaire* and although they were confident that she would be able to cope with looking after their guests in the Dairy Cottage, they didn't want to take her for granted. They planned to be back before the weekend to help with the changeover.

The following morning, leaving Alex with his Daddy, Mary went to see if any of her favourite dress shops had anything that would inspire her.

She finally found a dress that she loved. It wasn't a bridal gown, more an expensive-evening-out dress, but it was so close to what she had in mind, that she couldn't resist it. When she tried it on, she was a little disappointed. It needed to be close fitting to make the most of her figure, and it wasn't.

'Is it possible to have some adjustments made to this?' Mary asked a young sales assistant.

'I'm not sure. I'll go and find out,' the girl replied.

Mary was surprised when a man in his forties, she presumed, approached her.

'How can I help you?' he asked in a strangely soprano, camp voice.

'I love this dress, but it needs to fit better. Can you make adjustments?' Mary explained.

'Oh, dear. I can see exactly what you mean. It needs to show off your lovely figure. Do you mind if I make a few suggestions?'

Mary shook her head, and the man grabbed a tin of dressmaker's pins and started to make his way round her, delicately using the pins to pull in the gown where it was necessary. It took him nearly a quarter of an hour to complete his task, but at the end he had made the dress fit like a glove.

'Is that better?' he asked.

'That's amazing,' Mary said.

'Then if you take the dress off, madam, very carefully, then I will get our seamstress to make these changes permanent.'

'And how long will that take?'

'We usually manage it in a week. Do you have a deadline?'

Mary told him that she lived in France, but that she was getting married, hopefully, in Reading in a few weeks' time.

'I won't be able to come in for another fitting before the actual day.'

'Lucky you, living in France!' he said. 'Whereabouts?'

'The Loire Valley,'

'Oh my. How beautiful!' he exuded then continued, 'Unless you gain or lose a lot of weight, I'm certain that our seamstress will be able to get it right first time. I'll tell her the circumstances so that she can be extra meticulous. Not too many of those delicious French pastries, eh?'

He had done enough to persuade Mary and she paid for the dress. She said she would let them know the date of the wedding as soon as she knew it herself, and would pick up the dress on the morning of the wedding.

While Mary was shopping, Ben was making some phone calls. He had tomorrow set aside to meet with his business partners and with Maurice. By mid-morning, he had the appointments made, and decided to take Alex for a walk down by the river at Caversham. It was a dull day, but at least it wasn't raining, and the walk and fresh air would do them both good, he thought. It wasn't long before they were strolling along the towpath beside the River Thames.

Alex was excited each time he saw a boat going past. 'Bo!' he said time after time, long after the vessel was out of sight. They stopped at a small cafe and Ben ordered his usual coffee, and treated Alex to a glass of milk, which he dealt with enthusiastically. Not much of it went where intended.

Ben enjoyed being out and about with his son. He was such fun. Even the smallest of things was exciting to him, dogs being walked, people chatting, kids playing. He never seemed to miss anything and chattered away, most of the time indecipherably.

Alex didn't want to ride in his pushchair today. He was happier trying to push it in a straight line. On more than one occasion, Ben had to avert an accident, but people just smiled at Alex. Everybody seemed to love him.

'Shall we go back and find Mummy?' Ben asked when he considered they had gone far enough.

Alex shook his head.

'But Mummy will wonder where we are. I think we should go home.'

'OK.' Alex said reluctantly, sounding so grown up.

Ben's mobile rang as they were approaching Katie's house. It was Mary.

'I'm going to be a bit longer than I thought,' she said. 'You won't believe it but Ray has invited me out for lunch.'

'I wonder what he wants,' Ben replied.

'I thought that as well. He never took me out to lunch when I worked for him.'

'I bet he'll try to persuade you to go back to work for him. You won't will you?'

'Of course not. I'll get home as soon as I can. There's plenty of stuff in the fridge for your lunch. Is Alex OK?'

'Yes, he's fine. We've been walking down by the river. He'll probably sleep this afternoon. Don't worry about the time, and enjoy your lunch.'

'Thanks, I will.'

Ben prepared food for them both, and smiled when Alex slowly gave up. His head, heavy with all the morning's activity, nodded further and further down onto his chest until he fell asleep.

Ben gently lifted him out of his chair and took him upstairs for his afternoon nap.

He thought it was such a sensible thing to do, that he lay on the bed beside Alex and fell into a deep sleep, waking only when he heard Mary return.

## Chapter 26

Donald could do nothing more than wait. Wait for what? He didn't know. He was as close to Niels and discovering his part in the deception with Lucas as he would ever be. He couldn't give up now. He might never get another chance.

He tried to picture several scenarios but abandoned that no sooner than he had started it. It was impossible to imagine or invent what might happen.

He had brought his car from its previous parking space and was now parked a few hundred metres up the road facing the house. He was far enough away not to be noticed, but close enough to see any movements in and out of the house.

He watched as the guests emerged from the black limousines and made their way into the house, checking until he saw Niels, on his own, walking up the driveway.

As time went on, he considered walking down to the house on the chance that Niels might be outside having a cigarette or something. If he had any virtues at all, patience was not one of them but he decided that such an action would probably produce nothing and risk his being seen. He must wait.

Eventually his loitering paid off. Small groups of guests started to leave. Using his binoculars, he could see each person and after a short while, he saw Niels's diminutive frame appear and turn down the road away from the house. Donald started the car and waited for the right opportunity to drive slowly down the road, keeping Niels in his sight. At the junction of the main road, Niels turned left, and a short distance along the road walked into a small car park.

The space next to Niels's black left-hand drive Nissan was unoccupied. Donald drove into the space watching his target opening the door to his car. Jumping out of his car, he grabbed Niels by his arm wrenching his fingers from the door handle.

He bundled Niels into the back seat of the Mercedes, and slammed the door.

Niels looked mystified.

'Surely you remember me, Niels? We did some business in Amsterdam a few weeks ago.'

'I don't remember. Who are you? What do you want?'

'I'm sure you do remember, my friend. Lucas and I met you in Amsterdam, and you bought some South African diamonds from us.'

'Oh, yes. I vaguely remember now.'

'Of course you do, because you never paid us for the diamonds! You would remember that, wouldn't you?'

Donald started the engine, and pulled out of the parking space.

'Where are we going? I have to get to Harwich.'

'We're going somewhere a bit more private, so that we can have a heart-to-heart chat. It won't take too long.'

Donald felt good. His plans were working out and he felt in control again. The twenty miles or so to Wallingford took very little time, and Donald spun the car into the wide driveway to his house, parking it out of sight to the rear of the property.

Walking to the back of the car, he dragged Niels out and frog-marched him to the front door, glancing round every now and then to make sure they were not being watched.

'Up the stairs,' he ordered. 'Don't try anything clever. I'm a lot bigger than you and I won't hesitate to hurt you.'

Donald took the man into the room that was being used.

'Sit down, Niels.'

Niels meekly obeyed. He was terrified, the whites of his eyes showing against his dark skin.

'OK, Niels. The last time I saw you, I was looking at a computer screen showing my bank details and a very considerable sum of money that was being transferred to it.'

There was no noticeable reaction from Niels.

'You told me that the money would be in my account in about three days. Do you remember now? We're talking two million pounds here.'

'Two million? That much?'

'A bit more than that, to be precise. All I know is that the money did not arrive in my bank. Not in three days, not ever. So what I want to know is, where is the money? Did Lucas double-cross me and tell you to pay it into his bank? Or perhaps you kept it for yourself and didn't pay it to anybody?'

'I don't recall any of this. You gave me the diamonds?'

'No I didn't give you the bloody diamonds, Lucas and I sold them to you. Of course you remember!'

'And you have some proof – a receipt, an invoice, an agreement? I don't do anything without paperwork.'

'You didn't give me any paperwork, you little worm.'

'You say that you saw all this on a computer screen? So you came to my offices in Amsterdam?'

'No. We met with you in your big black vehicle, fitted out as an office. You had your laptop there.'

'So you are saying that you handed over two million pounds worth of diamonds to a man in a black van in the middle of Amsterdam and you didn't even get a receipt? That is absurd.'

'Lucas told me you were a trusted friend of his. It was he who arranged the deal with you, but the diamonds were mine.'

Niels was beginning to look more relaxed now.

'I haven't seen Lucas since – let me see – it must be four or five years ago. It is true we are – or were – friends and we have dealt in diamonds in the past, but not just weeks ago. I think you've got this all wrong.'

Donald lost his cool. He launched himself at Niels and had his hands round his throat in a flash.

'Listen. I'm already suspected of murdering a girl in South Africa, being involved in a contract killing in France, and even the death of Lucas. One more on the list is not going to make a lot of difference to me.'

'You killed Lucas?'

'Well, as it happens, the police don't think so. They think he died from natural causes.'

'But you killed him!'

'I said I was suspected of killing him. I didn't say I did. It's the same with the other cases. I'm simply a suspect. Nobody has been able to prove anything.'

'So you think you might just get away with killing me as well.'

Donald let go of the man's throat, and offered him a menacing smile.

Niels went to get his mobile phone from his pocket, but Donald's hand swiped it from his grasp and sent it flying across the room. He then retrieved the phone, removed the sim card and paced up and down the room for many minutes.

'OK,' he said at last. 'We're both businessmen. We both like to make a profit, and neither of us, it seems, cares very much how we do it. So ---'

'So what? I should come clean about something I know nothing about? I should offer you a share in a deal that never happened?'

'You know fucking well that this deal happened. You know that you've defrauded either Lucas or me out of a couple of million. Tell me where the diamonds are or the money, then I'll let you go.'

'That's so benevolent. I don't even know who you are, and you certainly don't know who I am so ---'

'Wrong again, Niels. I can find you through your car registration. So easy to remember, aren't they – Dutch number plates?'

Donald was thinking that this was becoming more and more like a game of chess, each of them trying to predict the other's next move. He sensed that his control of the situation was waning. He had manoeuvred himself into an impasse. The man he had so wanted to get his hands on was sitting in front of him. His car was twenty miles away, and Donald realised that he was getting nowhere. How could he get a confession out of this weedy little individual? He didn't have the wherewithal to inflict anything nasty on him. No drugs, no gun, not even a sharp knife was to hand. It didn't look like there was any possibility of negotiation or compromise.

What could he do next?

## Chapter 27

When Katie awoke later in the afternoon, still in her protective position, she was cold and shivering. It took her a few seconds to make sense of the situation. Why on earth was she curled up and naked in the corner of her bed? Then she remembered and trembled at the recollections.

She reached down beside her bed and retrieved the bedclothes that she had deposited there. They still smelled of Antoine's sweat and the evidence of sex, but she needed something to warm her up.

It took her just a few minutes to feel more comfortable, and only then did she venture out of bed and into the bathroom for yet another shower, trying desperately to rid herself of the still remaining sensation of dirtiness.

She towelled herself dry, and went downstairs.

Having put on a pot of coffee, she sat at the kitchen table, head in hands and deep in thought. She didn't want to stay in the cottage on her own tonight, but didn't know where to go, or who to contact.

Why Madame Delphine came into her mind, she didn't know nor did it matter. It was an inspired idea. She picked up the telephone and dialled the number of the restaurant.

The call was answered in French, but Katie was not deterred. She knew that most of the people there spoke some English.

'Can I speak to Madame Delphine?'

*'Oui. Moment.'*

Katie waited on the end of the phone. She had no idea what she would say, but she didn't have to wait long.

'Madame Delphine.'

'Oh, Madame Delphine, this is Katie. I need to ask you a favour.'

'Katie! How nice to hear from you. What can I do for you?'

'Do you have a room free for a couple of nights?'

'I have just one room vacant. It's not the best room by any means, but you can have that, if you like. Is it for you or one of your friends?'

'It's for me. I'm in a bit of a state. I just have to get away from the cottage.'

'My dear girl, whatever has happened? Is Ben not there?'

'No. He and Mary are in the UK. Please, can I come straight away?'

'Of course you can. Would you like me to send someone to pick you up? No, even better, I will come myself. You just wait there. It will take me just a few minutes to get there.'

'Oh, thank you, Madame Delphine. Please be as quick as you can.'

'I'm on my way now. Stay calm. I'll be there in minutes.'

While she waited, Katie packed a few clothes into a bag and did her best to hide the tell-tale signs of tears and anguish with a touch of blusher.

Madame Delphine was true to her word and Katie heard her sweep her open top sports car into the gravelled driveway. She went out to greet her.

They hugged tightly and the kisses Katie received were real, genuine signs of their friendship. All of Katie's efforts in hiding her feelings were futile. She burst into tears again, sobbing into Madame Delphine's shoulder. She could feel the warmth of the older woman's hands stroking her back until they separated briefly.

'Come on then, let me take you away from here, and when you're ready, and only then, you can tell me all about it.'

Other than Katie's snuffles, the journey was in silence. Katie didn't know how or when to start to describe what she had been through that afternoon.

When they walked into the restaurant, Katie was sure that everyone was looking at her. She averted her eyes, looking at the carpet pattern as she followed Madame Delphine into a small office behind the kitchens.

'Now, Katie, whenever you want to, please tell me what has happened,' Madame Delphine said as she helped Katie into a comfortable chair, placing a box of tissues on her lap.

'I've been raped!' Katie blurted out.

'Raped? Do you know who did it?'

'Oh, yes. I know him all right. So do you as it happens.'

'I know him?'

'He's a regular customer in your restaurant.'

'So are you going to tell me?'

'If you really want to know, it was Antoine.'

'Oh, my God,' Madame Delphine whispered as she walked over to pick up the phone from her desk.

151

'Please,' Katie said. 'Please don't call the police!'

'I'm not calling the police, Katie, but I know who I *have* got to call. I'll be with you in just a minute.'

Katie watched as her friend dialled a number. When the call was answered, Madame Delphine spoke in French. Whilst Katie could understand some of the language, when it was spoken at speed she was unable to decipher more than a few words here and there. Katie wondered who was at the other end of the call, but she didn't have to wait long to find out.

'*Merci, Gilbert. A bientôt!*' she said before returning to Katie.

'You were talking to Gilbert?' Katie asked.

'Yes. Do you know him?'

'Yes. I've met him a few times. Why did you need to speak to him?'

'If you know him, Katie, you will also know that Antoine is his best friend. Gilbert has looked after Antoine for as long as I can remember. I had to let him know what has happened.'

'Looked after him? What do you mean?'

'It's a long story, Katie, but Antoine has had a problem all his life. He has what is commonly called a split personality. He has had it since he was a kid. He is on medication, and he has had it under control for years now.'

'Oh, my God,' Katie said. 'I had no idea ...'

'How could you. As I say, it has been contained for a long time. However, he has just been to a new clinic in Rennes for a couple of weeks for his medication to be re-evaluated. I guess something has gone wrong. That's why I phoned Gilbert. He had to know immediately. Do you know where Antoine is now?'

'No. I feel awful now, but I cut up all his clothes and threw him and them out of the cottage.'

'I can't blame you for that. I just hope Gilbert can find him. I've asked him to come here so that he can talk to you first, and then we can start looking for him.'

Katie was speechless. This news explained Antoine's absence for two weeks and, to some small degree, mitigated his behaviour this afternoon.

'I should have guessed that something was wrong as soon as he arrived at the cottage. He was not his usual self. He was rough, violent. He really hurt me. It was horrible, and it took me completely by surprise.'

'Katie, you must not for one minute blame yourself. How could you have known anything about his past?'

'Will we have to involve the police? I don't want to press any charges. I wasn't going to anyway, but I certainly don't want to now.'

As they spoke, Gilbert came rushing into the office. He nodded acknowledgement to Madame Delphine, but came straight over to Katie.

'Oh, Katie I'm so sorry this has happened. I knew something was not right as soon as Antoine got back from Rennes. I could see a difference in him. But I never expected anything like this!'

He took Katie's hands in his, lifted one to his mouth, and kissed her knuckles tenderly.

'Madame Delphine has told me some of Antoine's past. I had no idea. What do we do now?'

'First of all, we need to find him. I don't suppose you know where he went when he left you, Katie.'

'I haven't a clue. All I know is that I doubt he will go anywhere public, because I slashed his clothes to shreds before I threw him out of the cottage.'

'Then I guess he would want to go home. Let's see if he's answering his phone.'

Gilbert dialled a number on his mobile but there was no reply. He left a message on voice mail.

'Antoine, this is Gilbert. Call me as soon as you get this. It's urgent I talk to you. Don't worry. Everything is OK.'

Katie watched Madame Delphine's raised eyebrows. She said what she was thinking without uttering a word.

'Can I come with you, Gilbert? Two pairs of eyes are better than one.'

'Are you sure, Katie?' Madame Delphine asked. 'You're still in shock. I don't know that it's such a good idea.'

'I'll be fine. Honestly. I want to help find him.'

'Mmm. I doubt whether he will want to see you,' Gilbert said.

'I don't care about that.'

'OK' Gilbert said. 'Let's go then.'


They didn't have to look far. They saw Antoine's car parked outside his house at the far end *Sainte-Justine.* Gilbert told Katie that the house belonged to his parents, but they were seldom there, so he had a free bachelor pad.

'I think it would be best if you stayed in the car for now,' Gilbert said, parking his car behind Antoine's. 'I've had to deal with this before, albeit several years ago, and I need to find out his present state of mind before I even suggest that he sees you. I hope you understand.'

Katie nodded in agreement. Now it came to it, she wondered whether she was quite so keen to meet with her rapist boyfriend. It was difficult to forget what he had done

154

to her only a few hours ago. It had left an after effect that would take some time to heal.

She watched as Gilbert knocked on the door, and for a second was able to glimpse Antoine's face when he opened the door. It was just a snapshot of a view. Both men immediately disappeared inside the house.

She had met Antoine and Gilbert on a double date a few months previously in Angers. They had taken her out to dinner on a boat, moored on the river beneath the impressive façade of the Chateau at Angers. It had been a magical evening and ended up by being one of the most exciting sex sessions she ever remembered. Both men had been involved, something she had not experienced before, or since for that matter.

She saw each of them a few times more, but it was Antoine that fascinated her. He was a gentle giant of a man. He treated her like a china doll, always making sure that she was happy, comfortable, relaxed about everything they did together. She always felt so safe when she was with him. He always seemed delighted to be with her - almost showing her off to people wherever they went.

Over the weeks and months, her fondness for him had developed into something deeper. She began to think that she could be happy sharing the rest of her life with this man.

No wonder that she was so shocked by his behaviour today. It was totally out of character, and she thought at one point that the relationship had come to a rapid, premature end.

Now that she was aware of the probable cause, she was able to contemplate that their friendship, somehow might be able to continue.

Gilbert returned to the car after about ten minutes, and sat beside her, taking her hand in his.

'I think he'll be OK,' he said. 'Like you, he's in a state of shock at what happened.'

'He remembers it all, then?'

'Oh, yes. He remembers. He's distraught. He hates the character that he was this afternoon. He had years of this earlier in his life. He was always in trouble, sometimes quite serious trouble. The other character was the exact opposite of him – vicious, violent and nasty. It wasn't until he underwent psychiatric treatment and was put on a course of powerful medication that he could control himself.'

'So what do you think happened in Rennes, then?'

'From what he's just told me, they changed his drugs. He told me that he knew things weren't right, but didn't want to pre-judge what they had prescribed for him.'

'What will happen now?'

'I don't know, but I'm taking him back to the clinic in Rennes tomorrow. He can't go on like this again.'

'I'm so glad I didn't castrate him like I wanted to!'

'You threatened him with that?'

'Yes. I had this kitchen knife in my hand. I had no intention of killing him, but I was tempted to do some damage to his genitalia. I told him that if he ever came near me again, I'd – well, you know.'

'Poor old Antoine!'

'Never mind poor old Antoine. I was standing there, naked, shaking with anger, very sore both inside and out, and bleeding. What was I supposed to do? Ask him to be a good boy and not to do it again?'

'Of course not. That's not what I meant. Look, I'll take you back to Madame Delphine's now. I'm coming back to be with Antoine. Is that OK?'

'Of course it is, Gilbert. You're a really good friend to him, and he needs you, I'm sure.'

They drove the short distance back to Angers without speaking and Katie walked back into the restaurant where Madame Delphine greeted her again.

'Did you find him?'

'Yes, he was at home. Gilbert went in to see that he was OK, but Antoine didn't want to see me – not today, anyway.'

'I think I can understand that.'

'Gilbert is taking him back to the clinic in Rennes tomorrow. I just hope they can do something to help him.'

'I hope so, too. I can't understand why they changed his medication, if that's what they did. He was doing so well as he was. Now, what can I get you to eat?'

B en set off early to meet up with his business colleagues. What had set out as an extremely lucrative Internet business had recently been in serious decline. The original idea was to help businesses reach the top spots in the search engines. They had found a 'back door' facility, which they sold to their clients.

The problem had arisen when the major search engines had plugged the loophole, and the once happy clients were suddenly becoming disenchanted and had started to drift away, slowly at first, but recently in much larger numbers.

Ben's two colleagues, both called Tony, were more interested in hearing about life in France than discussing the partnership's problems. Ben had brought a few bottles of wine with him, and the three men enjoyed tasting the samples of local wines from Angers.

Inevitably, the time came to turn their minds to more serious matters. The two Tonys had worked hard to come up with a similar product to replace the original, but had to admit that they had not been successful.

What they had managed to do, however, was find a buyer for the entire business. This came as a shock to Ben, as no mention had been made of this in any communications between them, and he made this plain to them.

'Ben, we had to do something. Our little scheme which had kept us happy over the last three years was going to dry up. We've found somebody who just wants our website and client list. We don't know what he wants to do with it, and we don't much care. The price he is willing to pay is astronomical, much more than we would have asked for, so we thought ---'

'You thought there was no need to ask for my opinion! I'm a partner, guys. I do have a say don't I?'

'Quite honestly, Ben, we thought you would be delighted. After all, it was you who warned us of what was happening. This way, we can take the money, and perhaps set up something new, something different. This 'cloud' business is beginning to catch on. We might be able to jump on that bandwagon for a while, who knows.'

'Oh, don't misunderstand me,' Ben replied. 'I could see that everything was collapsing a long time ago, and I agree with what you've done. It's just the principle – you didn't keep me posted. So exactly how astronomical is the deal?'

When he learned the price, he found it difficult to believe.

'That's almost a quarter of a million each!'

'It's the client list they wanted more than anything,' one of his colleagues said. 'Many of them are top grade businesses, and data like that is hard to come by.'

They handed Ben the agreement to peruse.

'Have you shown this to our solicitors?' he asked. Both of his partners nodded with wide smiles on their faces.

'No loopholes here.'

'Then let's get it signed and sealed,' Ben said. 'This is turning out to be a much better day than I had expected. Well done, guys.'

They each signed the document and decided that they deserved a celebratory lunch. The meal lasted much longer than Ben had expected. He had to phone Maurice to rearrange the time for their meeting.

Maurice had had dealings with Donald in the past, none of them pleasant, and Ben was hoping that there might be a chance that one or other bit of information from those meetings would serve as a starting point in his search for Donald.

The welcome he received from his ex-colleague was warm but by no means overwhelming. Ben had told Maurice of the reason for the meeting and was impressed that preparations had been taken prior to his arrival.

Sitting alongside Maurice in the comfortably appointed office, befitting a financial director of a successful IT systems organisation, was a young man, possibly still in his teens, who Ben did not recognise.

Maurice introduced him to Ben.

'This is Basheer. He's recently joined us and has a wide knowledge of computing and social media amongst other things.' Ben shook hands with them both.

'What exactly is it you are wanting to do?' Basheer said in a strong Indian accent.

Ben took his time explaining his concerns about Donald, including his belief that he was intrinsically involved with the attack on Mary.

'That's awful,' Basheer said. 'So what do you want us to do?'

'He has apparently disappeared into thin air,' Ben told him. 'I'm hoping that you might be able to trace him through his IP address or his computer transactions.'

Basheer smiled at Maurice.

'Shall I tell him what we've already done?' Basheer asked.

'I think that would be a good idea. That's what he has come to hear.' Maurice said, as if he were talking to a schoolboy.

Basheer ignored the remark and his face lit up as he looked into Ben's eyes.

'Do not ask me how I did it, as it is not entirely legal,' he said, waiting for Ben's agreement. Ben nodded.

'I have traced this man's IP address from the few bits of information Maurice had. He made just one small mistake by setting his 'Out of Office' facility on, so we had an auto response from his computer, and that was enough for me to be able to discover his IP address. I can tell you that at this moment, he is not using his computers, either his desktop or his laptop. As you say, he seems to have disappeared.'

'I could have told *you* that.' Ben said, showing a bit of frustration.

'Let me continue,' Basheer said. 'I would think that sooner or later he will boot up one or other of his machines, and as soon as he does, my computer will message me to say that he's live. Then I can start to pin point him.'

'Really?' Ben said.

'Oh. yes. I will also be able to tell you who he is talking to, and what he is talking about.'

'So you will be hacking his computers?'

'Yes, and if you want me to, I should be able to copy stuff from his hard drive, so we should be able, for instance, to get a list of his contacts.'

Maurice looked at Ben.

'He's good isn't he? Every IT company should have a hacker on board, don't you think?'

'Absolutely, Maurice. So all I have to do is to find a way to make him open his laptop. Is that it?'

'Exactly,' Basheer said, looking rather proud of himself. 'If you can do that, we can get things moving immediately.'

'So, when are you coming back to join us, Ben?' Maurice asked. 'You're clever little wheeze with the search engines seems to have come to halt, doesn't it?'

'Yes it has, unfortunately.'

'So?'

'Sorry, Maurice. My partners have managed to sell the website – well, the business, I suppose – for an amazing sum, and I've agreed. The money will allow me to expand my little empire in France. As much as I enjoyed my time here at SRX, it would take an awful lot of persuasion to entice me back, I'm afraid.'

'Oh, well. That's what I expected to hear. It's a shame, though. I could use you here at the moment. Your admin skills were first class, and we've not managed to find anybody, so far, to match them.'

'Look, guys, I'm very grateful to you for your help in this. I'm confident that I will find him, and then we have to bring him to justice for the things he's done. I won't rest until I have. Meanwhile, if either of you fancy a break in the Loire Valley, just make contact through our website. Oh, and no hacking, please.'

As Ben drove back to Katie's house, he couldn't help but smile. It had turned out to be a very successful day. He was considerably richer than he had been when he left this morning, and he now had a team of hackers waiting to feed him information just as soon as Donald switched on his computers. A very good day's work, he thought.

He arrived home just as Mary was laying the table for the evening meal. He retold everything that had happened, trying not to miss out any important points. He could see that Mary was pleased for him, but she felt nowhere near the excitement that he did.

'I didn't ask you why Ray wanted to take you out to lunch yesterday. What's he up to?' Ben asked.

'You were right about the job. He did ask me if I fancied working for him again.'

'I thought he would. That's both of us with back-up jobs if we need them!'

'But there was something else.'

'Go on.'

'It was about Georgina.'

'Why would he want to talk to you about Georgina?'

'The girls have been meeting up with her. You remember the old Friday evenings?'

'I remember them all right. You were always full of the gossip when you got home. But I still don't understand...'

'As I say, Georgina has been meeting up with the girls from the salon, and they have been a bit concerned about her. They reckon that she's changed – is trying to be something that she isn't.'

'That's not necessarily a bad thing is it?'

'No, but the girls say that it's not a healthy kind of change. She's trying to be somebody different, and it's not working. She has been looking very moody and despondent recently and Ray wanted to find out if I knew the cause?'

'What did you say?'

'I told him what had happened in France, and how she had left in floods of tears.'

'I see.'

163

'Ray's a really nice guy and he cares about people who have worked for him. I think he just needed to know what was troubling Georgina so that he might be able to help her in some way.'

'Do you think there's any way we can help her? Should we meet up with her while we are over here?'

'Like, no!' Mary said. 'I don't think seeing you again would help her at all. No, better leave well alone I think.'

The following morning the trio went to see the registrar in Reading, complete with passports and birth certificates.

The meeting was brief and to the point. By the time they left, they had confirmed that they would be able to marry in the UK whilst residing in France. More importantly, there was an afternoon spot on a date that suited them, which they snapped up.

'OK,' Ben said, once outside, 'I think our little visit has been very successful. Now we can go home knowing that everything is in place and ready to roll.'

'Ben, I feel like a silly kid. I'm so happy - I want to jump up and down and scream! These have been the two most exciting days of my life. I love you so much, I can't tell you.'

They drove back to Katie's house, giving Mary the opportunity to phone the dress shop to confirm the date that she would be collecting her dress. She also phoned Ray to say that she would be at the salon shortly after midday on the big day.

As soon as they had finished packing their bags, they drove the now familiar journey to Portsmouth to catch the next available ferry to Caen.

## Chapter 29

Commissaire Claude Boulet met up with Lizzie just before lunch.

'What's the latest?' he asked

'Well, there were three incendiary devices placed on the second and third floors.'

'Three! Whoever it was meant business then.'

'Right. But only two exploded. The third one has been recovered, and is undergoing forensic scrutiny right now.'

'What about your man? Do you think he is involved?'

'I can't be sure. I'm not often wrong in my suspicions, but if he did play a part, he's clever. Other than visiting the British Consulate, he was with me all the time. In fact, I think he quite fancied his chances with me.'

Claude smiled. 'So you've been using your *Mata Hari* tactics again. You should be more careful, Lizzie. You don't know who some of these characters are.'

'No need to worry, Claude. Once they're hooked, they are like lambs.'

'To the slaughter?'

'Something like that. Anyway, Matt was a nice guy.'

'Matt?'

'Yes, my suspect. He's called Matt.'

'No he isn't, Lizzie. His name is Charles Masterson. He has a record as long as your arm; spent many years in prison, but recently he seems to have reformed.'

'Are you sure?'

'Absolutely. The British Consulate sent his basic details, and Europol furnished the remainder of the information.'

'So he's not the man I thought he was, in more than one sense.'

'When do you expect to hear from forensics?'

'Later today. I can't say any more than that.'

'OK. I'll hang around for a bit. I'd like to find out more about this Bear character. How much do you know?'

The two officers decided that it was time to eat, and Lizzie took her senior colleague to a nearby bistro where they continued their conversation. Lizzie reiterated that Bear had been close to being charged on many occasions, but he had brilliant lawyers working for him and each time the case was dismissed before reaching trial; usually on a technicality or lack of substantiating evidence.

'All the more reason' Claude said, 'that we get it right this time. I've a feeling that your fan, Charles Masterson, might well be able to help us if, indeed, he is in any way responsible for the fire. You don't go around razing buildings to the ground without a very serious motive. Let's hope forensics can find something which will link him to this somehow.'

An hour or so later, Claude went to the site of the fire. Lizzie didn't join him, as her cover and position of trust was sacramental to her. She could not allow herself to be seen entering the building with anybody that could ruin that. She enjoyed her job and her lifestyle too much.

She did, however, text him when she heard that the forensic report on the third device was available at the police station.

'Whoever it was,' Claude Boulet said to Lizzie before he sat down at a spare desk, 'they made a bloody good job of it. They knew exactly what they were doing.'

'Except the third device didn't work.'

'Yes, except that. All we can hope for now is that he has been a little careless, and left something on that third device.'

'Forensics will be here in a minute or so. I'll get some coffee. Sugar?'

'Not for me, Lizzie. Make it a strong one.'

While she was gone, Claude took a long sweeping look round the room. He had not been here for several years, but had spent his earlier years as a police officer in Paris and had visited this station many times during that period. Then it was all typewriters and stacks of paper. Now it was dominated by computer screens, but the stacks of paper remained, albeit less prolific.

Only a few of the desks were attended. There were just six young officers, two women and four men, gazing intently at the screens in front of them.

Lizzie returned with a tray holding four large mugs of coffee, and sat down alongside Claude at the desk, followed by two smartly dressed young officers who positioned themselves opposite Lizzie and Claude.

They produced a thick polythene evidence bag and laid it on the table.

Claude waited for a few seconds before saying brusquely 'So?'

The two officers looked up.

'So, what are the results of your investigations?'

'Absolutely nothing, sir. It's a very simple, basic device, but there are no signs of prints, no signs of anything. It's as if the thing was manufactured in a factory.'

'May I see?' Claude enquired.

'Of course, sir. We have finished with it now.'

Claude carefully took the device, which looked like a normal pack of playing cards. He undid one end of the pack, and slid the mechanism out.

'I haven't seen one of these for a few years. They used to be popular with arsonists. Now, of course, it's all electronics and mobile phones.'

Claude studied the apparatus.

'What time did the fire start? Do we know?' he asked Lizzie.

'Early hours of the morning, I'm told. The fire service was called out at 2.30.'

'This timer is limited to twelve hours, so the packages must have been placed in the store after three o'clock the previous afternoon, I would think. Is there any CCTV?'

'Only inside. We've looked at that and there is no sign of anybody acting suspiciously. I can only guess that the first thing the person did was to check out CCTV cameras and avoid being in range. Once again, it points to this being a professional job.'

Claude studied the device again,

'Is there any way I can talk to some detectives?'

'That shouldn't be a problem, sir,' Lizzie said. 'Give me a few minutes.'

'I understand that there were three of these things involved in the fire,' Claude said to the forensic officers.

'That's what the fire service think.'

'Think? Are they not sure?'

'Sorry. That's what the fire officers say. There were two distinctive sources of the fire.'

'And they consider that the two sources would have been activated by similar devices?'

'There doesn't seem to be much doubt about that, sir.'

Claude looked up to see Lizzie walking back into the room with a tall, well-built man who she introduced to Claude as Commissaire Louis Armand. The two men shook hands.

'I have a handful of detectives that you can talk to, if you care to come this way. Lizzie has given me brief details of the case, but you can fill in the details.'

Waiting for them in another room were six detectives of various ranks. Each one of them looked as if they hadn't slept for days. They were bleary-eyed, unshaven, and generally unkempt.

They didn't react to Claude's entrance until their own Commissaire had spoken. He told the assembled officers that Claude wanted to speak to them about matters related to the recent fire in Rue de Maubeuge.

Claude held up the incendiary contraption, explaining that such devices had been the cause of the fire.

'Forensics have found nothing of interest on this one, which did not ignite.'

There were mutterings amongst the detectives, which were indecipherable to Claude, but which he put down to the lack of respect between the two departments.

'So,' he continued, 'we need to find out where the component parts were purchased. I would suggest that they were bought fairly locally. So, take for example the watch that has been used. It should be simple enough to find out who sells this make of watch. It should be equally simple to track down a sale of three such items.'

The device was now being passed round for inspection among the detectives.'

'These are sold by *Intermarché*,' one of the detectives announced. 'My brother bought one last weekend.'

'OK,' Claude said. 'Let's start there. Contact every *Intermarché* and see if somebody bought three of these things.'

'I think I might be able to shortcut this,' Lizzie said. 'The person I think is responsible for this spent most of the day prior to the fire in the Madeleine area. He had his passport stolen and went there to get papers to allow him back into the UK. If I remember rightly, there is a big *Intermarché* quite close to the British Consulate. I should make that a starting point. It might save a lot of time.'

'Good thinking, Lizzie. I would like to get this tied up as quickly as possible, as I'm convinced that a number of other crimes are linked to this fire and to the person who started it.'

Commissaire Louis Armand assured Claude that they would be on to it immediately.

'By the way,' Claude said just before he left the office, 'Does anyone know the whereabouts of Bear? Has he been informed of the damage to his property?'

There was a unison of shaking heads.

'Well, someone must know. Can we get onto that as well? He, too, is deeply involved in all of this, I'm sure. At this moment in time, we have a young man being detained in Angers for his part in a failed assassination attempt. He says that he was acting on Bear's instructions. However, the boyfriend of the victim insists that the whole thing was orchestrated by a man called Donald O'Hanlon from the UK.'

'How seriously do you take his assumptions?' one of the detectives asked.

'I'm pretty well convinced. So we have a connection between our detainee and Bear. It seems we now have a link between Bear and Lizzie's suspect, who is also a Brit.'

'So we need to find an association between Lizzie's suspect and this Donald man, is that it?'

'In a word, yes. You all know that we have been trying to get Bear to trial for much too long. If we can bring this all together, I think, this time, we might succeed. He like all the others involved would be charged with attempted murder. So you see how important this is. Speed is important, but let's get it right this time. Keep impeccable notes – dates, times – you know the drill. I don't want this one to have any cracks in the evidence.'

As he turned to walk out of the office he halted and turned back to the detectives, and addressed the Commissaire.

'If it's OK with you, sir, can I ask that Lizzie is kept updated with everything. We are in constant contact and I want to be kept fully informed.'

Commissaire Armand agreed and thanked his colleague from Angers for his time and support.

Once outside, Claude bid Lizzie goodbye with a kiss to both cheeks. As he walked away from her, Claude wished he had someone like her working for him in Angers.

# Chapter 30

As they drove into the circular drive of *La Sanctuaire*, Ben said, 'That's strange.'

'What's strange?' Mary replied.

'The place feels deserted.'

'Katie's probably indoors.'

'Maybe, but it's unusual to drive in here and for her not to run to greet us.'

'To greet *you*, maybe.'

'Whatever. I'll go and see if she's in the garden. You take young Alex indoors. He's probably very hungry after the journey.'

Ben walked round to the entrance to the garden, and down the path to the stream at the far end, but he knew she wouldn't be there. He sensed from the minute they arrived that something was not right. He turned round and redoubled his pace back to the cottage.

Mary was waiting outside the front door.

'There's no sign of her in here,' she said. 'I've looked in her room, and it's in a bit of a mess.'

'Let's go and have another look,' Ben said, and together they made their way to Katie's room. Mary was right. Either she had had one truly wild sex session, or something was seriously wrong. When Ben found the kitchen knife on the floor, and discovered the stained bed covers with flecks of blood, he knew it must be the latter.

'Perhaps she's with Antoine.' Mary said. 'Have you got his number?'

'Why should I have his number?'

'I just thought ---'

'I don't even know his surname, so I can't try directory enquiries.'

The phone made them both jump when it rang. Ben picked up the receiver.

'Oh, good, you're back.'

'It's Madame Delphine,' Ben whispered to Mary.

'Nice to know that you missed us,' Ben quipped, but there was no humorous reply from their friend.

'Ben, I've got Katie with me. She stayed here last night. Something horrible has happened to her.'

'Horrible? How horrible?'

'Rape, Ben. That horrible.'

'Can I talk with her?'

'She's sleeping at the moment, but I think the best thing, now that you're home, is that I bring her back to the cottage. Is that OK?'

'Of course it's OK, Madame Delphine. Thank you for taking care of her. What happened, then?'

'I think it's up to Katie to tell you the details. I'll wait for her to wake, then I will drive her over. She'll be so pleased that you're back home.'

Mary had been trying to listen in on the conversation, but when Ben spoke with the ex-Folies Bergère dancer, they often spoke in French, so she understood very little.

'What's happened, Ben? Is Katie alright?'

'No, she's not. She's been raped.'

'When? Here?'

'I don't know, Mary. I don't know any details. We'll have to wait until she gets home. Madame Delphine has been looking after her and she's going to drop her back here as soon as she wakes up.'

'Oh, my God. What is it with this place, Ben? First me. Now Katie. I think, maybe, you should think of another name for it. It certainly doesn't seem to be much of a sanctuary to me!'

'I know what you mean. In the meantime, I suggest we go and tidy up her room. She won't want to come home to anything that will remind her of her ordeal.'

'I'll do that, Ben. Can you get us all something to eat – and drink!'

'Red or white?'

'I'll have a chilled white with a slight soda topping, please.'

'Philistine!'

'I'm not a Philistine. I just want something refreshing.'

Ben went into the kitchen where Alex was waiting patiently in his high chair, for something to eat. Ben mulled over what Mary had said about the name of the cottage. He had to agree that recently, there had been little to suggest that it was a sanctuary. In the past however, the name had been well suited. It had been a sanctuary for Katie when he had rescued her from her captors in Germany, and surely Mary had not forgotten how apt the name was when he liberated her from Donald's evil grasp. It was surely a sanctuary then.

*La Sanctuaire* was intended to be a place of safety and security for whoever lived here; a place of peace and tranquillity. And it would be again. He would make sure of that.

In a few weeks' time, he and Mary would be married and they could begin to plan their future in a more permanent way. They could start to shape Alex's education at nursery and primary schools. When Mary first came to France, one of the things that impressed her was the superb educational facilities at their disposal, now they could start to experience it for themselves.

He had pacified Alex with some French toast spread with a little honey. Within seconds, the little boy was a completely sticky mess, spreading the effects over everything he touched.

Mary came into the kitchen with Katie's bedclothes and put them in the washing machine.

'Ben, what have you given him?'

'Toast and honey. He loves it!'

'Yes. I can see that. It's your job to clear up after him. I'm not doing it. Why is it that men do such stupid things?'

Ben didn't react. He was enjoying the spectacle of his wife bending down to load the machine. She still had a great figure, and it was still good to have little fantasies every now and then, wasn't it?

'D'you know, Mr Coverdale, I can tell when you're staring at my backside. Just behave yourself – your son's watching.'

'Sorry. Just can't help it. You have such a gorgeous bum and I'm only human.'

When she straightened up, they kissed and Alex stretched out his arms for his kiss.

'No way!' Mary said. 'If I kissed you now I might be stuck to you for ever. Ben. Get some warm water and sort him out.'

Ben decided that the simplest way was to take Alex for a shower. He would deal with the high chair later. Alex loved the shower. In fact, it was true to say that he enjoyed water in any shape or form – the stream at the bottom of the garden, the evening bath time and especially the sea. How he loved the waves along the Atlantic coast!

It was a struggle to get him out of the shower, but having done so, Ben took him down to the stream, and Mary brought their food and drinks to enjoy in the afternoon sunshine.

It was good to be home. They were both experiencing a mountaintop experience, having at last got the wedding planned. Love was well and truly in the air today. Even the news of Katie could not douse their feelings of excitement.

After a leisurely, basic lunch of brie, salad and baguettes, Ben and Mary unpacked their bags while Alex discovered toys that he had not seen for a few days and played happily.

Were they not waiting for Katie to return, Ben would have been tempted to suggest a little sexual celebration, but he knew that was not on the cards. It would have to wait until later.

They heard Madame Delphine's car pulling up outside the cottage sending a shower of gravel everywhere. For a woman in her sixties she sometimes behaved more like a teenager. She was an attractive lady and had enough energy and *joie de vivre* to put many a younger woman to shame. Ebullience was her second name. She had taken to Ben from the first day he arrived in France and had become a good friend. Her taking care of Katie, then, did not surprise Ben at all. That is what she does.

Ben went to open the door and watched as Madame Delphine led Katie slowly towards the cottage. When Katie saw Ben waiting, she did her best to run to him, flinging her arms around his neck and kissing him; not the French kiss-on-the-cheeks but very much the British kiss-on-the lips.

Mary caught Madame Delphine's eye and shrugged. There was still something special between her husband-to-be and Katie. Until recently, it had worried her but lately her doubts had diminished. Katie had found herself a man, and in a few weeks' time, Ben would be her husband. Why should she worry any more?

The embrace went on for what seemed minutes before Katie broke away from Ben.

'Ben, why weren't you here when I needed you? You've always been here for me, and the very time I need you most, you're not here!'

Ben was lost for words.

'If I'd have known that you were in danger, I would never have left you here on your own, but there was no way I could have known that, was there?'

'I know,' Katie said tearfully, 'but I still wish you had been here. You're the only person in my life that I can really trust. You were there for me when I found myself in Germany. You brought me back here and took care of me, helped, loved ---' she stopped abruptly at the last word and turned away from both Ben and Mary, tears streaming from her eyes once again.

'Awkward,' Mary muttered under her breath before Madame Delphine took her arm and guided her into the garden.

'I'm sure Katie will tell you everything in due course and in her own time, but the basic fact is that she was severely raped right here in the cottage.'

'Do we know who did it?'

'That's the terrible bit, Mary. It was Antoine.'

'I don't believe it.'

'But it's true. However there are some things you ought to know so that you can be of help to Katie.'

Madame Delphine told Mary of Antoine's past problems with schizophrenia and how it seemed that his medication had been changed – for the worst.

'Oh, wow,' Mary said. 'I suppose that's the end of a very short romance, then.'

'No. I don't know that it will be. Katie is a remarkable girl and I get the impression that she will do all that she can to support him.'

'Really? I'm buggered if I would.'

'I don't know that I could either but that, it seems, is the way she wants to go. He must be very special for her to be able to even think about sticking with him.'

'So she's not pressing charges?'

'No. She told me that she wouldn't have taken action anyway, but that she certainly won't be pressing any charges now that she knows the circumstances.'

'Well, all I can say is that she's made of much sterner stuff than I am,' Mary said. 'I think I may have misjudged her all these years.'

'She's going to need your support as well as Ben's for a while. She'll need another woman to talk to about things she can't discuss with Ben. Are you up to that?'

'Yes, I think so. I've never considered myself to be a counsellor, but I'll do my best.'

'Good. If you need help, I'm always there.'

They walked back into the coolness of the cottage to find Ben and Katie sitting side by side on the sofa, Ben's arm round the girl's shoulder, and her head on his chest. Katie looked up at Mary.

'Sorry, Mary. I just had to borrow him for a few minutes. I just needed him. I guess we've become soul mates over the last year or so.'

Ben was watching Mary's face to gauge her reaction but there were no signs of the usual distrust. She seemed genuinely concerned for Katie.

'Well you're home again now, and you can borrow him whenever you need to. Just remember he's mine and I'm marrying him in a few weeks.' Mary said with a friendly smile on her face.

'I must go now,' Madame Delphine said. 'I've got a business to run.'

Mary was the first to hug her, followed by Ben and finally Katie.

'Thank you so much,' Katie said. 'I don't know what I would have done without you.'

'You just concentrate on getting better, Katie, and you,' she said looking at Ben and Mary, 'take good care of her.'

The little party went out to the garden, and watched as the red sports car sped off through the gate back towards Angers.

## Chapter 31

Donald tried his best to recollect exactly what had happened. One minute he and Niels were sitting staring at each other, each trying to guess the other's next move. The next moment all hell had broken loose. Niels had complained about feeling hot and removed his black tie. Then, suddenly, the scrawny little man had leapt up from his chair. Before Donald had time to take evasive action, Niels had pushed him backwards onto a wooden chair and used the tie to secure his hands behind his back. The loose ends of the tie were used to secure him firmly to the chair.

'Car keys?' Niels snarled. 'Where are the fucking car keys?'

'In my pocket,' Donald replied more feebly than he intended.

Niels delved into Donald's trouser pocket and drew out the bunch of keys.

'Thank you. I used to have a Merc, myself, but I found them a bit too ostentatious for my taste. I'll leave it at the car park in Kintbury. I have a ferry to catch.'

'You won't get away with this,' Donald said.

'Really? I don't see why not. I think, at this moment, my friend, I have all the trump cards.'

'I mean you can't get out of here. It's all securely locked.'

'But I can break a window or two, can't I?'

'That would alert the police.'

'Exactly. And you don't want that, do you? Have coppers sniffing round your house? No. You've been so careful, so clever to avoid that happening. Whichever way you want, I'm leaving now. You can tell me how to deactivate the locks, or I will happily smash my way out.'

Donald knew he had lost this round. Niels was absolutely right. The last thing he wanted was an interview with Thames Valley police.

'There's a doofer over there,' he said, gesticulating as best as he could to the table in the corner of the room. 'Press the green button at the top.'

Niels did as he was instructed. There was a series of electronic beeps from somewhere downstairs. He wiped the doofer with a tissue before returning it to the table.

'Thanks,' Niels said with a false smile on his face. 'It's been a pleasure meeting up with you again - for me, anyway.'

'You haven't heard the last of me,' Donald snorted. 'Nobody treats me like this and gets away with it.'

He was wasting his breath. Niels was half way out of the room, carefully avoiding touching anything with his bare hands. Donald listened to the sounds of the little man running down the curved staircase to the atrium. He heard the heavy front door open and slam shut.

Niels slowed down to a casual pace once outside and walked to the rear of the house, clicked the key fob in his hand and heard the smooth mechanical sound of the central locking opening the car's doors.

He familiarised himself with the layout of the dashboard and only then realised that the car boasted an automatic gearbox, something he was quite unfamiliar with.

Gently, he pulled the gear paddle to the 'R' position and pressed gently on the accelerator. The car shot backwards much faster than he was expecting and he had to brake frantically to avoid reversing into the wall behind.

Unperturbed, he put the car in forward and gingerly drove down the side of the house, along the tree-lined drive and out through the wrought iron gates onto the road. He soon got used to the gearbox and the power of the big diesel engine and began to enjoy the drive back to Kintbury, where he would pick up his own car.

As he swung the car into the car park, he miscalculated the proximity of a low wall and scraped the front offside of the car along the full length of the obstacle.

He got out to inspect the damage. It would probably be costly to reinstate, but there was no serious damage. Anyway, what did he care?

He wiped all the surfaces he had touched inside and outside the car and tossed the keys into the glove compartment.

Once he had reversed out of the car park, he sighed with relief and wondered whether he would ever be able to get his hands on any of the two million that he had transferred to one of Lucas's companies in Madeira. He doubted it, but it might be worth a try.

The last thing Donald wanted was for his car to attract any attention. He had to get to Kintbury as quickly as he could.

He struggled to try to free his hands, but only tightened the knots. The only way he could free himself from his trusses was to topple the chair over and hope that it disintegrated. Not as easy as it sounded, he realised. One of the legs had snapped off so now he could no longer use the chair to sit on. Not one to give up, he stood up with the remains of the chair attached to his arms behind his back, made several attempts at jumping and finally managed to ease himself and the chair onto the table and threw himself off.

The chair landed on one of its remaining three legs and smashed into a heap of pieces that looked like an Ikea flat pack.

His injuries were troubling him. He decided to take a shower, and only when he looked in the mirror did he realise how badly he had damaged himself. One of the chair legs that had split had gouged his right arm and there was a nasty gash just above his right eyebrow, which would probably benefit from a stitch or two. He cleaned the wounds as best as he could, using tissues to stem the bleeding and was pleased that things weren't any worse.

Donning some suitable disguise – his black woollen hat, jeans and the ubiquitous dark glasses, he left the house and walked to Wallingford centre, from where he took a cab to Kintbury.

It was a short walk from the town centre to the car park near the church. He was relieved to see his car sitting there waiting for him.

He didn't notice the damage to the offside wing and drove back to his house as rapidly as he could, parking his car in the confines of the garage.

He made his way back up to the single room and poured himself a large Scotch.

He was furious and humiliated by the fact of being trounced by such a diminutive man. It was the speed at which it happened that had taken him by surprise.

For the time being, he resigned himself to the thought that his dealings with Niels were over for now. He may have lost this round, but the fight was by no means over.

## Chapter 32

Katie joined Ben, Mary and Alex for a late breakfast the following day and apologised if she had appeared to be off-handed when she arrived home with Madame Delphine.

'I just want to say that I do appreciate your concern for me, but I really don't want you fussing over me. It is just something that happened. I'd have preferred it if it hadn't, but it did, and I can get over it. No worries.'

'Madame Delphine did tell me briefly what had happened. It must have been awful for you. You know, somebody you thought you could trust,' Mary said.

'Of course it was, but it turns out that there were extenuating circumstances that go a long way to explaining his actions.'

'And you accept that?'

'I'm keeping an open mind. If this does turn out to be the end of a friendship, it will be his decision, not mine. I think he might have more difficulty dealing with this than me. My hurt was mainly physical. His are deep and psychological, I'm sure.'

'And you're not pressing charges, I understand.'

'That's right. I wouldn't have done anyway. You can imagine how the lawyers would have dealt with me and my past sex life, can't you?'

Ben was looking out of the tiny window and saw the yellow post van stop at the gate.

'I'll go and get the mail,' he said.

Mary tried to continue helping Alex with his breakfast of fruity cereal, but Alex had other ideas. He pointed toward Katie.

'Kay,' he said. 'Kay.'

'Well that's a new one. That's today's word,' Mary said.

'That's brilliant. He can say my name!'

'And I think he wants *you* to help him.'

'My pleasure. That's really made my day, Alex.'

When Ben returned with a handful of post, Katie told Ben enthusiastically about his son's latest word.

'Something new every day with him,' he said ruffling Alex's curls.

Ben handed Katie her official-looking letter with a UK postmark and watched as she opened it.

'Something wrong?' he asked.

'Not exactly,' she replied, 'but it's something I could do without right now. It's notification of the trial of my kidnappers. I have been summoned to appear as a witness.'

'When?' Ben asked.

'It's the Monday of the week before your wedding.'

'So you'll want your house, won't you, if you're staying on for the wedding.'

'No, not at all. I've told you the house is yours. I can't wait to get rid of it. I'll be happy to stay with Dave's father, Mark, as planned. Just means that I'll stay a few extra days.

I wouldn't be surprised if he offers to come with me to the trial.'

'That would be good,' Mary said. 'I wouldn't fancy going through that on my own. At least you can still get to the wedding.'

'I wouldn't miss it for the world, Mary. Where are you having the reception?'

'I don't know.'

'Don't know? How can you not know?'

'Ray from the salon where I worked is organising something for us, but he won't tell me what.'

'That's nice. I didn't realise that you and he were such good friends.'

'Nor did I, Katie. It seems that he's really missed me since I left the salon. He's offered me my job back three times now.'

'So you'll find out more on the big day, is that it?'

'So it seems. Knowing Ray, it will be something special.'

All this time, Alex was enjoying his breakfast. When Katie took her attention away from him, he grasped her wrist and pulled the spoon back to his mouth.

'Changing the subject,' Ben said. 'I wonder what's happening with Tommy. I'm surprised we haven't heard anything.'

'Can you ask the judge?' Mary suggested.

'No. I don't think that would be wise. If she wanted to talk to us, I'm sure she would have contacted us. No. I just wondered, that's all.'

\*\*\*\*\*

Lizzie lazily stirred from her bed, looked at the clock and checked her phone. *Touch base at ten,* the text read. She had just fifteen minutes to shower and get to the police station. She hated this kind of start to a day and flitted from one room to another, multi-tasking as she went. She left her apartment with her bag slung over one shoulder. Pulling the door to behind her and munching on a yesterday's croissant she ran down the road.

For all her efforts, she was more than five minutes late and entered the room to see her superior officer and some of her colleagues turn and stare at her unkempt appearance as she bundled her way to a vacant chair.

'Sorry,' she said, still panting from her exertion. There was no response.

'OK. Now we can get on with the business. Lizzie, you will be pleased to know that your idea of checking at the supermarket at Madeleine was spot on. The management were very keen to help us, and we found that one customer had bought three of the watches. We were also able to see what else he had purchased. Every item on the list could be associated with the incendiary device.

'He was being as careful as he could not to be caught on CCTV, but he wasn't quite clever enough. He was caught three times – well four to be exact, but one was too blurry to be of any use. Lizzie, you need to see the tapes to verify that he is the man we're looking for, but I think we have enough evidence to suggest that the devices that started the fire at the furniture store were built by this man.'

'When can I see the tapes?' Lizzie asked.

'Straight after this briefing.'

'The other helpful thing, of course, is that we have the unexploded device, and the materials bought match exactly to those in the device we have.'

'The one thing we don't have is proof that he planted the items in the shop. He may have bought the materials, but we don't know that he built the finished articles or that he planted them,' Lizzie said.

'That's true, Lizzie. He does not appear on CCTV in the store, and as yet nobody has come forward as a witness to say that he was in the building. You said he was with you in the evening. From what time was that?'

'He arrived at my apartment just before five.'

'So that means that he must have placed the packages sometime after two and before five if the maximum delay is twelve hours, and the fire started round about two o'clock the following morning. So we have a window of three hours during which the deed was done.'

One of the detectives asked whether any of the staff noticed anything strange.

'No. Apparently not. But now we can get some prints from the *Intermarché* CCTV tapes, we can ask the staff again if anybody recognises him.'

'And people in offices overlooking the store.'

'Yes, and even people who work in the area who might have been walking past at the time and caught a glimpse of him,' Lizzie added.

'OK, guys. Let's not hang around. We'll get the mug shots to you in less than half an hour, and I want you out there asking a lot of people a lot of questions. Lizzie you come with me.'

Inside the Commissaire's office, Lizzie sat opposite him across his impressive crescent-shaped desk. He handed her a box of tapes.

'Numbers twenty seven and thirty seem to have him captured,' he said. 'There may be more if you have the time to search through them.'

Lizzie nodded.

'I've been talking with my colleague in Angers.'

'Claude Boulet?'

'Yes. It seems that the man we're interested in could be a large piece in an even larger jigsaw puzzle. Is that how you see it?'

'Absolutely, sir,' she replied. 'There is obviously a connection between our man and Bear. Bear, we think is involved in an unsuccessful contract killing of a woman in Angers. The boyfriend of the woman who was attacked is convinced that is the case, but he cites another man as being more likely to be the instigator – a Donald O'Hanlon. Now, I think our man could well be the link to Donald.'

'That means that it is very important that we get solid evidence that our man is the arsonist. If we can do that we can bring him back to answer questions and see if we can persuade him to reveal his link with Mr O'Hanlon, Bear and hopefully the attempt on the woman in Angers.

'I know that you cannot be seen to be any part of this. It is important that we maintain your cover, but I want you to keep your eyes and ears open. For one thing, try to find out where Bear is. I'm certain that he must have heard of the fire by now. It's strange that he hasn't returned.'

'I agree. The fact that he disappeared following the bungled attempt to get rid of the woman in Angers convinces me of his involvement in it. I'll try to find out more. If we can find out where he's likely to be, we can issue photos of him and try to flush him out.'

'Who's taken over his drug dealing business? Can you find a reason to bring him in?'

'I can try. I don't know much about him. I'll concentrate on that as a starting point. In fact I'll get on to that right now,' Lizzie said, as she rose to leave the office.

'And the tapes. Don't forget them. We need you to confirm our man's identification.'

'No sooner said ...' Lizzie said, leaving the sentence unfinished.

## Chapter 33

Mary and Ben, carrying large trays, walked to the patio at the far end of the vegetable gardens, followed by their little boy who was pulling a piece of wood on the end of a piece of string. It was his 'dog', and currently had to go everywhere with him. It was a hot, sultry afternoon at *La Sanctuaire* and with the exception of Alex, nobody felt over energetic.

The garden was overflowing with produce. So much so that their guests were told to pick as much as they wanted. Katie's horticultural efforts had paid off and now, in late September, much of the crops were ready for harvesting. They had even started to supply Madame Delphine's restaurant with a wide range of soft fruits and vegetables.

During the summer, Katie had planted border plants along the edge of each raised bed, bringing some vivid colour to the overall look of the garden. Today, she was removing the ones that were fading.

'Come on, Katie,' Mary said as she walked down the pathway. 'I've got us some lunch. We're going down by the stream. It might be a bit cooler down there.'

'I'll just wash my hands, and I'll be with you,' she replied.

Mary laid out the meal on the white patio table which was shadowed by a large parasol. She had prepared salad,

191

freshly picked from the garden, with a selection of cheeses ranging from local soft camembert and brie to harder cheeses which were becoming more popular in France recently. English ham was still a rarity, and the closest Mary could find was a softer *jambon*, which they all liked. A selection of breads, baguettes and dressings finished the savoury spread.

In the centre of the table was a large bowl of fruit that Mary had chilled in the fridge which looked mouth-watering as the frosting turned to tiny beads of dew-like water. Ben had brought out some white wine and chilled beers to quench their thirsts.

Katie ran back to join them.

'You guys must be getting so excited!' she said. 'Is everything ready now?'

'Not everything but the important things are in place,' Mary said enthusiastically 'We've decided that we will go over on the previous Saturday, once our guests have left. Among other things, I want to collect my car so that I can bring it back here after the wedding.'

'By the way,' Katie said, 'are you doing anything special for Ben's birthday on Saturday?'

'Well, I thought ---' Ben started only to be interrupted by Mary.

'You're not paid to think,' she said, 'but I'm told that something is being organised. You will be around won't you, Katie?'

'You bet. Sounds good. If I can help at all ---'

Katie's mobile played its jolly ring tone and she walked away to take the call. She could see on her handset that the call was from Georgina.

'Hi!' she said once she was out of earshot. 'Great to hear from you. How are things going?'

'Not bad at all. I think I've come to terms with my life again – almost back to normal. And you?'

'Yes, me too. I've had a rather nasty experience recently but I think I'm getting over it.'

'What happened?'

'I don't want to go into details. It was just a nasty and very unexpected incident. Maybe I'll tell you more when the right time comes. For the moment, like you, I've got to come to terms with it.'

'Sorry about that. How's Alex?'

'He's as lovely as ever. He's so tanned now and his hair is so blonde, he looks absolutely great. He can say my name now. He calls me Kay. Isn't that sweet? Aren't you going to ask about Ben?'

'Should I?'

'Well, if you think you've got over him, I would have thought you would.'

'OK then. How's Ben?'

'Not much change there, but you should know that he and Mary are getting married next month.' There was such a long pause that Katie thought Georgina had hung up on the call.

'Are you still there?'

'Yes, I'm still here. That came as a bit of surprise. Maybe I'm not so 'over him' as I thought. But, hey-ho, something else I've got to accept and get used to.'

'Sorry,' Katie said, 'but you did ask about him.

'Only because you said I should, remember?'

'Do you think you would be able to come to the wedding?'

'I don't think so. I don't think that would be a very good idea, do you?'

'I think Ben would be delighted to see you there.'

193

'And Mary?'

'Yes, I think she would be happy- for Ben anyway. It would kind of put everything in its place wouldn't it? For everyone – you, Ben and Mary. And I tell you who else would love to see you.'

'Alex?'

'Absolutely.'

'You're beginning to persuade me, Katie. I'll give it some serious thought. Now let's change the subject.'

The call went on for several minutes more with Georgina asking about everything and everybody. Only when she ran out of credit did the call end and Katie made her way back to the patio by the stream.

'Who was that?' Mary asked.

'Georgina,' Katie replied watching the reaction on their faces. She thought Ben was going to choke on his baguette, but it was Mary who spoke again.

'What did she want?'

'She just wanted to ask how everyone was, really. She said she still misses *La Sanctuaire* and was catching up on the news, that's all.'

'Did you tell her about the wedding?'

'Yes, I did.'

'And how did she take that?'

'Pretty well. She says she's come to terms with things and is getting on with her life again. She said it was something else she would have to accept and get used to – her words, not mine.'

'That's brilliant. It's good to know that she's getting over her infatuation, isn't it Ben?'

Ben looked up, his mouth full of food and merely nodded. He didn't like the word infatuation.

Katie wondered what he really felt and, in an attempt at easing the situation, turned to Alex to help him with his lunch.

Midday meals at *La Sanctuaire* were fast catching on to the extended French lunches, lasting anything up to two hours. Mary had been surprised when she discovered that car parking was free for the hours of midday to two o'clock, to allow for the long lunch hours. The only down side was that most shops, and even some banks, were closed for that period as well. It was all part of French life, she supposed, and so she tried to introduce it at home as well.

They were just coming to the end of the meal when Katie heard a car pulling into the driveway at the front of the cottages.

'Who's that?' Mary asked.

'I'll go and find out,' Katie offered and ran up the garden to see Gilbert walking towards her.

'Hello, Katie,' he said cheerfully as he gave Katie a warm hug and the obligatory kisses to her cheeks. 'How are you doing?'

'I'm fine, Gilbert. You?'

'Yes, me too. I thought I would come and get you up-to-date on Antoine. I presume you want to know how he's doing?'

'Too right. Is he back home?'

'No. The doctors suggested that he stayed up there for a few days while they monitor his state of mind.'

'What did they say?'

Gilbert gave her a full report of what they had told him. They admitted that the change in medication was probably a factor in his behaviour and would consider reverting to his previous treatment once they had reassessed his condition.

'I don't understand why they changed anything. His old medication seemed to be working well, didn't it?' Katie said.

'I agree,' Gilbert said. 'I wouldn't be surprised if they were trying to save a few Euros. Some of these drugs are very expensive. On the other hand, it could be that there are new products on the market, which are supposed to do the same thing. Anyway, I've told Antoine to make sure he's happy with what they are doing for him before he leaves the clinic, and I will certainly have a word with the doctors before I bring him home.'

As they spoke, Ben and Mary came back from the garden with empty trays and Alex, still walking his 'dog'.

Gilbert had to repeat most of what he had told Katie and a few minutes later, drove off, leaving Katie feeling relieved that something positive was being done for Antoine. She could hardly believe it, but she was missing him.

## Chapter 34

Commissaire Boulet lived an organised life with his wife and two daughters. If you asked his wife, she would tell you that he was exasperatingly meticulous in everything he did; a perfectionist. How she wished, sometimes that he would let go and do something reckless, but she doubted that he ever would. Even their holidays had to be planned to such a degree that they knew, before they set off, exactly where they would be each day, the exact time of departure and arrival and precise details of hotel rooms and hire cars. If anything were to veer from the plans, he would immediately show signs of tension until things were back on track.

This desire for perfection was evident in his police work as well. He expected the same degree of precision from his officers, whatever rank they may be. However, he had but a handful of officers who came anywhere near his expectations. The one officer who he would be delighted to have working alongside him was Lizzie, but he knew that would not happen. She was too happy carrying out her undercover work in Paris. She was a hands-on woman but her policing skills were worth as much as half a dozen of his men in Angers. She was attractive, too, but he would never consider getting too close. Any kind of romantic relationship, however tempting it might be, was definitely not on his agenda.

Having opened his mail and sorted it into three categories – immediate, today and delegate, he stirred his coffee that his secretary had, as always, brought to him five minutes after his arrival. Only then did he switch on his desktop computer.

A rare smile lit up his face when he saw that there was a lengthy report from Lizzie. He decided to come back to that after he had scanned his other emails.

Once the daily round of interruptions had ceased, he went back to Lizzie's report. It was lengthy, detailed - much as he would expect from her.

In her report, she reaffirmed that there was indisputable evidence that Masterson had purchased most of the items used in the devices from the *Intermarché* store at Madeleine. She had inspected the CCTV tapes and confirmed that the man at the checkout at 14.05 was, indeed, the man who had stayed at her apartment for two nights.

She said that there was no evidence that he had constructed the devices, but there was little doubt that he had. They were still attempting to trace his steps after he left *Intermarché*. However, they had had a breakthrough in that they now had images of him entering the store on Rue de Maubeuge at 16.24 on the day before the fire. An external CCTV camera, a short distance up Rue de Maubeuge, had picked him up. Although the images were blurry, the camera was a modern, state of the art piece of equipment, and it was a simple matter to enhance the images. Masterson could be seen wearing a grey hooded jacket entering the store.

There were no pictures of him inside the store. He must have observed where the cameras were, and avoided them, her report said. And, strangely he was not seen leaving the premises.

Her conclusions were that they had proof of him buying the parts and also being on the premises within the required window. In her opinion, there was enough evidence to make a good case against him.

Finally she asked Claude Boulet to let her know if she had omitted anything of importance.

The Commissaire sat back in his red leather swivel chair and smiled.

In his opinion, there was sufficient impelling evidence to request an extradition order so that they could charge Mr Masterson with arson, and hold him in custody while they endeavoured to discover the links between him and Bear and possibly Donald O'Hanlon. The opportunity was too good to miss, but it must be handled quickly. The normal procedures, through Interpol, could take some time so he had to call in a few favours.

His first telephone call was to his counterpart in Paris, Louis Armand.

'Did Lizzie let you have a copy of the report she sent to me?' he asked his colleague.

'She did indeed.'

'Good work from your men, Louis.'

'I agree. How can I help you?'

'Do you agree that we have enough evidence to call Mr Masterson in for questioning?'

'You mean extradition?'

'Exactly.'

'I guess we have enough evidence, but an extradition order for an arson attack? Seems unlikely.'

'Louis, I just want him back in Paris. I want to interrogate him in respect of all the other bits of this unsavoury jigsaw. I'm not all that interested in the arson charge. It's just a way of being able to talk to him about other things. We might be able to offer a reduced sentence for the arson if he cooperates with us. What do you think?'

Louis Armand could see that it would be good to solve more than one case by using this man.

'The question is, Louis, do you know anyone in the UK hierarchy who could help us bypass Interpol? Does anybody owe you any favours?'

'Not in the UK, but I think I know somebody at Interpol who could maybe get round the red tape.'

'Can you get in touch and let me know if it's a goer?'

'For sure. How would you like to handle it?'

'What I would *like* is to be able to talk directly with the Chief Constable of the appropriate area. I think it would be Thames Valley police. I doubt whether that's possible, but that's what I would like.'

'I'll see what I can do, Claude.'

'Great. Don't forget to stress that it's not really the arson charge we are interested in. We might be able to solve a number of other cases.'

'Of course. I'll get back to you as soon as I can.'

Commissaire Claude Boulet usually played everything by the rules. This was quite audacious behaviour for him but he could see that the right result would far outweigh any risk he was taking. He replied to Lizzie's message, telling her what he was attempting to do and congratulated her on her efforts.

Within a few minutes, he received a reply from her saying that she couldn't wait to see Mr Masterson's face when he discovered who she was.

Claude heard from his colleague sooner than he expected.

'I've managed to arrange a direct link for you with the head of Thames Valley Police Special Branch,' Louis Armand said. 'I have given them basic information about the case, but said that you had full knowledge of the background.'

'Do I just phone him, or does this entail going to the UK?' Claude asked.

'Initially, it is merely a phone call, but I guess it may well result in your having to go over there. Is that a problem?'

'No, not at all. I just wanted to be prepared, that's all. This is all above board, isn't it, Louis?'

'Of course it is. It happens all the time. I think it would be wise to record your conversations with the Special Branch man. They have been known to be a bit slippery.'

'Slippery?'

'You know, denying conversations when it suits them. A bit like the security services over here, I suppose.'

'I take your point. I'll make sure my calls are logged and recorded. Thanks again, Louis. I owe you one.'

It was late in the day, and Claude decided to leave the call until the next day. He wanted to make sure that he had everything that he needed to hand before talking to the UK police. He called his secretary on the intercom.

'Marie, can you get me all the files on Tommy Williams, Mary Willson, Ben Coverdale as well as anything we have on file for this Bear character in Paris.'

He then put in a call to Mme Bervois, the judge who was handling the Tommy Williams case.

'Monsieur Boulet, what can I do for you?' she replied.

Claude told her of the latest developments in Paris.

'What I need to know is what stage the Tommy Williams case is at. Are you allowed to tell me that?'

201

'I shouldn't, but I will,' she replied. 'The fact is that I am in no great hurry to get him to trial. I wonder sometimes whether he should be going to trial at all, but at the moment that is what is planned. However, it will be some time yet. Why do you ask?'

Claude told her of the arson attack, and that they had strong evidence that it had been carried out by an English man and they were trying to arrange his extradition.

'We are convinced that he is connected with a man called Bear. The same man who Tommy Williams has told us instructed him to carry out the attack on Mary Willson. So the extradition is an excuse to get him back to Paris for questioning about a few other matters. I'm simply trying to get everything as up-to-date as I can before I talk with the English police tomorrow.'

'Then I wish you luck, Claude. I hope it goes well for you.'

Claude bade her goodbye and wished her a good evening just as Marie knocked on his door and walked in with a pile of files that she put at the end of his desk.

'Some good bedtime reading there, sir,' she said with a wicked smile.

Her boss looked up at her with a more half-hearted smile at which she turned and left the office.

## Chapter 35

Ben had nagged Mary all week to tell him what was being planned for his birthday but to no avail. He had tried his best to obtain some clues, but when the day arrived, he had no more idea of what the day might entail than he did a week ago. Neither she nor Katie were able to enlighten him as they didn't know, either.

'What do I need to wear?' he asked over breakfast.

'Anything you're comfortable in,' was the only answer he received.

'What time is the "do"?'

'There is no "do", Ben. Well not really. Perhaps I'll give you a little clue once our guests have left,' Mary said.

'That's a couple of hours away. Do I have to wait that long?'

'Actually, I think they're planning to get away quite early, so it might not be *that* long.'

'And next week's visitors are not arriving 'til quite late,' Katie added.

'So it's an all-day thing, then?'

'Ben, you're wasting your time. We're not going to tell you. You're like a little boy, wanting to know everything. Just wait, and all will be revealed,' Mary said in her best motherly voice.

Time dragged for Ben. It was true, he couldn't cope with secrets. Eventually, the family who had been staying in Dairy Cottage for the last two weeks, emerged with their luggage, settled their bill and made a reservation for the same two weeks next year.

Alex was left with his Daddy as the two girls cleaned the cottage and changed the bed linen ready for next week's guests. It was a little after eleven o'clock when the quartet left *La Sanctuaire* and drove the short distance to Angers. Still, Ben was no wiser as to what was happening. He was happy to go along with it.

He parked the car near the Chateau, and they walked down to the river, where the surprises started. Waiting for them was Madame Delphine with one of her chefs, François, the lawyer who had helped Ben through the buying procedures for his cottages, and his wife, Michelina. Walking along the path toward them were four of Ben's best friends and, to Katie's delight, Gilbert.

There was a melange of kissing and hugging and it was ten minutes or more before the party walked a short way along the path by the river to where a traditional wooden ferryboat was moored.

The owner of the boat welcomed them and helped them aboard.

The craft was mainly open to the elements except for a small covered area toward the bow. There were bench seats along each side of the boat, and a trestle that was going to constitute a table ran down the centre.

Once everybody had settled into his or her seats, bottles of wine and glasses appeared out of nowhere, and the sound of popping corks filled the air.

Once the 'captain' had gone through the regulatory information of where lifebelts and rafts were stored, the small engine burst into life and the ferryboat ventured slowly away from its mooring, and made a U-turn heading away from the shadows of Anger's impressive chateau.

Within minutes, the animated chatter of all on board drowned the sound of the engine.

It was a beautiful autumn day, the sun glinting on the water and a warm breeze wrapping its arms around them. The river was lined on either side by trees that were showing off their autumnal colours.

Ben insisted in regularly changing seats so that he could talk to as many people as he could, frequently rocking the boat quite violently. Katie was quite happy to feel Gilbert next to her. She had no intention of moving.

Before they knew it they were approaching a small town called Saint-Gemmes-sur-Loire. There was a large grassy area bordering the river, and the boat gently pulled in alongside.

Ben wondered if that was it. A pleasant little ride along the Loire, but he hadn't noticed the silver van parked on the grass, and he had taken little notice of the small marquee alongside it.

Madame Delphine and her chef were the first to disembark and make their way to the tent, the others following at their own pace. Passing to the right of the van, they saw, laid out under the canvas roof, a cornucopia of savoury and sweet foods. The colourful presentation was almost as good as the taste of the foods. Smooth patés, roasted chicken joints and spicy pastries; green and Caesar salads and even a platter with peppers of varying degrees of heat. There was such a choice that it was doubtful anyone could try everything. Needless to say, wine was flowing freely. Rich red, chilled white, delicate rosé, and iced water with mint and lemon to quench the thirst. Ben couldn't believe his eyes.

'Who's idea was this?' he asked Mary when he eventually had a chance to speak with her. She and Alex had become the centre of attention once again. Everyone was anxious to know how she was recovering from her ordeal and intrigued to see how Alex was growing.

'You'll have to ask Madame Delphine,' she replied. 'It's nothing to do with me. I'm just following orders.'

When Ben met up with Madame Delphine, he asked her the same question.

'It wasn't my idea, Ben. I'm not *that* generous. This was ordered and paid for by someone unknown.'

'So you don't know who arranged all this?'

'I have no idea, Ben. All I know is that I was delighted to prepare it for you.'

Ben looked around his guests. Which of them could have organised this? Which one of them could afford it? He went back to the marquee to see if he could catch a snippet of conversation that might give him a clue. All he heard were other people asking the same questions – who had laid on a birthday party like this?

Soon, the tables were reset with sweets and desserts. It looked like a patisserie with tiny pastries, rich chocolate cakes, ice creams and a bowl of Chantilly cream. Ben was getting worried about being sea sick, but overcame his concern by eating more.

The lunch party lasted over two hours. It was good to catch up with news from people he hadn't seen for a while. As he and his guests made their way back to the wooden ferryboat, he presumed that they would be returning to Angers. Once more he was wrong.

The boat continued chugging its way along the river. The scenery was becoming more beautiful the further they went. Tranquil hardly described it. The sound of the water splashing against the side of the craft, the swish of the breeze blowing through the trees that overhung the banks of the river and the myriad echoes of birdsong made the journey both therapeutic and soporific. Ben noticed that more than one of the passengers was beginning to doze.

He, on the other hand, was still trying to puzzle out who his benefactor could be. He had to quiz Madame Delphine again. He had to discover who had organised this amazing day out. He made his way across the small craft to sit next to her. Across on the other side of the boat, Katie was still with Gilbert, although he had noticed more than one of his friends trying their best to engage her in conversation. Nothing new there, he thought.

Madame Delphine was deep in conversation with François. Ben awaited his opportunity.

'Hello Ben,' she said. 'Are you enjoying your day?'

'I can't remember a better day,' Ben replied, 'but I'm still intrigued as to who organised it.'

'Oh, that's simple, Ben. I organised it. I had *carte blanche*. Whoever it was that ordered it merely told me to plan something special. It didn't matter how much it cost, just do it.'

'Just like that?'

'Just like that, Ben. I have no more idea of who ordered it than you. I'm just glad you are enjoying it. I thought you might. I think I know your tastes quite well now.'

'That's obvious,' Ben said and moved to go back to his seat.

'Oh, by the way, Ben, it's not over yet. There's more to come.'

Katie, whilst seemingly in deep conversation with Gilbert, was watching Ben intensely. She knew what he was attempting to discover, but there was no way that he would find out. She felt good inside, seeing him enjoying himself. This was the first time that she had got one over on him and she was so pleased with herself, she was almost giggling inside.

Ben had been so good to her in the last few months and until now, she had never been able to repay him; firstly because she didn't have the money but also because he wouldn't let her. It was different now. She had become a wealthy young woman since her husband's untimely death and it was giving her great pleasure to be able do something special for him on his thirty seventh birthday.

She had known Ben for a number of years, and had once tempted him into bed with her. He was the first man ever to turn down sex with her, all because he was fixated on Mary Willson. She had never quite forgiven him for that.

As the little boat prepared once again to moor at the side of the river, Madame Delphine stood up and addressed them all.

'This lovely little town,' she said, 'is Les Ponts-de-Cé. We have come here, specifically, for Ben, Mary and Alex. I will be taking them to a rather special place. You are all welcome to join us, or you may explore this lovely place at your leisure.'

Ben and Mary glanced at each other, not knowing what was going on. Alex had shared his time between his parents, Katie and Michelina, but now Mary grabbed him to herself as they made their way off the boat.

The whole party decided to join with the family as they walked up the typically French high street with stone and whitewashed buildings on either side. Various banks, the ubiquitous Spar shop and a wide range of small stores and offices as well as cafes and *tabacs* were there to be seen.

At the top of the street, where a fountain played in the centre of a roundabout, the party crossed to the left.

'This is where we must leave you, I'm afraid,' Madame Delphine announced taking Ben, Mary and Alex with her into a short driveway leading to a pretty white fronted house. 'We shouldn't be more than thirty minutes or so.'

'Let me explain,' she said to Mary and Ben, as they reached the building. 'This is an *École Maternelle*, – what you would call a nursery school. But this is probably the best in the area, and I've arranged for the proprietors to meet with you to show you round. They are friends of mine. That's why they are happy to meet you here on a Saturday afternoon.'

This was not something Ben or Mary had expected, but they followed their friend into the house and were warmly greeted by the owners and shown round, room by room, to see what the children did. There was the usual artwork, a maths room with numbers and simple sums on the walls, a language room with lists of verbs and conjugations, and then the kitchen. Kid-size sinks and cookers, a wide range of highly polished utensils and tiny table and chairs filled the room.

'But now come and see the garden!' they were told. 'You see, we encourage the children to grow the vegetables that they cook – within season, of course.'

The tour took more than the half hour that Madame Delphine had suggested, but then there was one more surprise.

'We would like to invite you and your friends into the garden at the back of the house. We have done our best to provide you all with an English tea. We hope you will enjoy it,' the proprietor announced.

Madame Delphine returned to the front of the house, brought back the other six travellers along with the boat's captain, and took them to the back of the house where tables had been positioned under parasols and pots of tea and plates of triangular sandwiches were laid out among a selection of cakes. These were not the usual French pastries found in any patisserie, but iced buns, cupcakes and Viennese fingers.

'These were all made by our children,' the proprietors boasted, 'with, of course, a little help from the staff.'

Even Katie was not expecting this. Madame Delphine had used a big chunk of poetic license with this, but it was a fitting end to a lovely day.

It was into the evening before the party boarded the ferryboat once more and listened to the chugging of its engine as they made their way back to Angers.

It was late into the evening when Ben's mobile phone buzzed in his pocket. Reluctantly he switched it on and read the text message: *Thought you ought to know, Ben, that Tommy Williams was found dead in his cell this morning. Suspected poisoning. Talk soon, Claude.*

# Chapter 36

The Wednesday morning briefing was already underway when Lizzie entered the room. 'Sorry,' Lizzie said, but her apology was ignored by all present. They would have been surprised if she *had* been on time. She always arrived a few minutes late, but nothing was ever said about it. If it had been any of her colleagues, it would have been a different matter. She settled into her seat, and the briefing commenced.

'It appears,' her Commissaire began, 'that our friend Bear is back. Nobody has seen him, but the signs are there. You agree with this, Lizzie?'

'Yes, sir. As you say, I haven't seen him, but I'm sure he's around somewhere. We all know how good he is at not being seen when it's necessary for him. The addicts are behaving differently, so I presume they are being cared for again.'

'So, it is important that we keep a good look out for him. Obviously, he can't return to the furniture store, so he must have settled somewhere else – probably somewhere local. Find out where that is. The other thing that makes me think he's back in action is that a young man called Tommy Williams, who was being remanded in Angers pending trial, was found dead in his cell at the week-end. Now, if we believe that this guy was hired by Bear to assassinate the

211

woman, Mary Willson, a few weeks ago and it all went wrong, it is probable that the latest death is connected to those facts. In fact I have little doubt about it.'

There were a few questions asked about Tommy's death, but the Commissaire had little information other than the cause of death appeared to be poisoning.

'It's bad news for us, because he had agreed to testify against Bear about the attack on Mary Willson. Now, of course, he can't. However,' he continued, 'we do have progress in respect of Mr Masterson. I have informed my colleague in Angers that it looks extremely likely that we can obtain a swift extradition from the UK. Commissaire Boulet is talking directly with his counterpart in Special Branch in the UK.'

'There is more good news,' Lizzie announced. 'The leads that you boys picked up in Madeleine have brought us what we wanted. The woman who said that she recognised Masterson said that she had seen him outside of Église Saint-Roch. When we sent in sniffer dogs to search for phosphorus or sulphur, the dogs found traces of both on a pew in a corner of the church. Yesterday the same dogs were used in my apartment and picked up the scent there as well. Very little, but enough to connect it to Masterson. Great work, guys.'

'Yes, indeed. We now have a consolidated case against Masterson for arson, and we will be able to put some heavy pressure on him regarding Bear. He must know that arson can carry a long prison sentence in this country which gives us considerable bargaining power. You've all worked well on this case. Now we need to know where Bear is. Go find him, but don't let him know that we know.'

\*\*\*\*\*

Chas was in a deep sleep in his pretty semi-detached cottage in Theale, a few miles west of Reading. He jolted into life. There was heavy knocking on his front door and it sounded urgent. Glancing at his bedside clock, he saw that it was just after six o'clock. His heart pounding from the shock awakening, he donned his dressing gown and went down to the front door. The knocking was incessant.

'OK, OK, I'm coming,' he shouted above the noise.

As he opened the door he saw a police officer running towards the front door with a battering ram.'

'What the fuck ...?'

'Police, sir. May we come in?'

Chas held the door open and four plain clothes officers walked in.

'Charles Masterson, I presume? I'm detective inspector Robson, and this is detective sergeant Belover.'

'I'm so pleased to meet you,' Chas sneered.

'I'm here to arrest you on behalf of the Paris police on a charge of arson. If you would like to pack a bag---'

'Hang on. Arson? Paris? Pack a bag? What is this?'

'I need you to come with me to the police station, where you will be formally cautioned and the necessary paperwork can be filled out. You will then be accompanied by two police officers to Paris, where you will be handed over to the Commissaire who is handling this case.'

'I don't know anything about arson.'

'But you have recently been in Paris, haven't you, sir?'

'Well, yes, I can't deny that. I had my passport stolen and had to obtain papers to get back to the UK. Yes, I was in Paris. That doesn't mean that I set light to anything.'

'The French authorities tell us that they have indisputable evidence that you did, sir, and that is why they want to ask you some questions.'

'And what if I don't want to answer their bleeding questions? Do I not have any rights?'

'This is an extradition order, sir. We are merely carrying out orders. Now we can handcuff you and take you to the station, but I can't believe you want that. Or you can come voluntarily and make things easier for everyone.'

'I want a solicitor.'

'I'm sure that can be arranged for you at the station, sir. So, what's it to be?'

For all his bravado, Chas was a worried man. He had been so meticulously careful. How could anybody trace the fire back to him? The place was trashed. There were no clues, no evidence. He didn't make mistakes like that.

'I'll pack a bag, then. Hang on just a few minutes.'

Chas went to his bedroom, hoping he would be alone long enough to call Donald, but one of the constables accompanied him. He hurriedly threw clothes and toiletries into a large holdall and went back to the detectives. As they escorted him to their car, Chas noticed a few neighbours looking out from behind their curtains. He felt like giving them all two fingers, but decided against it. A hand was placed on his head as he was helped into the back seat.

'Do you get some kind of perverted satisfaction from doing this?' Chas asked as they drove off. 'Do you have to wake the whole bloody neighbourhood? Do you have to use a liveried police car? I guess you must enjoy embarrassing people, whether they are guilty or not.' There was no reply from any of the officers.

'And if I hadn't have opened the door when I did, were you really planning to smash it in? For Christ's sake, this

214

isn't a murder enquiry. I'm not a suspected paedophile or a terrorist. You people are way over the top.'

But he was talking to himself. He imagined that they had heard all this a thousand times before.

Arriving at the Thames Valley Police headquarters, he was shown to an interview room, and soon afterwards, two men from the special squad came in to guide him through the procedures.

He was allowed one phone call. He dialled the only mobile number he had for Donald, but the call was not answered. He could not think of anyone else to call. The officers then confiscated his mobile and kept it with his other possessions for the French police to deal with.

Later that day Chas was escorted to Heathrow Airport on his way to Paris.

*****

It was breakfast time on Sunday. Ben did not disclose the latest news about Tommy Williams to either Mary or Katie yesterday. He didn't want to spoil their enjoyment of his birthday in the same way that the text from Claude Boulet had for him. This morning he had to tell them both.

'Dead? How can he be dead?' Mary screamed. 'He was in police custody.'

'I know. It seems impossible, but that, according to the text I received, is the case. I'll get in touch with Claude on Monday to see if I can find out more.'

'Tommy always said he was scared of what might happen if he testified against Bear, didn't he?' Katie said. 'It seems he was right, poor bugger.'

'Claude won't be well pleased, either. He was counting on Tommy's testimony to get Bear into court.'

'Did Tommy have any family?' Mary asked.

'Not that I know of. He may have done before he became hooked on drugs, but I really don't know. I can ask. The police should have his next of kin details.' Ben said. 'In the meantime, Mary, I don't want you out of my sight, not even for a minute. Or Alex. I think I'll see about getting an alarm system fitted, and possibly CCTV. I thought by coming to France I was getting away from all this.'

'It's all my fault, really, isn't it,' Mary said. 'If I hadn't been stupid enough to get involved with Donald, none of this would have happened.'

'That's all water under the bridge, Mary. We probably would not be living here at all if it weren't for him, so there are good parts to it as well.'

'Yes, but ---'

'But nothing, Mary. It's our future I'm concerned about at the moment, not our past. Let's just agree that for now, none of us goes out alone. OK?'

'Agreed, but it's making me nervous,' Mary said.

*****

'There's going to be a full enquiry into this, Ben, I can assure you of that. I want to know how this could have happened. If Bear instigated this, it implies that there must be a leak somewhere within the police force or the prison service. That worries me. I need to know how Bear found out that Tommy Williams was being held in Angers.'

Commissaire Claude Boulet was hopping mad when Ben contacted him on Monday morning.

'Will Tommy's death make a lot of difference to the case as a whole?' Ben asked.

'I don't know, Ben. It would have been good to have Tommy there as a witness, but we have his signed statements which we can use in court. But I doubt you've heard the latest news.'

Claude told Ben about Masterson's extradition from the UK to answer charges of arson.

'We will be pushing him hard to tell us what his link with Bear is and why he set fire to Bear's premises. We think that he might also be the missing link between Bear and Donald O'Hanlon. So, you see, it's not all bad news.'

'When will this be happening?'

'For all I know, Ben, he may well be in Paris already. If that is the case, he will be interrogated very soon. There are time limits in matters of this nature, and we cannot hold him for long without charging him with something. I will keep you informed, but I must go now, Ben. There is much to do.'

Ben thanked Claude for all his help and relayed the latest news to Mary and Katie.

'Do you know anything about this other man, Masterson, Ben?' Katie asked.

'Nothing at all, but the police in Paris are convinced that he is linked to Bear in some way. Why else would he burn Bear's property down? All we need them to do now is to link him back to Donald.'

Katie was more nervous on the day of the trial than she could ever remember being. She had travelled over on the Saturday and Mark, her late husband's father, met her at Southampton airport and drove her to his lovely home in the village of Wheathampstead. The grandeur and size of the house was more than she remembered from her previous visits. The surrounding gardens and woodlands looked magnificent in their kaleidoscope of autumnal colours.

Mark was his usual affable self. She wondered how Dave, his son and, for a short while her husband, had managed to go off the rails while being part of such a lovely family.

Dave had been murdered in Albania by bandits because of his involvement in human trafficking. What Mark must have gone through when he learned about it from the police, she couldn't imagine. Somehow, between them, they had come through the trauma together and had grown closer as a result.

Her first few stays had been nervy and apprehensive but now she actually looked forward to her visits. Each time she stayed with him, she wished that she had had a father like him.

The weekend was very relaxed. Katie went out with him on Saturday afternoon to his local Waitrose store, and helped him choose food for the weekend. It was rather more expensive shopping than her own, regardless of the fact that foodstuffs in France were generally more expensive than in the UK. Mark enjoyed the best quality in whatever he did, and shopping was no exception.

They rose late on Sunday morning, and had a leisurely breakfast.

'I'm going to church,' Mark announced after eating. 'Would you like to join me?'

Katie was somewhat surprised by the invitation, but said she would be happy to join him. They walked the short distance to the village church where, not so long ago, she had married his son. Her emotions as they entered the church were a mixture of nostalgia, sadness and anger. She could so easily recall the big day; she was the happiest girl in the world. She had never considered being married, but she had found in Dave everything she wanted – and the sex was sensational.

What she had never understood was why, if he loved her as much as he said, he had taken the risks that he did. How could he gamble their relationship by working for a human-trafficking gang? She had never come to terms with that. That was why, when she heard of his death and the reason for it, she had aborted both him and any relationship they ever had from her life.

She found it difficult to concentrate on the service. She stood when everyone else stood, kneeled when they kneeled, and did her best to sing the hymns that she knew. She was also aware of Mark watching her, and on one occasion when they sat down, she welcomed his arm round her shoulder. It was a warm, friendly, parental gesture, nothing more and she felt safe.

The same feeling was there on Monday as they drove to the County Court in Reading; a fusion of terror at having to face her abductors again with the comforting knowledge that Mark was there in the court with her, albeit not by her side.

The waiting outside the courtroom was the worst part. Katie's heart was pounding, wondering how the defence lawyers would be questioning her. These people had the knack of being able to make the most innocent of witnesses somehow feel guilty. She was determined not to be belittled in any way. Mark encouraged her resolve by reminding her that she was here to give evidence and if her evidence were true, then the perpetrators would be brought to justice.

Nevertheless, when the waiting was over, and her name was called, she was shaking with tension and had to hold tight to the rails that led into the witness box to maintain her equilibrium.

She looked around the court, at the jury, the press and others in the room but was interrupted when the first question was put to her by the prosecution barrister.

'Mrs Atkinson, can I ask you to look around the court and tell me if you recognise anybody.'

Katie slowly cast her eyes around, looking at every face. And then froze.

'Well,' the barrister continued, 'do you recognise anybody?'

'If you mean the men in the dock, sir, I can't be certain that I recognise them.'

'You can't be sure. Why is that?'

'For most of the time during my kidnap, it was dark and they were wearing balaclavas. I cannot truthfully say that I recognise any of them. But there is someone in the court that I *do* recognise.'

220

'Can you point out that person?'

Katie turned towards the jury and pointed to a smartly dressed man in the back row.

'You have seen this man before?'

'Yes. Only briefly, but I met him in Frankfurt where I was being held captive.'

'He was part of the gang that captured you?'

'Not exactly. But he knew the men who had. It was this man,' she said, pointing at the man again, 'who threatened to sell me as a prostitute or sex slave or something like that. I remember his exact words – "you are a very beautiful girl, and you could easily earn enough to pay your husband's debts."'

'Are you absolutely sure that this is the same man?'

'Yes, sir. I wouldn't forget that face in a million years. He made me look right into his eyes. He terrified me more than any of the others.'

'My lord,' the barrister said, approaching the judge, 'may I suggest we have a short recess while we discuss this development.'

The jury was told to retire and the lawyers and the judge left the courtroom only to return a few minutes later, whereupon the jury was called back into the courtroom. They were then dismissed and the case adjourned. The police arrested the man that Katie had pointed out and took him away for questioning. Katie was told that she could go, but would be required to stand as a witness again at a future date. She didn't need a second telling and almost ran from the courtroom.

Her barrister caught up with her and explained the ramifications of what had happened. The case had to be adjourned and would be scheduled for a later date with a newly elected jury.

'If we can prove that he was there illegally,' he said, 'it could almost certainly change things to our advantage. I'm hoping that we might be able to get the defendants to plead guilty to all the charges. That would be a good result.'

Katie thanked him for what he had done. Then she saw Mark approaching her from the visitors' gallery, and ran over to him and gave him a hug.

'That's going to make the news this evening, I think,' Mark said. 'Well done, Katie. That took some guts.'

'I'm still shaking,' she replied. 'When I saw him sitting there, I couldn't believe my eyes.'

'You have no doubts about it?'

'Absolutely not. He held my face in his hand when he said those words. Our faces were inches apart. There's no way I can be mistaken about him. He was posh, and smarmy – and English!' she said. 'I'll swear on my life about him. What I can't understand is how he came to be on the jury. Was it just coincidence?'

'Oh, I doubt it, Katie. One way or another he was there in an attempt to swing the jury. I imagine he may well be facing a long prison sentence for perverting the course of justice, if nothing else.'

'Can we go and get a drink somewhere. I need to get out of here,' Katie said.

'Of course,' Mark replied, and putting his fatherly arm around her once again, guided her out through the foyer into fresh air.

'Let's go and have some lunch. I know a nice little place just round the corner.'

'I'm not sure that I'm hungry,' Katie replied.

'I think you'll change your mind when you see the menu,' Mark said.

That evening when Katie was contemplating going to bed, her mobile rang. She didn't recognise the caller's number that showed on the screen.

'Hi,' she said tentatively.

'Katie?' She knew the voice immediately, and her heart missed a beat.

'Hello, Antoine,' she said.

'Katie. I've managed to find you. I'm in London. I couldn't wait another week until you come home. I've come over especially to see you. Can we meet?'

'Well, not tonight. I'm just about to go to bed.'

'Tomorrow then? I must see you.'

*****

Donald was fast becoming a hermit. He had not ventured out of his room during the last four days. Now he had run out of food, he had no alternative but to venture out - or starve. He didn't understand why he was so reticent to leave his house. He had not had any visits from the police. In fact, as far as he knew, nobody had tried to make contact with him. His desire to 'vanish' seemed to be working.

Nevertheless, he took every precaution he could whenever he undertook an outing and today was no exception. He made a tour of the upper floor of the house, staring at length from each window into the grounds surrounding the house. Only then did he go downstairs, unlock the doors from the central security board, and let himself sample fresh air at the top of the flight of steps which led down to the driveway.

Using his small 'doofer' to secure the house, he made his way to the double garages where his silver Mercedes

Benz had been left. As he went to open the driver's door, he noticed some damage to the offside front wing.

He presumed that Niels must have caused the deep scratches when he took the car to Kintbury, and cursed the little man once again. He made a note to get the car to a garage as soon as he could.

His mission today was to stock up his larder so that he had enough to eat for a few more days. To ensure the best anonymity, he headed straight to his local Tesco and parked the car in the quietest section of the car park.

He hated shopping, hated being hustled by determined women with their bulging trollies and obnoxious kids, hated queuing whilst the girl on the checkout was conversing with her colleagues instead of looking after the customer. It had never been a favourite pastime, but now that he wanted it to be done in the minimum time possible, it became even more of a nightmare. Why did they have to move things around? He thought he knew exactly where to find the items on his list. Instead, he found himself weaving his way up and down each aisle as if in some kind of treasure hunt. What should have taken him fifteen minutes at the most was going to take him twice as long.

Almost an hour later, when he arrived back at his house, he let out a sigh of relief, made himself a large mug of coffee, and sat down to watch the news channel. When the financial news came on, he was surprised to see that there had been some improvement in the value of the Euro. He wondered what effect that might have had on his inter-currency dealings. This tempted him for the first time in weeks to open up his laptop. His first stop was the Forex site, where he saw confirmation that things were at last moving in the right direction for him.

His heart was beginning to pound as he keyed in the password for his investment portfolio.

This was the best day he had had in a long time. He had given up on his daily check on the currency market. It had depressed him too much recently. He was not in such a serious situation as he had imagined. Clever transactions now could put him in a much more comfortable position, and in a much happier frame of mind.

Not having a printer attached to his computer, he made copious notes on trends and future estimates to enable him to make informed decisions as to when to make a move.

Basheer was slaving away at his workstation, working on new security measures for SRX Solutions. Being a seasoned computer hacker, he was able to incorporate high levels of protection that other experts would not consider. He had found it so easy in the past to gain access into computer systems of some major organisations that he was almost embarrassed by the lack of meaningful security being used by them. SRX was one such business. If anyone wanted to, they could, with the minimum of hacking experience, be able to corrupt or sabotage files enough to bring the whole system crashing down. His skills were now being used for the good of the company.

As he worked, a series of bleeps came from his computer speakers.

*"Donald on line."* flashed in red at the bottom of his screen.

Basheer immediately logged off from what he was doing and became a hacker again. In less than half a minute he was in contact with Donald's laptop. A few seconds more, and he could see that Donald was searching a financial site. The figures didn't mean much to Basheer, but that was beside the point. He had tracked the computer, and now had to use his skills to locate the machine.

As quickly as it had arrived, the *"Donald on line"* message disappeared from his screen. Donald had logged off.

'Damn,' Basheer said aloud, 'but he'll be back. I'd bet on it.' He decided against contacting Ben Coverdale. There was nothing to report until he could locate the computer.

## Chapter 38

Commissaire Louis Armand was seldom the most amiable of police officers in Paris, but today he was putting on a good show of being a kind, genial man.

'Thank you so much, Monsieur Masterson, for agreeing to travel back to Paris.'

'I didn't exactly choose to come. I wasn't given any option.' Chas said. He was ignored.

'There are just a few things you might be able to help us with in our investigation into the fire at a second hand furniture store close to Paris Nord station. I believe you were in Paris – in the proximity of the fire in fact – when the fire took hold on Thursday night, three weeks ago.'

'I can't deny I was in Paris,' Chas said, 'but I don't think I was in that particular area at the time.'

Louis Armand offered Chas a long hard stare.

'Are you sure of that, Monsieur Masterson?'

'When did the fire break out?'

'Approximately two-thirty in the morning.'

'Well, I would have been asleep at that hour.'

'Where?'

'Where what?'

'Where were you asleep at that time?'

'I was staying with a friend.'

'His name?'

'It was a young lady. Her name was Lizzie.'

'Surname?'

'I – er – I don't know her surname.'

'A lady of the night, perhaps?'

'No. She helped me after I was attacked, and she said I could stay there a couple of nights.'

'But you don't even know her name.'

'She just introduced herself as Lizzie.'

'And you introduced yourself as Matt, I believe. Why was that?'

'No. I think you've got that wrong. My name is Chas.'

'Our witness is quite adamant that you said your name was Matt.'

'Sorry, they're mistaken.'

'Perhaps we'd better ask her, then.' Louis Armand pressed the button on his intercom. 'Can you ask Lizzie to come in, please?'

Chas's face went several shades paler, as he saw Lizzie walk casually into the office.

'How can I help?' she asked, and then merely glancing at Chas, said 'Hi, Matt.'

'It's Chas.'

Lizzie smiled at Chas. 'It may be Chas today, but when you stayed at my apartment it was most definitely Matt. You told me that your name was Matthew, but said most people call you Matt,' she said.

Chas said nothing.

'Thank you for clearing that up, Lizzie,' her Commissaire said, and Lizzie disappeared from the room as quickly as she had entered it.

Chas still had no idea of Lizzie's part in this. He presumed that she was just a witness.

There was now an icy silence in the room. Chas was trying to figure a way out of the pit into which he was falling.

Louis Armand opened a file on his desk and slowly and deliberately spread out several separate piles.

'You do realise how seriously we take arson in France, Mr Masterson.' It wasn't a question, more a statement of fact.

'You are presuming that I am guilty of arson, but I'm not.'

'I wish I could believe you, Mr Masterson, but the evidence I have here on my desk suggests otherwise. It suggests that you purchased the necessary parts for the incendiary devices from an *Intermarché* store at Madeleine, then you went to Église Saint-Roch where you manufactured the devices before returning to Rue de Maubeuge and placing the devices on the first and second floors of the store.'

'Sounds a bit circumstantial. But it wasn't me.'

'The problem was, you see, that one of the devices failed, and we were able to trace where all the components – or most of them – were purchased. Purchased by you, Mr Masterson. CCTV footage shows you at the checkout at *Intermarché*. We found traces of the explosive materials at Lizzie's apartment, and we have witnesses who saw you enter the store that afternoon. So, once again, I don't believe a word you are saying. We have unquestionable evidence that you were totally responsible for the attack on the store belonging to a man called Bear.'

Chas said nothing.

'What I want to know, Mr Masterson, is why you did it. What is your relationship with Bear? What has he done to you to make you do this?'

'I have nothing to say,' Chas said quietly.

'Then I am going ahead with this case, and will demand the highest punishment for such a deliberate act of vandalism. You should expect a prison sentence of five or maybe even ten years.'

Chas felt a chill run down his spine at the mention of Bear's name. He needed some time on his own in order to figure out the best way forward, if there was a way forward, or at least to work out the best damage limitation he could. He was in trouble, and he knew it. He was relieved when he heard the Commissaire say, 'I am detaining you for further questioning, Mr Masterson. I suggest you spend the time considering your position. As of now, things do not look good for you.'

The two police officers who had entered the room took Chas to his cell.

Ben was pushing Alex around the small supermarket in *Sainte-Justine*, helping Mary with the shopping when he felt his mobile buzz in his pocket.

*"We've got him, Ben. Check your emails, Basheer."*

Under normal circumstances, Ben would have been excited, but he replied, *"Thanks, Basheer. I'm getting married in a few days, so won't be doing anything about it for the time being. Can you just keep a tag on him?"*

*"Certainly can. But read the email anyway – quite interesting."*

Ben didn't reply. He returned the phone to his pocket and caught up with Mary. Alex loved it when

Ben pushed him fast, and there were squeals of laughter as they nearly crashed into the back of his Mum.

'Who was that?' Mary enquired.

'Nothing important. Do we need some more of these nappies?'

'We do, but not that size. Do you not notice these things?'

'Obviously not,' Ben replied sheepishly.

When they arrived at the checkout, Mary said that she thought she had everything they needed. Ben looked at the heaped trolley, and said that it certainly looked that way. Alex was doing his best to twist round in his seat to grab a packet of chocolate covered biscuits he had seen but was unsuccessful.

'Biss,' he said, looking hopefully at his Mum.

Unpacking the shopping when they arrived home took a little longer than usual because Mary was having to separate the things that were going with them to the UK at the weekend from the normal, everyday items.

Only when everything was put away in the right places, did Ben boot up his computer. Amongst the usual spam, there were two items which interested him. One was from Basheer, the other from Katie.

He opened the latter first. She was simply asking him to call her when he had a spare minute. The one from Basheer was, indeed, interesting. If what Basheer was saying were true, Donald had returned to the house in Wallingford. He was, apparently, spending a considerable amount of time checking exchange rates between Sterling, Euros and American Dollars. There were also a few transactions between the currencies.

That seemed accurate enough information for Ben. He knew that Donald had dealings in such things. He had seen the screens in his office on the day that Donald attacked him with an antique sword. He replied to the email, and thanked Basheer for his efforts, but reiterated that he had more important things on his mind at the moment.

Mary was always the more organised of the two, and as Ben shut down his computer, he heard her calling from upstairs that she needed his help.

'I'm in Katie's room,' she said as Ben ran up the stairs.

Laid out in neat piles on Katie's bed was everything she was planning to take with them to England.

'Have a look through this,' she said, 'and see if you think I've missed anything.'

Ben stood there staring at the orderly array of clothes and toiletries.

'You can't do it by just looking at it, Ben. See if I've chosen the right shirts and trousers for you. See if you think I've included enough changes of clothes for Alex.'

Ben started to thumb through the piles.

'We're only going for a few days,' he said. 'You've got enough stuff here for a few weeks.'

'You reckon? I don't want to forget anything important.'

He took his wife-to-be by the shoulders and turned her round to face him.

'The only important thing to take is you. If you forget anything else, it really doesn't matter, Mary. I'm sure everything that we need is there. Just relax. The last thing I want is for you to get all tensed up.'

They hugged.

'Me 'ug. Me 'ug,' they heard from below them, and Alex was there with his arms held up to join them.

'I've just had an email from Katie asking me to call her,' Ben said.

'What about?'

'I don't know until I call her. I'll go and do it now.'

Ben went to make the call while Mary started to prepare the evening meal with Alex in tow.

The call lasted longer than Ben had expected. Katie told him of the outcome of the trial, that it had been postponed, and the man in the jury who she had remembered so clearly from her time being held in Frankfurt, had been arrested. Ben just listened. How does this girl always seem to get herself into these scrapes? She also told him that Antoine was in London and they were meeting up tomorrow.

'Do you think I'm mad, Ben? I've agreed to see him, but I'm wondering whether I should have.'

'I think you are probably crazy, but I know how much he means to you, so I guess you have to meet up, don't you?'

'That's what I feel, too. I'm excited, scared and – I don't know what else. I'm in a right mess, Ben. I'll let you know how it goes.'

Returning to the kitchen, Ben recounted everything to Mary.

'What is it with that girl?' Mary said. 'Everything she does seems to be a drama. She should write a book. So is she staying over there now until the wedding?'

'Yes. She says she's enjoying her stay with Dave's father. From what she's told me, Mark has taken on the role of a father figure and she's extremely excited about meeting with Antoine.'

'Why doesn't anything surprise me about that girl?' Mary said as she began to lay the table.

## Chapter 39

Donald was becoming more encouraged by the day. It was amazing how a few percentage points in exchange rates could make so much difference to his financial wellbeing. Each time he turned on his laptop there was another movement, and a high percentage of the movements were in his favour.

He played his cards very carefully, moving modest amounts from one currency to another, sometimes for just a few hours. The thrill and excitement of playing his game was back. He had less to play with than in the past, but what he did have was improving in value by the day.

He wasn't aware that Basheer was also quite impressed by what he was doing. A track was being kept on every move, every transaction. Basheer so wanted to interfere, to tamper with the figures. It would be so simple to drain away a little of the funds each day, but that was not in his remit. His instructions were to watch what Donald O'Hanlon was up to, and as far as he could see, he was simply playing the currency market.

Oblivious to the fact that each keystroke was being monitored by SRX's hacker, Donald became more adventurous. He at last broke silence in order to find out how his dwindling money laundering business was performing. There were no surprises there. There was money coming in from his 'boys' but barely enough to maintain the kind of life style which he enjoyed a year ago. Something had to be done.

He sent a brief email to Chas asking him to make contact.

Then it was back to Forex, back to making a profit on the exchange rates.

He found himself a plastic cup and opened a bottle of Tesco's special offer Cabernet Sauvignon. Thank God for screw tops, he thought, realising that he had forgotten to buy a corkscrew. For the first time in many weeks, Donald leaned back in his uncomfortable chair and slowly drank the whole bottle.

Tomorrow, he told himself, he would start transferring the balances from some of the other bank accounts. He would need as much liquidity as he could get hold of to make the most of what was happening in the currency markets.

*****

Ben was getting daily reports from Basheer as to Donald's activities, and whilst he really wasn't interested in his undertakings, he was very interested in his location. He passed on his thoughts to Basheer, asking him to ensure that he kept an up to the minute record of Donald's geographical position.

It was Saturday morning. By ten o'clock, everything was packed into the car. All they had to do now was wait for their guests in Dairy Cottage to depart. It seemed that they were reticent about leaving, and it was well past eleven o'clock before Ben, Mary and Alex could leave *La Sanctuaire* on the most exciting visit to Reading that they had ever made.

They could feel each other's exhilaration. The tension was almost palpable, the elation showing on their faces, and even Alex seemed to get into the mood. Whereas he would normally fall asleep as soon as the car drove off, today he was fully awake, alert and animated. They hardly noticed the countryside as they drove north although it was at its most beautiful with breath-taking autumnal hues. Golden leaves fell like feathers from the trees. Beech hedgerows shone in their newly acquired winter colours and farmers were already beginning to tear up fields that had been host to crops of wheat, barley and maize.

Ben fixed his eyes on the long, straight, undulating roads that made driving in France so pleasurable. They knew all the villages and small towns on this journey well. They had driven this road so many times before. They knew the places that they could stop for refreshment - and the places they wouldn't.

They were running late. Ben knew that they had to drive fast to have any chance of catching the afternoon ferry at Caen. There would be a long wait if they didn't. There would be none of the usual leisurely stops today; just brief toilet stops at suitable *Aires* where they could get drinks, feed Alex and drive on.

As luck would have it, the roads were clear and they reached the port with half an hour to spare before the ferry departed. Still half an hour later than they should have been but it didn't seem to matter. Their documents were examined, and they joined the queue. Alex, as always, was hungry. Mary found a few things for him to eat amongst the pile of luggage in the boot, and he was soon happy again.

Normally, Ben would have been at the stern to see the French coastline disappear, thinking only of the return journey. His love of France had not diminished regardless of the catastrophes that had beset him and his family and friends. He could never imagine leaving *La Belle France.* For him, it had lived up to all his desires.

Today, however, he was not to be seen leaning on the rails at the back of the boat. Today, he was on his way to England for a very precious event. The girl with him, who had caused him so much heartache in the past, was finally going to be his wife. A huge new chapter in his life was about to start.

Once under way with the powerful diesel engines throbbing in the depths of the boat, they followed the usual routine of making their way round the shops and play areas for Alex to see. On this occasion, he was showing all the signs of being tired – he had been awake for most of the car journey – but still sufficiently awake to take an interest in all that he saw. Soon enough, when Mary had fed him a jar of banana and custard pudding, he fell asleep in his pushchair, and Ben and Mary made their way to the ships elegant restaurant to enjoy the rest of the crossing in comfort.

'I'm looking forward to getting my car back,' Mary said during their meal. 'It will be nice to have a bit of independence again.'

'Do you mind if we go straight to Katie's house tonight, though. I'm really tired, and we can go over to Goring Heath in the morning to collect it. Betty does a great Sunday carvery as I recall.'

'Fine by me. I think tomorrow is going to be a long enough day, waiting for our big day on Monday, so it would be good to have something to do for part of it.'

For the umpteenth time, they went over the plans for Monday. Ben was looking after Alex while Mary went into Reading to pick up her dress and have her hair coiffured by her old friends. She would travel straight from the salon to the Register Office where Ben would be waiting with Alex. After the ceremony, they and the few guests would be taken to... to what? They didn't know what to expect. Ray had given no clues as to his part in the proceedings. They admitted that they were intrigued to discover what he had put together for them.

The crossing was quiet and Alex slept for the whole journey. The drive from Portsmouth to Reading was not so easy. Even late at night the amount of traffic, the incessant traffic lights and the claustrophobic feeling of the built up areas made driving difficult. By the time they arrived at Katie's house they wanted nothing but to get to bed.

But now Alex had woken up.

## Chapter 40

Chas had hardly slept at all; not because of the discomfort of the cell, but for the reason that his brain would not shut down. He went through every scenario he could think of and whichever one he examined, the outcome was the same. Whether from the French police, from Bear, or from Donald or maybe all three he was in deep trouble. As things stood at the moment he was the fall guy for everything and everybody. If he gave away any information on Bear, he was probably a dead man, yet they knew he had a connection with the man.

What else did they know? Would they know that he was instrumental in the planned killing of Donald's ex-girlfriend, Mary? If he admitted to knowing Bear, the police would want to know how. If he told them anything, he would instantly be involving Donald. It was he who had given him the instruction to put out a contract on Mary. When that had failed, the orders to 'do what has to be done' also came from him, which in Donald's language meant trashing Bear's place.

Of course, he could put his hands up for everything, and get Donald and Bear embroiled. What had he got to lose? He was sure he was facing a lengthy jail sentence. What were a few more years? Another chill went down his spine. Knowing the influence both Bear and Donald had in the criminal fraternity, he doubted he would ever get out of prison, other than in a box.

Chas was living a nightmare. A nightmare that wasn't going to disappear when he woke up. This was one bad dream that he was somehow going to have to live through.

No sooner had he dozed off than he was served with a bowl of strong black coffee and two croissants. Chas didn't like coffee at the best of times, but served black and in a bowl was little more than an insult. He ate the croissants and found them boring and tasteless, but he had to eat something or he felt he would pass out.

Half an hour later he was collected from his cell and taken into an interview room. It was devoid of anything other than essentials. In the centre of the small area was a vinyl-topped table with two wooden chairs on each side. He was instructed to sit down, facing them.

Sitting opposite him was Commissaire Armand and, to his surprise, Lizzie. No explanation was given as to Lizzie's presence as the questioning began again.

'How much do you know about Bear?' he was asked.

'I told you. I don't know the man at all.'

'Wrong answer,' Lizzie said. 'When we first met you told me that you knew him. You were doing some kind of business with him. You said you had come over specially to meet up with him.'

Chas looked at Lizzie, but her eyes were cold and unfriendly.

'Well, yes, that's true, but I don't know him personally. We have never met.'

'So what was your business with him? Was it drugs? Was it under age prostitution?'

'No, absolutely not. I'm not into anything like that,' Chas said.

'What about assassinations?' Lizzie asked. 'Are you into that?'

Chas swallowed and knew that Lizzie had noticed.

'Let me tell you, Mr Masterson, where we stand at the moment. A young man, a drug addict, attempted to murder a young woman by the name of Mary Willson in a village near Angers a few weeks ago. Fortunately, he didn't succeed, but he caused serious injuries for which he was charged.'

'I don't know anything about that,' Chas stated.

'I'll continue,' Louis Armand said. 'There are two more things you should know, Mr Masterson. Firstly, the young man, Tommy Williams, told us during questioning that he was instructed by Bear to carry out the killing.'

'I don't know any Tommy Williams or Mary whatever-her-name-was. Why are you telling me all this?'

'Because we think you are in some way implicated in this. We think you came here as a direct result of the failure of Tommy Williams to carry out his instructions. You were here to confront Bear, but when you found he had gone away, you vented your anger by setting fire to his business.'

'Rubbish!' Chas shouted. 'Absolute crap. This is all in your imagination.'

'Secondly,' Louis Armand continued, 'Mary's boyfriend has told us that he thinks that another man,

241

Donald O'Hanlon, is the actual instigator. Do you know Mr O'Hanlon?'

'Why would I know him?'

'You tell me,' Lizzie interjected. 'At the moment we're not so sure about Mr O'Hanlon, but we are sure about Bear. We've been watching him for months, if not years, and we know he's into anything unpleasant and illegal, including killings. But as yet, we've never been able to bring him to trial. He has clever lawyers – criminals in their own right – who have managed, so far, to get him off on technicalities.'

Lizzie looked Chas in the eyes without blinking. Chas noticed a glimmer of a smile.

'Can I ask why Lizzie is part of this interrogation? I thought I was here to talk to the police.'

'You are, Mr Masterson. Lizzie is a senior detective and a major part of this operation. Of course, you didn't realise that when you were hoping to jump into bed with her, did you?'

Now Lizzie *was* smiling. The smile he had seen on her face before, a welcoming, suggestive, tempting smile. She had well and truly deceived him. He cursed himself for being so gullible.

'So, let me see,' Louis Armand said, 'You don't know Bear, you don't know Mr O'Hanlon, and you know nothing of Tommy Williams or Mary Willson. Is that right?'

'That's right.'

'So, I'll just charge you with arson, then. We have enough evidence on that charge to put you away for a long time. There's just one last thing I should tell you. Tommy Williams, who was adamant that his instructions came from Bear, has been found dead in his cell in Angers. What do you have to say about that, Mr Masterson? An innocent, if stupid, drug addict is contracted to kill an equally innocent woman. He fails in his task and now, even while in police custody, he is murdered.'

'It's sad but it has nothing to do with me.' Chas answered nervously. 'Are you implying that I had any part in this?'

Lizzie exchanged glances with Louis Armand.

'I think what the Commissaire is trying to say, Chas, is that if Bear feels threatened by anyone, he will stop at nothing to take them out of the equation.' Lizzie said in a menacing voice. 'Just think what he might do if he got news of your being here – the possibility that you might give evidence about his activities to us. It hardly bears thinking about, does it?'

'I'm not grassing on him, though, am I?'

'Now I know that, Lizzie knows that, but Bear doesn't, does he? He will have worked out by now that it was you who burned down his business. It's probable that he already knows that you are back here being questioned.'

'You see,' Lizzie continued, 'with only the charge of arson against you, we cannot offer you any extra protection. We will do our best to see that you are safe, but we can do no more than that.'

She was now staring at Chas, mesmerising him with her wicked bedroom eyes.

'If, however, you were helping us with our enquiries regarding Bear and Donald O'Hanlon, things would be quite different. We could arrange twenty-four hour personal protection for you. We know, Chas, that you have many of the answers we are looking for. Your failure to co-operate with us could land you with a much longer sentence than you will get for arson. Is it worth it? Wouldn't you like to see people like Bear and O'Hanlon put away for the rest of their lives? You, Chas, have the key in your hands. You can make this happen.'

'OK, that's all for now, Mr Masterson,' Louis Armand said. 'Go back to your cell and think about what we've said. We will talk again this afternoon, when another Commissaire, Monsieur Claude Boulet, will join us. He is in charge of this case at the Angers end, and I'm sure he will be eager to talk to you.'

With that, Louis Armand and Lizzie rose from their seats and left Chas, alone and increasingly frightened, in the interview room. Would he dare to expose Donald and Bear? Could he take the risk? He had baulked at the thought of an innocent girl being killed when Donald had told him to 'deal with her'. It was different when other criminals were involved, but she had done nothing to deserve what was suggested. Yet he had done his boss's bidding, and instructed Bear to organise the elimination of Mary Willson. He had even arranged the payment to Bear. Now the poor sod who Bear had chosen to do the work was dead as well.

Can I live with all this on my conscience? Is this the one chance I have to do something right – something good in my life?

He didn't hear the two police officers come into the room. They took him back to his cell.

**Chapter 41**

Donald was delighted how things were going for him. Three days in succession had seen his finances climb. He had now transferred extra funds into his trading account to make the most of the current trends.

He couldn't remember the last time he had felt so animated, so buoyant.

This was a game of cat and mouse, trying to out-guess the market, transferring balances at exactly the right moment. A few seconds could make all the difference to an outcome. Get the timing wrong and you lose out. Donald, at the moment, was getting most of his transfers right, and watched his assets grow by the hour.

His next plan was to get Chas to motivate his 'boys' in order to bring in more funds to add to his working capital while the trend lasted. Why couldn't he find Chas? He wasn't replying to emails. Whilst he was feeling more confident recently, Donald didn't want to go live on the mobile network. However, he had now reached the point where he had no option but to turn on his mobile. There was just one missed call. No one but Chas knew this number, so why had he called? There was no way he could find that out. He turned off his phone as quickly as he had turned it on.

The only other way to get in contact with Chas was from a payphone. That would be difficult for anyone to trace. Donald left his laptop turned on and walked as nonchalantly as he could into town to the only payphone he knew of. He put the minimum amount of coins into the box and dialled Chas's number. His phone was turned off.

He had never known Chas to turn his phone off before. What was going on?

With his brain working overtime, Donald realised that he was most secure in his single room in the mansion that had once been his home and walked briskly back to it.

He made himself a large mug of coffee and went back to his computer to settle down to more money transferring. Down in the bottom right hand corner of the screen was a message, flashing in red.

*"Gotcha!"* it said.

Donald tried everything to remove it. In the end he turned the machine off. This was unnerving. When he re-booted, it had gone, but a few seconds later, it was back. *"Gotcha!"*

Clicking on the message revealed nothing. Highlighting it and trying to delete it had no effect. It was permanent. Dare he continue using the computer if somebody was watching? He thought about it for some time and decided it was probably a virus so he ran the anti-virus software embedded in his machine.

*"Gotcha!"* It was still there.

Whatever program he moved to, the message sat, flashing in the corner of the screen.

'Go away, you little bastard!' he yelled at the message. 'I've got work to do.'

Then, as his blood pressure continued to rise, the message disappeared.

'Thank Christ for that!' he said, and returned to his Forex site once again.

*****

Katie walked the short distance from Charing Cross Underground station, doubting her sanity but curious to find out what Antoine had to say. She spotted him as soon as she entered Trafalgar Square. He was sitting casually at the base of the statue of Sir Henry Havelock, just inside the square. He had a can of Fanta in his hand and was watching the cosmopolitan crowd of tourists milling around, some feeding the pigeons, others studying guidebooks and many more taking souvenir photographs of the icons within the square. He didn't see her walking towards him.

Katie had to wonder what was going on in his mind. If she felt nervous, what must he be feeling? She didn't go directly to him but walked round the perimeter of the square, glancing at him every few yards.

He looked lonely, disconsolate.

The more she watched him, the more she had to question her actions. Could she ever be absolutely sure that he would never turn into a monster again? What if he forgot to take his medication? What if the person lying beneath the Mr-Nice-Guy façade was the real Antoine? What if covertly, he enjoyed the occasional foray into the depths of depravity?

After circling the square twice, she sat at the base of Nelson's Column considering what she should do.

She saw him looking around, probably searching for her, but she was hidden from his direct line of vision. She could observe him, but he couldn't see her.

She watched as he produced his mobile phone and dialled a number. The phone in her bag buzzed and she promptly turned it off.

Half an hour later she saw him rise from his concrete seat and slowly walk away from the square in the direction of The Strand.

Part of her wanted to follow him, to embrace him, to tell him that everything was going to be fine. But her overwhelming sense of self-preservation won the day. She wandered to the south side of the square and made her way to a sandwich bar and bought herself a ham and salad baguette and a large latte coffee.

She could see most of Trafalgar square from where she sat, and wondered whether Antoine might return. But if he did, she didn't see him.

With a multitude of emotions still in her mind, she made her journey back to Mark's house. It took her a lot longer than she expected, and by the time she arrived at the mansion, she was tired, moody and confused.

Mark was in the kitchen when she arrived and called out a welcome to her. She threw her coat on the bottom stair, and went to find him. She was never so pleased to see anyone. Here was a man who she knew she could trust. If she had been able to choose a father, he would have been the one. In fact, Mark was the only good thing to have come out of her marriage to his son, Dave.

They had shared the outrage and shame of what he had become, and they had shared the grief of his death when he was murdered in Albania not so long ago.

Now she was cradled in Mark's arms. There was no suggestion of anything more than a comforting cuddle.

'Is there something wrong?' he asked quietly.

Katie looked up at him with tears welling up in her eyes.

'Actually,' she replied, 'there's quite a lot wrong.'

'And do you want to talk about it?'

'Maybe later, Mark. I need to sort things out in my head first.'

'Of course. Whenever you're ready, I'm here to listen.'

'Thanks, Mark. I think I'll go and have a long soak in the bath. That quite often helps me unwind.'

'Would you like to take a drink with you?'

'No thanks. I'll just go and chill out. See you later.'

Katie was half way up the stairs when Mark called up to her.

'Oh, by the way, Adrian's coming round this evening. Hope that's OK.'

'That's fine. It'll be nice to see him again.'

She was lying. For her it would be more of an embarrassment. On two occasions in the past, she had made a fool of herself with Adrian. The first time was at her wedding. She shuddered when she remembered her outrageous behaviour on that day. Adrian had been dancing with his beautiful, raven-haired girlfriend and the more she watched them, the more horny Katie had become. In the end she took over the dance and had her time with Adrian.

When the dance finished, she went to kiss Adrian but held her hand behind his head and pulled him towards her for a full-on, lingering wet kiss. The poor

249

boy wasn't expecting that, and pulled away as quickly as he could and scampered back to his girlfriend.

More recently, she had met up with Adrian again. They went out for dinner and Adrian confessed that as beautiful as she was, his girlfriend was far from forthcoming with sexual favours. That night they both stayed at his Uncle Mark's house and Katie had the honour of introducing Adrian to the delights that her body had to offer.

There were several "action replays" during the ensuing week or so, and Katie could see him wanting to get more serious. He was several years younger than she was and she couldn't see any way that such a relationship could work for either of them.

When she returned to France after Dave's funeral, Adrian pestered her with texts and telephone calls, telling her how much he loved her. In the end, she had to be cruel and tell him that it was over. She heard him crying on the phone that day.

Now he was coming to dinner. How was she going to handle that?

It was just one more thing for her to deal with. Her love life had never been problem-free. Now she had to contend with the aftermath of Antoine, plus the added awkwardness of meeting Adrian again.

This bath had better be good. She poured in some lavender oil, climbed into the steaming water and rested her head on the rolled end of the bath.

It was good. By the time she got out from the bath and had dressed she felt that she could talk to Mark, and even face meeting with Adrian later on.

Mark was sitting in the lounge watching golf on TV. He immediately turned it off and got up to greet her. Katie refused his offer of a cup of tea.

'I'd really like to talk to you. I need an honest opinion on something.'

Mark raised his eyebrows but didn't speak.

Katie told him everything that had happened between Antoine and her, ending with the episode in Trafalgar Square.

'The thing is, Mark, I don't think I want to go back to France now. I would be bound to see him and I don't want to have to deal with it all over again. Do you think I'm being a bit paranoid?'

'That's the last thing I'm thinking,' Mark said. 'What an ordeal for you. I don't blame you at all for wanting to avert any embarrassing meetings. Anyway, you still have a lot of things to sort out over here, so it might be a wise decision for you to return here for a while – or permanently if that's the way it turns out.'

'You're right about that, Mark. And it would give me a genuine reason to offer to Ben. The busy season is over now, anyway, so I'm sure he will be able to cope without me.'

They continued their conversation in the kitchen whilst they prepared the evening meal, and, as was so often the case when Katie talked with Mark, she felt much more relaxed and ready to face Adrian.

As it happened, she didn't have anything to worry about. It was as if he was meeting her for the first time. He seemed delighted to see her again, and the evening was a great success.

Katie made a mental note that Adrian could be another good reason for her to return to England.

## Chapter 42

Ben and Mary went, as planned, to Goring Heath to collect her red and white Mini-Cooper. Betty, the proprietor of the pub, had welcomed them and they stayed for a gargantuan Sunday roast after which, they told Betty all that had happened and the news of their marriage the next day.

'Congratulations!' Betty enthused. 'You should have said. I would have been only too happy to put on a reception here for you. It would have been my pleasure.'

Sometime after three o'clock Ben and Mary left in their separate cars and drove back to Reading through strong winds and driving rain.

'Ben, I swear it was him. I know that car,' Mary said to Ben as soon as they arrived back at Katie's house.

'It might have been his car, Mary,' Ben said trying to mollify her. 'It didn't necessarily mean it was him driving it. It was a lease car, after all, wasn't it?'

'Ben, I saw him. We pulled up alongside each other at some traffic lights. He's grown a beard, but I could still recognise him. It *was* him, I swear.'

'OK, let's say it was. Did he see you?'

'I didn't see him looking at me. I was too scared, but my car does stand out a bit, doesn't it, with the white stripes right across the roof? He must have recognised my car. If he didn't he must be blind.'

'It was pouring with rain and dark enough to be the middle of the night. If he didn't look at you, then he probably didn't see your car. He might have had other things on his mind, and you know how it is, you often don't see somebody because they are out of context, as it were. You were the last person he would expect to see in Reading. As far as he's concerned, you're hundreds of miles away in France. I really shouldn't worry'

'Easy for you to say, Ben. If I remember rightly, he tried to have me killed when I was "hundreds of miles away in France". I know it was him.'

'Then can I suggest that we change our plans for tomorrow. Alex and I will come with you in the morning.'

'No, I don't want that. I really want to be on my own when I try on the dress and have my hair done. Thanks, but no thanks, as they say.'

'OK. It's up to you, but the offer's there if you want to change your mind.'

'I'll be as careful as I can. I can keep the car locked from the inside while I drive to the car park, and after that I will be with someone – the dressmaker, and then the girls at the salon. Then I'll be coming to the Register Office in Ray's car. He'll look after me.'

'That's true. OK, we'll leave everything as planned. The sooner we get away from here, the better.'

Ben thought that it was good that he could at least presume where Donald was living if anything were to happen.

\*\*\*\*\*

253

Claude Boulet, Louis Armand and Lizzie spent a considerable amount of time discussing how to approach Chas Masterson. Under Interpol regulations, they had to charge him with the arson attack today or release him back to Thames Valley police in England.

The main point in question was how he was going to respond to the grilling he had received yesterday. They had clearly shaken him when they revealed how much they already knew, and he was equally scared at the possible consequences of not admitting his involvement. All three officers were convinced that he was a major link. The problem was whether he was ready to confirm that. They considered both outcomes. If he persisted in claiming his ignorance and innocence, they could see both Bear and O'Hanlon getting away with yet another serious crime. If he were to co-operate, and confess to his part in all of this, then they could pursue both men with a good chance of convictions for both of them.

Chas was ushered into the interview room by a young woman police officer and was shown to his chair and left to wait. He was nervous, not knowing what to expect today.

First to arrive was Lizzie who asked whether he had slept well.

'What do you think?' Chas replied curtly.

'Some people seem to be able to sleep well in our cells. But you didn't?'

Chas didn't answer. He still had visions of this police officer walking around her flat wearing little more than a smile. Now she was sitting across the table from him, waiting, no doubt, to fire more questions at him.

'You might not believe this, Chas, but I'm sorry it has turned out this way. I quite liked you and your impertinence. I like a guy with some spirit. I hoped I had got it all wrong, and that you were only connected with Bear in some small way. Unfortunately, especially for you, my instincts were spot on, and here we are. Shame, really. I think we might have had something going between us.'

Chas wasn't going to react to this. She wasn't going to get anything out of him by being nice, that was for sure.

'Do you have a wife, Chas?'

Chas shook his head.

'Were you ever married?'

No response

'A girlfriend back in England, perhaps?'

'No. No wife, no girlfriend.'

'Is that by choice or is it that women don't go for you?'

'I don't think that's any of your business, do you?'

'I just thought that might have explained your keenness to get it on with me. You thought that at last you'd found someone who liked you. Was that it?'

'No, it fucking wasn't. Can we change the subject?'

'Sure. Let's change the subject. What's your view of women then. Chas? Does it embarrass you, for example that you are being questioned by a woman?'

'No. Should it?'

'What do you think of women, Chas. Do you just like to look? Do you give us marks out of ten? Or are you a chauvinist, or even a misogynist? Do you not really like women at all?'

'I'm none of those things. I like women as much as the next man. What are you getting at? You think I'm gay or something?'

'Oh, no, I don't think that, Chas. I'm trying to find out how you could get involved in the attempted murder of a totally innocent woman like Mary Willson. You say you like women, yet you can be part of a plan to kill a beautiful girl who you've never even met. That really is sick, Chas. That's really as low as a man can go. Just try to tell me why you did it, why you arranged to have her murdered, for that's what it was, Chas, cold bloodied murder. Christ, Chas, she had a little boy – not a year old. Just tell me. How could you do that?'

Chas could see tears welling up in Lizzie's eyes. She was getting very emotional. This was cruel. He thought he was going to be quizzed about the fire, again, not this. He didn't have any answers to her questions. She had raised issues which had already disgusted him, things that he hated himself for.

'I was following orders,' he said before realising it.

'I wish I could believe that, Chas. You have now acknowledged that you *were* involved in the attempted murder of Mary Willson, but you are trying to say it wasn't your idea. Someone else was to blame. You surprise me. I thought you were more of a man than that.'

Lizzie waited for a response, and when there was nothing more coming from Chas, she rose to leave.

'That's fine, then. Chas. We can add the charge of attempted murder to the arson charge. Thank you for co-operating with us so willingly.'

Lizzie moved towards the door.

'No, wait!' Chas said. 'I'm serious. I was given instructions. I didn't want to carry them out, but I had to. It was more than my life was worth to ---'

'I've heard enough, Chas,' she said and left the room.

Left on his own again, Chas muttered 'Now what the fuck have I done?'

\*\*\*\*\*

Bear's recent travels had taken him round the world. After enjoying two weeks on his small Greek Island, he had visited his producers in Colombia and The Balkans followed by suppliers in the Caribbean and Portugal. At every point he had smashed down the prices he was being charged. Everyone complained, but none of them was willing to lose the lucrative contract which they had with Bear.

Back in Paris, Bear was now comfortably ensconced in a five-bedroom houseboat, moored on the banks of the River Seine. He was aware of what was going on. He had reliable sources within the police force in Paris. They had kept him out of trouble in the past and he had no doubt that they would in the future. Information received by them had always kept him one step ahead of the authorities and, because of them, he was still a free man.

He had been told very soon after his arrival back from his travels that Tommy Williams was about to give evidence against him at his forthcoming trial. He had dealt with that promptly and effectively.

Now he was hearing that Chas Masterson had been extradited from the UK on charges of arson. Bear had

257

guessed it was Chas who had torched his building on Rue de Maubeuge. And he knew why. He also knew who had issued the order. Chas didn't have the guts to do it off his own bat. Poor old Chas – always the loser. Now he faced a few years behind bars. One thing was for certain. He would never dare to involve anybody else. That would be the end of him.

Bear, therefore, was happy to keep his head down for a while so that the arson business could be cleared out of the way. After that, it would be business as usual and with a substantial improvement in profits.

When he looked up, he saw Mariana coming into the lounge area. She was his latest acquisition. Hispanic and beautiful, her tanned body, tumbling black hair and lithe young body turned him on every time he looked at her. He didn't know her exact age – he had never asked – but he doubted she was older than fifteen and possibly younger.

She sauntered over to him in her white miniscule shorts and bright pink top, and knew what she had to do. She peeled away the two small pieces of cloth from her body, tantalisingly unhurriedly and then went over to where Bear sat. As slowly as she had rid herself of her shorts and top, she started to unbutton Bear's shorts, pulling them off his strong athletic legs to the floor.

*****

Claude Boulet and Louis Armand had been listening to the conversation between Lizzie and Chas.

'She's good,' Claude said.

'Oh, yes. She's clever. She knows how to get under a man's skin. That's why she's so good at her job – why she's so valuable to me.'

The two men ceased their compliments as Lizzie walked into the room.

'I think that might do the trick,' Lizzie said with a grin on her face. 'He won't know what to do now.'

'Before we go any further, can I say that I want all dealings with Chas to be between us three.' Claude Boulet said. 'We all know that there is a leak somewhere. I'm not saying that it is here in Paris, it may well be at my end. I don't know. But for security's sake, Chas Masterson is here to answer questions about the fire. Nothing more. The last thing we want is another tragedy.'

'Agreed,' Louis Armand said, and Lizzie nodded.

There were just eight hours left before they had to charge Chas or let him go. The three officers agreed that, whether he confessed to anything else or not, they would charge him with the arson. That would also send the right message to Bear.

'Do we know where Bear is?' Lizzie was asked.

'Yes. He's living rather comfortably on a houseboat. We are keeping watch, but we haven't seen anyone going on or off the boat. He seems to have a young girl with him, but we don't know who she is. We might be able to use her, if necessary, but I don't think she's allowed off the boat – that's how it looks.'

'OK. Can we tap into any phones or anything?'

'We can try. I'll look into it. I'd have to have permission before I can do that, though.'

'Consider it done, Lizzie.'

Chas was left in the interview room for nearly an hour before Claude Boulet went to meet him.

'Mr Masterson, Lizzie has told us of your little chat earlier. I tend to agree with her reaction to your suggestion that you were ordered to carry out the attempted murder of Mary Willson. I don't believe you.'

'No, listen. It's true. I was following orders.'

'Enough, Mr Masterson. We don't believe you.'

'It was the same with the fire. I was told to deal with Bear.'

'I said enough! I am charging you with arson, Mr Masterson. I do not want to hear any more about your not being responsible. We have more than sufficient evidence to take this to trial, and that is what we are going to do.'

'I'll make a statement. I'll tell you everything.'

'Not now, sir. You will be charged with arson, and perhaps we will talk about these other accusations another time. For your own safety, you will not mention anything else to anyone. Do you understand?'

Chas nodded.

Claude Boulet called in two police officers, and instructed them to charge Chas with the arson attack on Rue de Maubeuge and walked out.

When Chas had been charged, the officers were about to take Chas back to his cell when Lizzie entered the room.

'Thanks, gentlemen. I'll take Mr Masterson to his cell. I just want a word with him first.'

She sat down opposite Chas and looked straight at him.

'Who gave you the instructions, Chas?'

'My boss, Donald O'Hanlon. He told me to arrange the killing of Mary Willson, and he also told me to carry out the arson attack.'

'Thank you, Chas. Let's get you back to your cell, shall we?'

## Chapter 43

Strong winds and storms are to be expected during October in the UK, but the night before the wedding, the weather excelled itself. Torrential rain accompanied by winds of up to sixty miles per hour whipped around Katie's house, keeping Ben and Mary awake for a good part of the night.

When they roused from their sporadic sleep, they were surprised to see that the sun was trying to break through and the wind had all but ceased. Outside there was a carpet of leaves and small branches from the trees that lined the road and Katie's garden, unkempt at the best of times, had taken a severe battering.

'What time's your dress fitting?' Ben asked.

'I've said I'll be there about eleven. That will give me plenty of time to get to the salon, spend some time there while they try to make me look gorgeous, and still be on time at the Register Office.'

'Actually, I don't know why you're bothering with all that. I'd be happy to marry you right now, just as you are.'

'With my hair looking like this? In my nightdress?'

'Absolutely.'

'OK, then. I'll come with you like this. It'll save a lot of time.'

Ben pulled her to him in a solid embrace.

'I just want to know that you're my wife,' he said. 'That's all, really. But I want you to have a day to remember, so I guess it had better be the dress and hair-do after all.'

'And I thought it was women who were supposed to change their minds.'

Mary left the house a few minutes before eleven o'clock.

It was nice to have her own car again. She was proud of her red Mini Cooper with the two white racing stripes going from front to back. She had spent some of the profit from the sale of the flat that she and Ben owned, and had bartered outrageously to get it at a good price.

She settled herself comfortably in the wrap around driver's seat and drove the few minutes into the centre of Reading, heading for the multi-story car park close to where she wanted to be. She would pick it up after the reception. She still wondered what Ray had got in mind for that, but she knew that he wasn't going to tell her. She would just have to wait and see. Already, her nerves were jangling.

The car park was almost full. She stopped at the barrier to obtain her entry ticket. There were only ten places left, and she had to find out where they were. Things were made more difficult because the sun had come out and she was driving in and out of the brightness and into the shade. Eventually she saw a space, and waited while a few cars slowly made their way past her on their way out.

*****

It was a long time since Ben had worn a suit, and he was concerned that it might not fit him any more. He thought he may well have put on some weight since moving to France. He was surprised to find that, if anything, he had lost weight. He recalled this suit being well-fitting last time he wore it, but today, it hung nicely on him. His crisp white linen shirt and his newly acquired grey and mauve tie looked good against the mid grey suit. Polished black shoes finished the outfit, and he was pleased when he inspected himself in the mirror.

He partly undressed again while he attended to Alex. Mary had bought him a long sleeved white shirt, a grey, clip-on bow tie and long grey trousers. Alex wasn't too keen. He, like his father, was used to much more casual attire and he struggled all he could to avoid being dressed up. He pulled at the sleeves on his shirt, he tugged at the bow tie and he was none too happy about the trousers either.

Ben decided he had to compromise. He removed the bow tie and opened the shirt at the neck by one button and then he rolled up the shirt sleeves. Alex still wasn't happy, but he seemed to accept his Dad's attempts to make things better. Ben put the bow tie, along with the wedding ring in his suit pocket before re-dressing himself.

Mary had left a list of things that he mustn't forget, and he checked them off carefully.

Everything was ready. His mobile buzzed as he made for the front door. He took it from his pocket.

*You'll be pleased to know that D...*

The text was the latest report from Basheer on Donald's activities. He shut his phone down, picked up his son and the bag containing Alex's stuff, locked the front door carefully after him and made his way to his car which had been parked on the road overnight.

He drove directly to the Register Office and arrived half an hour before the two o'clock start. He sat in his car with Alex until a few people started to arrive.

His two partners, the two Tonys, arrived first, then a few minutes later about a dozen of the staff of SRX Solutions came into the car park. Ben was surprised by that. It was something he hadn't expected. Maurice, the accountant, was among them, and came over to shake his hand.

He was even more surprised when Katie arrived with Mark, and with them was Georgina. As she got out from the back of Mark's limousine, she looked over towards him with a big question mark look on her face. Ben made his way over to her.

'You don't mind, Ben, do you?'

'Mind what?'

'Me being here. You don't mind, do you?'

'Of course not.'

'That's what Katie said you'd say. I thought I might be the last person you would want at your wedding. Do you think Mary will mind?'

'I guess she'll be as surprised as I am to see you, but I don't think she'll mind. It's nice to be surrounded by my three favourite women.'

'Really, Ben!' Georgina said. 'It's your wedding day. Behave yourself.'

At that point, other people were coming over to talk with him, so Ben left Georgina, who walked back to be with Katie and Mark.

The previous wedding party was now leaving the Registry Office, and an official came out to ask Ben's guests to take their place inside. Ben handed Alex to Katie who took him with her and sat in the front row alongside Mark and Georgina.

The Register Office was pleasant enough with light wood furniture and comfortable seating. Piped music was being played, and Katie thought the flowers looked as if they were plastic or silk, but said nothing. After a while, people started to look at their watches. Five minutes went by, then ten.

Ben was standing outside waiting for his bride. But she didn't come. He called Mary on his mobile but there was no reply.

Inside, Georgina turned to Katie.

'She hasn't done it again, has she?' she whispered.

'What do you mean?'

'Let him down. She couldn't, she wouldn't, would she?'

'Of course not, Georgina. She's most likely held up in traffic or something like that. She'll be here in a minute.'

Ben was getting worried, too. He went into the Register Office, and made straight for Georgina.

'Do you have the salon's number?'

Georgina knew it by heart and gave Ben the number, whereupon, Ben went back outside, followed by Georgina. She saw him punch in the number, and watched as his face went pale.

'What is it, Ben?'

'She hasn't been to the salon. They haven't seen her,' he said.

'Oh, my God,' was all that Georgina could think of to say.

'Was she going anywhere else before the salon?'

'Yes, to her dressmaker, but I don't know who that is. I've no idea, and without going round every women's outfitters in Reading, I don't know which one it is.'

Georgina wanted so much to hug him.

'I'm sure there's a good explanation,' she said, trying her best to be positive whilst trying equally hard to think what such an explanation could be.

At that moment, Ray, the owner of the salon, emerged from the Register Office.

'What's happening, Ben? Is there anything I can do?'

'Not unless you know where Mary was getting her dress from,' Georgina said.

'I don't,' Ray replied, 'but I bet the girls at the salon do. Hold on a minute.' He opened the flap on his phone and dialled his salon. Collete answered the call, and confirmed that she did know the dressmaker. She found the number and dictated it to Ray who immediately called the number she had given.

'No,' the shop owner said. 'She was expected about eleven, but she hasn't turned up. No word, no anything. Her dress is here waiting for her.'

Ben and Georgina listened in on the call. Ben turned away and sat down on a low brick wall, his head in his hands.

'I guess that's it, then,' Ray said quietly to Georgina. 'We'd better tell the guests inside.'

While Ray went to inform the guests that there was not going to be a wedding, Georgina went and sat next to Ben on the brick wall. She didn't touch him, though every part of her wanted to, but merely sat with him. She hoped that he could sense what she was feeling without her having to say anything audibly.

Minutes later Ray came back, followed by a group of dazed guests, none of whom knew what to do or say, and took command.

'Look, this might be well out-of-order,' he said to anyone who wanted to listen, 'but I have arranged something rather special for you all, and it's a shame to let it go to waste. Can I suggest that we meet back here in about half an hour? That will give Ben time to recover his thoughts a bit, and if he wants to, we can still have something of a get together.'

The party of guests started to drift away, leaving Ray, Katie, Alex and Georgina with Ben.

'I'm going to take Alex for a walk,' Katie said. 'I don't want him to see his Dad like this. If anybody can help him at the moment it's probably you, Georgina. I'll be back in a little while.'

Making sure that he was out of earshot, Ray took it upon himself to phone the two local hospitals.

## Chapter 44

Poppy was hanging on to the sides of her seat as the silver Audi, travelling at far more than the safe maximum speed, careered down the ramps of the multi-storey car park in the centre of Reading.

'Shane, slow down. You're going to kill us all,' Poppy screamed.

The tyres were screeching at every corner, and there was a strong smell of burning rubber invading the interior of the car. The two other girls in the back seats were being tossed about in every direction, screaming.

'Shane!' Poppy yelled. 'Stop the car. Stop the fucking car!' There was little she could do other than yell. 'You do know that you hit that car up there, don't you?' Shane had apparently gone mad. It was supposed to be a bit of fun when he had invited Poppy and her two friends for a spin. That was OK but this was not a spin. This was lunacy. This was a suicide trip.

The car hit the ground floor level with a thud, the exhaust pipe scraping along the ground, sending a shower of sparks into the air. He stopped only to shove the ticket into the machine. The barrier rose, and he drove off again at reckless speed. His passengers were terrified. They tried to get out of the car while he was at the barrier but by the time they had fumbled with their seat belts Shane had driven off again. He was only too aware that he had collided with a red Mini Cooper on the second floor down and wanted to get away before anybody could do anything about it. It was only a bump, he thought, but he didn't intend to hang around to find out more. Six months into a year's driving ban and without insurance –he would be in real trouble.

He continued his wild drive onto the A4, persistently breaking the speed limits.

'I want to go home,' Poppy said, crying and realising that her friend had just thrown up over the back seat.

'OK,' Shane said. 'Soon. I just want to go for a drive.'


Mary was about to make her way into the parking space that she had spotted when she was aware of the screeching of tyres coming from her left. She looked to see where the noise was coming from, but it was too late. As she pulled out from the ramp towards the space opposite, the speeding car had spun round the corner to her left and was careering straight towards her. She tensed herself for the impact. The boy racer had caught her car on the front wing and shunted it sideways into a concrete pillar. The driver's door was severely damaged and jammed against the pillar. The front airbag had inflated, but she had been flung against her door, and her head had smashed against the support just behind the driver's seat.

She could feel the blood running down the side of her head. The pain in her stomach and right shoulder was excruciating, and then everything around her slowly faded to black and white. She could vaguely make out some people trying to open her car door to get her out. But she had locked the car internally for her own protection.

The last thing she remembered was the agonizing pain in her stomach.

People continued to try to get her out. Two burly young men managed to lift the car away from the pillar. They tried to smash the windows, but didn't have the right equipment to achieve their goals.

By the time the paramedics arrived, Mary was dead. Drenched in blood, her terrified, staring eyes were wide open.

The police were quickly on the scene and took statements from the few people who were near the accident spot, but nobody could give any clear details.

'All I can remember,' said one bystander, 'was hearing this car, racing down the slopes. I heard a bang, but I didn't realise at first what had happened. Not until I saw this poor girl stuck inside her car.'

'Can you remember anything about the car?'

'No, I didn't actually see it. I just heard it.'

'It was silver,' an older man said, 'but I'm not sure of the make. German I think – BMW, Audi, Merc - but I wouldn't swear to it.'

Mary's body was eventually cut out of the car, and taken by the ambulance to the Royal Berkshire Hospital where she was pronounced dead.

*****

'I wonder if you can help me,' Ray said to the receptionist at the first hospital he called. 'Have you had a young woman brought in this morning? Her name is

Mary Willson, with two ells, she's in her thirties with dark hair and brown eyes.'

'One moment sir. I'll put you through to A and E.' It felt like several minutes before Ray heard a man's voice at the end of the phone.

'How can I help you?'

Ray repeated his description of Mary.

'Was it an RTA?

'What's an RTA?'

'Road traffic Accident.'

'I don't know. She seems to have gone missing. I'm just checking the hospitals.'

'Hold on one minute, sir.'

One minute turned to five before the voice returned.

'Are you a relative of Mary Willson, sir?'

'No, but her fiancé is here. I can go and get him. Just wait a moment and I'll put him on the phone.'

Ray walked as quickly as his mind was racing over to Ben.

'Ben, I've got the Royal Berkshire Hospital on the line. They need to talk to you. I think Mary is there.'

Ben took the phone from Ray.

'Hello. My name is Ben Coverdale. I'm Mary's fiancé.'

'Mr Coverdale, your fiancée was brought into A & E at eleven forty-five this morning.'

'And?'

'I'm sorry to have to tell you this, sir, but she was dead on arrival. A nasty car accident. Can I ask where you are? The police would also like to talk to you.'

'I'm outside the Register Office in Reading. We were due to be married this afternoon.'

'Sir. I'm so sorry.'

Ben handed the phone back to Ray and sat there with a blank look on his face, shaking his head slightly. He vaguely heard Ray speaking to the man on the phone, but his head was full of other sounds. Sounds like fierce winds and rushing water, of screeching birds and smashing glass.

Katie came over to Ray and asked him what had happened.

'Mary's dead,' he told her. 'The hospital has just told us.'

'Dead?' Georgina said having overheard what Ray had just said. 'Are they sure?'

'I don't think there's any doubt about it. The hospital said they were trying to trace her next of kin.'

Georgina ran over to where Ben was sitting on the wall.

'Oh, Ben. My dear, dear Ben' Georgina said. 'This is so dreadful. Oh, my God. How did it happen?'

Ben sat with his head in his hands. He still couldn't speak.

'The police are on their way here at the moment, Ben,' Ray told him. 'They want to talk to you. You'll be able to ask them for more details.'

A police car drove into the car park as he spoke and a uniformed officer came over to Ben.

'Mr Willson?' the officer said.

'No. I'm Ben Coverdale. Mary Willson and I were getting married today.'

'I'm so sorry, sir. Perhaps it would be better if we talked in the car?'

Ben nodded, and went with the officer and sat in the back seat of the Range Rover with him.

273

'How did it happen?' Ben asked as soon as they had settled in the car.

'We're a bit short on details, Mr Coverdale, but it seems that Ms Willson's car was hit while she was trying to park. A hit and run accident from what we can make out. People saw a car speeding down the ramps, but there are no details of the car.'

'And the car, was it silver by any chance?''

'Yes, sir. It was. We're certain of that.'

'And German, yes?'

'Right again, sir. How comes you know this?'

'Because I know who did it.'

'Sir?'

'There's a man. His name is Donald O'Hanlon. He has attempted once before to have Mary killed, but it failed. Mary said she saw him in Reading yesterday and now she's dead. I'll bet my life on it. He's tried to kill her again, and this time he has succeeded. Would you like his address?'

'We'd certainly like to talk to him. That name rings a bell, actually. Something to do with a death on a ferry?'

'That's right, but on that occasion the police decided that there were no suspicious circumstances and nothing more was heard about it as far as I know. I think the police in South Africa would like a word with him, too, about the death of a young coloured girl a few years ago.'

'All the more reason why we should have a chat with him.'

'You'd better get over there quick,' Ben said, 'because if you don't, then I will be over there as soon as I feel up to it, and I'll probably kill him.'

'I'll pretend I didn't hear that, sir.'

Ben informed the officer of Donald's residence in Wallingford, and a call was put out immediately to get somebody over there to apprehend and question him.

'Will you be alright, sir? Have you got anybody who you could stay with tonight?'

'Yes, I'll be OK. My friends are all out there waiting for me. By the way, if he does not appear to be at that address, keep trying. I have been reliably informed that he is there, but I doubt he'll want to see you guys.'

Ben felt no better after his conversation with the police officer. He got out of the car and walked over to where his wedding guests had congregated with forlorn looks on their faces. They tried to hide their feelings as he approached.

Ben didn't want to share the details of his talk with the police and returned to where Georgina was playing with Alex. He slumped down onto the wall, and stared into space.

He was surrounded by people who cared about him but he wasn't aware of them. He felt as though he was the only person left on the planet. Alone in a now monotone, silent world. He knew there were people milling around him but nothing registered. He knew there was noise, but all he heard was white sound. Reality had morphed into a capricious world where nothing made any sense, nothing happened, nothing mattered.

It felt very similar to the two occasions in his life when he had passed out. That feeling of floating, seeing faces but not registering them. Maybe this was the body's way of getting him through this, but he was not sure that he wanted to get through. His life was on hold.

Only when he realised that Alex was trying to climb onto his lap did any feeling come back. He leaned forward and pulled his son up to him, hugging him as the tears cascaded from his eyes.

Georgina, who had been entertaining Alex, came over to Ben.

'I don't think this is good for Alex, Ben. I think the best thing we can do is to get you back to Katie's house where you can lie down, and Alex can do whatever he wants.'

Ben didn't agree. Alex was the only part of Mary that was left. He held the child close to him.

Georgina didn't move, didn't react. It was Alex who eventually put his arms in the air, asking for a cuddle from her. Ben looked up and reluctantly handed his son to her.

'Ray has offered to take us home,' she said to Ben. 'Let's do that. We can't sit in a car park. At least we can have something to eat and drink there.'

Ben nodded.

'Would you like me to come with you? I could look after Alex for a while.'

Ben slowly stood up and walked over to Ray's car. Nothing was said. There were no words that would have any meaning in these circumstances.

'I don't really want anyone other than you two around me at the moment.'

'I can understand that,' Georgina said. 'I'll tell the others that is what you want. I'm sure they'll appreciate that as well.'

It was Ray who explained to the other guests that Ben was going home and wanted to be left in peace before driving Ben, Alex and Georgina to Katie's house.

'Where's Katie?' Ben asked when they arrived.

'I'm not sure, but I guess she's gone home with Mark. Shall I get us something to eat?'

'Please,' Ben said. 'I think Alex must be hungry by now. Better see to him first.'

'I will. I think it would be best if you took yourself to bed. Have a rest for an hour or so. I'll take care of things downstairs and I'll bring you something to eat in a while.'

When she did get around to taking a snack up to Ben's room, he was fast asleep.

## Chapter 45

Louis Armand called Lizzie into his office later the same day.

'I think we've got enough evidence now to bring Bear in,' he said. 'We have Chas Masterson willing to give evidence to the fact that he paid Bear to have Mary Willson killed and we have the testimony from Tommy Williams to show that Bear gave him the instructions to carry it out.'

'There's more,' Lizzie said. 'Chas told me this morning that he could prove that money was given to Bear, delivered by courier. So, I agree, I think we've got a good case against him this time.

'Who's the girl on the boat? Do we know anything about her?'

'No. Nothing. She's very young and pretty, but I know no more than that.'

'Then let's bring her in as well. Not at the same time, though. We don't want Bear to know that we're talking to her. She might know something that we don't. I want to tie him up in knots this time.'

'He has his lawyer, don't forget,' Lizzie said.

'I know that well enough. This time I think we're much more likely to make something stick. I don't care what it is. A motoring offence, a parking ticket, anything. I want him in custody so fast that he doesn't have time to think.'

Two hours later, while Bear was being shown into an interview room and was being guarded by two uniformed officers, the young Hispanic girl was brought in separately. Lizzie took her into another, more comfortable room where they sat side by side.

'There's no need to be scared,' Lizzie said. 'You haven't done anything wrong. Can you tell me your name?'

'Mariana,' the girl replied so softly that Lizzie could hardly hear her.

'And where do you come from, Mariana?'

'I come from Mexico but I have no family there any more. My mother and father were both killed by drug traffickers and my two brothers have disappeared.'

'So how did you come to live with Bear here in Paris?'

'I was brought here by some men, and they put me with Mr Bear.'

'And he looks after you?'

'Yes, he's a good man. He gives me food and nice clothes and some booze.'

'Some booze?'

'Yes. He's nice to me.'

'How old are you, Mariana?'

'Eighteen.'

'You don't look eighteen. Is that what you were told to tell us?' Mariana nodded shyly.

'It's OK. But I would like to know the truth. It's just between you and me. So, truthfully, how old are you?'

'I will be sixteen in two weeks' time.'

'That's more like it. Tell me what do you do all day? Do you stay on the boat all the time?'

'Yes. Mr Bear says I'm to stay there because I could be in danger if I go out alone so I read and watch TV most of the time.'

'And are you happy with that?'

'Well, I would like to go out, but if it is dangerous for me to go out on my own, it's better if I stay with him, isn't it?'

'I guess so. Do you and Bear have sex together?'

Mariana looked shocked and embarrassed by this sudden question. She nodded her head.

'Do you want to have sex with him?'

'Yes. I like the feeling it gives me. Mr Bear taught me how to do sex.'

'Does he ever force you to have sex even if you don't want to?'

'No. I enjoy it. Why would I not want to?'

Lizzie thanked Mariana for being so honest, and left her in the company of a woman police officer. She found Louis Armand walking along the corridor to his office.

'Looks like we might get Bear for under-age sex, as well,' she said. 'The girl who is staying on the boat is only fifteen, and they are having regular sex.'

'Nice one, Lizzie. That might take him by surprise as well. He's bound to say that she said she was older, but the fact remains, she isn't. What are you going to do with her now?'

'I'll have to get welfare to look after her,' Lizzie said. 'I'll do that right away.'

*****

280

Insistent banging on his front door woke Donald from his sleep. As he forced his eyes open, he glanced at the clock by his bed. It was two-thirty in the morning. Quickly, he got his head into gear, dragged himself from his bed, made his way, silently, to the front of the house, and peered out of one of the windows.

The scene that presented itself was what his nightmares were made of.

There must have been five, maybe six, police cars parked in his drive and along the road, blue lights flashing like a fair ground attraction.

The banging on the door was loud and furious. Now a loud hailer burst into life.

'Mr O'Hanlon. We know you are in there, and we are prepared to force our way in if you do not open the door.'

Donald didn't have time to think straight.

Why were they here? What was so urgent that they were threatening to use force to get in? How did they know he was here? The questions kept coming, but he had answers to none of them.

'Two minutes, Mr O'Hanlon, then we are coming in.'

There was nothing he could do. There was no way out. He had no alternative but to open the door. He threw on some clothes and made his way down the grand staircase to the front door. As he opened it, he heard a woman's voice shout, 'Sir, I think you ought to see this.' She was calling from the area to the right of the house.

The officer in charge went to where the woman was waiting, and she took him into the garage. Using her torch, she showed him what she had found. There was damage to the right front offside of the silver Mercedes saloon, and signs of red paint running a small distance down the wing. She was told to take samples of the red paint and photographs of the damage.

Donald stood in the doorway, still bleary-eyed from his rude awakening.

'What's going on?' he asked.

'Mr O'Hanlon, we are arresting you on suspicion of the murder of Mary Willson. We would like you to get dressed and accompany us to Police Headquarters in Reading.'

'Are you mad? Is this some sick joke?'

'Negative to both questions, sir. Please do as we ask.'

'And how am I supposed to have murdered this woman?'

'We can talk about this at the station, Mr O'Hanlon. Please get dressed.'

Two uniformed officers directed Donald back into the house. He splashed some cold water over his face, got dressed and was led back downstairs and thrust into the back of one of the cars.

At the police station, the real questioning began.

A constable put his head round the door and announced that Donald's solicitor had arrived. He was asked to show him into the interview room.

Donald breathed a sigh of relief and stood up to welcome the tall, overweight man. His skin was the colour of mahogany, his forehead furrowed with deep lines. On the right side of his face were the remains of a scar.

He sat down alongside Donald and spoke, first to the interrogating officer.

'I need to know the reason for my client's arrest,' he said in a soft, velvety voice.

The young detective informed him that he had been arrested because they had reason to believe that he had deliberately driven his car into the Mini Cooper belonging to Mary Willson that had resulted in her death.

'Thank you for being so succinct. I would like to have a few minutes with my client in private.'

Ten minutes later, the interview began in earnest. Donald's lawyer was sitting by his side, and was guiding him as to what he should say and what he should not.

'Where and when was this accident supposed to have happened?' Donald asked

'Yesterday morning at about eleven o'clock, in the multi-storey car park in the centre of Reading,' he was told.

'But I wasn't in Reading yesterday. I didn't venture out all day,' he told them.

'And you can verify this? Can anybody confirm that you were at home all day?'

'No. I was alone.'

He was then told that they also wanted to question him in connection with the attempted assassination of Mary Willson in Angers. Again, he protested his innocence. Likewise, when he was told that the South African police would like to talk to him about the death of a coloured girl in Kimberley, he said he knew nothing of such a girl.

'And then there is the matter of the death of Lucas Berber. You don't deny you knew him, do you?'

'Of course not. We were good friends.'

'You were in South Africa together, is that right?'

'Yes, some six or seven years ago.'

'Not more recently than that?'

Donald shook his head.

At that point, the officer terminated the interview, turned off the recording machine and informed Donald that he would be held in custody until the morning, when he would be questioned again.

'If I were you, Mr O'Hanlon, I would consider your position very carefully while you have the opportunity,' he said as he left.

By the time Donald was taken to his bleak cell, a new day was dawning. He was astounded that so many accusations were being thrown at him. He was convinced that he had covered his tracks well. How come then, that suddenly all his misdoings should be produced at the same time. Not only that, but he was being accused of murdering Mary when he was not even in Reading at the time. He thought he had glanced her the day before, but he was not sure that it was her. It certainly looked like her car, but he couldn't see her face through the windscreen because of the heavy rain. Now he presumed that it *had* been her, and she had probably seen him, but the fact remained that he was not in Reading yesterday.

Another thought came to him. How did the police know where he was? Nobody knew his whereabouts. But there was that 'Gotcha!' message on his computer screen. Had somebody tracked him down? The question remained – who told the police? There could only be one answer. It was her bloody boyfriend, Ben. Once again, he was the fly in the ointment, the bane of his life.

He should have got rid of him the first time they met, when he came to announce that Mary was leaving to live with him. Ben, the bastard, that's who it was. That's who knew where he was and told the police. That's who has had these accusations piled on his head.

He had to wonder how much evidence Ben, the bastard, had uncovered. Had he traced the link through Chas to the failed attempt on Mary's life? How could he have done that? There was no traceable link back to him. And Laila, the girl in Kimberley, surely he had not been able to uncover anything bordering on proof of her demise there. As for poor Lucas, the greedy one, the police themselves said that there were no suspicious circumstances surrounding his death.

No, he told himself, this must all be supposition based on Ben's determination to have his revenge. Nothing more; nothing less. There was little point in losing sleep over it.

\*\*\*\*\*

The next morning's interrogation started rather badly for Donald as he sat once again, with his solicitor in the interview room.

'Good morning, Mr Kruger.'

An older detective was addressing him. There was a pile of folders on the desk, which the officer was inspecting, slowly turning over the pages.

'Should we be addressing you as Mr Kruger or Mr O'Hanlon – or even Mr Martin Holden-Smith?'

'My name is Donald O'Hanlon.'

'For most of the time you are in this country, it seems. However, according to newspaper reports that I have in front of me, you are known as Jan Kruger in South Africa. Is that right?'

'No comment,' Donald said.

'I take that to be a yes, then,' the detective said. 'I'm happy enough to call you Mr O'Hanlon today, if that makes it easier for you.'

Then the questioning began for real. If he had not been in Reading on Monday, how was it that there were smudges of red paint that matched exactly the paintwork of the dead girl's car? Could he explain the damage to the front wing of his car?

He refused to answer.

The grilling then centred on his trip to South Africa.

'We know you were travelling with another man – Lucas Berber – but we would like to know the reason for the journey. My sources say that diamond smuggling was involved. Is that the case?'

Donald said nothing.

'OK, Mr O'Hanlon, let's turn our attention to France for a minute. The French police in Paris and Angers have been working on the case of Mary Willson, and her attempted murder. They have done well. They are, as we speak, interviewing two men who they believe had a part in the assassination attempt. I believe that you know both of these men.'

'I don't know which men you are talking about,' Donald said firmly.

The detective was showing signs of impatience and decided that he was not going to achieve anything by continuing the interrogation.

'Interview terminated at eleven twenty-three,' the detective said as he and his colleague left the room.

Once the door had been closed, Donald's lawyer turned to him.

'You've really dropped yourself in it this time, my friend. How the fuck have you got into this mess?'

Donald told him that he had no idea how this had all come about. How he had not been in Reading on the day in question and how he was surprised that all of the accusations should have been made on the same day.

'The problem is, Donald, that everything they have told you this morning is true. They are holding Chas in Paris and another man by the name of Bear who I don't know. I'm afraid your links to these two men have been blown open.'

'But you can find a way to ...'

'To be honest, Donald, I'm not sure that I can this time. If this were a game of chess, it would be close to check-mate. Obviously I will do all I can, but to change the metaphor slightly, I don't think we have many trump cards up our sleeves. We'll just wait for them to make a few errors, and have the case thrown out.'

'But all the evidence they have is circumstantial. They don't have any facts, do they?'

'If you combine what is happening in France with the circumstantial evidence they have here, the picture changes considerably, Donald. When the questioning starts again, I will help you all I can. Just don't dig yourself into a bigger hole than the one you're already in.'

Donald had no option than to agree, and when the interrogation began again half an hour later, he referred to his counsel before answering any of the questions.

At the conclusion, the police were not satisfied with his mitigation, and charged him with the murder of Mary Willson.

**Chapter 46**

Katie went back with Mark and later asked him to drive her over to her house in Reading. When she arrived, she found it eerily quiet. Georgina was playing games with Alex in the lounge, but there was no sign of Ben.

Alex looked up as Katie entered the room. 'Kay!' he said, running over to her.

Katie picked him up and gave him a cuddle.

'So he knows your name, now,' Georgina said. 'How great is that? I guess he'll have more difficulty with my name.'

'He'll just abbreviate it,' Katie replied. 'Is he OK?'

'He seems to be, but he won't be able to understand, will he? How do you tell a one-year-old that his Mum's been killed?'

'I haven't a clue. Sooner or later he's going to ask where Mummy is, and I suppose that's when somebody has got to try to explain.'

'And what about Ben?'

'I don't really know, Katie. He's tucked away inside himself. I don't think there's anything we can do at the moment. I think he's got to decide for himself when he wants to talk. Until then, I think it's best to leave him.'

Katie said that the best thing they could do for now, is to find something to eat, and went to look in the fridge and freezer to see what was available. She came back into the room to say that there was very little food there.

'I suppose not,' Georgina said. 'I guess they were expecting to eat at the reception, and I think they were planning to go back to France straight away, or tomorrow at the latest.'

'I'll pop down the road and get us a pizza or something; will that be alright for you? I'll get an extra one in case Ben feels hungry when he wakes up.'

'What about Alex, did you find anything for him?'

'Yes, he's catered for. There are several jars of food in the fridge. Anyway, he'll eat almost anything these days.'

Twenty minutes after Katie had left, Ben wandered downstairs and found Georgina helping Alex with his tea. He just stood in the doorway and stared at the sight. Alex seemed to be happy enough with Georgina looking after him. Ben guessed that as long as there was food, Alex didn't mind all that much who prepared it. Ben, too, was wondering when he would have to answer the big question – 'Where's mummy?' He would not lie to his son, but he didn't know how he was going to tell him the truth.

'Oh, hello,' Georgina said, looking up at a rather dishevelled Ben. 'I thought I'd let Alex have his tea. He's tired and hungry, and he needs to go to bed.'

'Thanks,' Ben said. 'Did I hear Katie just now?'

'Yes, she came over a while ago. She's gone to grab some pizzas for us. I guess she'll be back again soon.'

'Right. I need to talk to her. I'm going to have to stay here for a while. There's the post mortem and possibly an inquest before I can go back to France – and the funeral, of course.'

Katie returned as they were talking.

'I picked these up from Domino's,' she said. 'Hi, Ben. Silly question I know, but how are you feeling?'

'Numb,' he replied. 'I'm still having difficulty registering what has happened. It's so unreal, so bizarre.'

'I can imagine, well no, I can't actually. I suppose I came close to it when Dave died, but we were never as close as you and Mary.'

'I think the only way I can get through this is to concentrate on things that have to be done. When are you planning on going back to *La Sanctuaire*, Katie. It's just that we left in a bit of a hurry, and there is a family arriving on Saturday.'

'I'm going back to Mark's this evening, and I was reckoning on going back to France on Wednesday. That would be OK, wouldn't it? That will give me plenty of time to get the cottage ready.'

'Yes, of course.'

Inside, Katie was frightened of being on her own at the cottage in France, but she wasn't going to tell Ben that. But there was something she did have to tell him, she felt it was only fair.

'I'm happy to look after the cottages while you are here, but I have decided, after talking with Mark, that I should return to England.'

'For good?' Ben asked, shaken by the news.

'I don't know that, Ben, but there are so many things to be sorted out here that can't be done from France.'

'Well that's bit of a bombshell, Katie. I wasn't expecting that!'

'Sorry to have tell you today of all days, but I thought you should know. Obviously, I will look after things over there for you for as long as it takes. I guess you'll be staying on here for a while,' she said. 'I suppose there will have to be a *post mortem*. Do you think there will be an inquest as well?'

'I've no idea, but, yes I'll have to stay on until it's all dealt with. I can't say I'm looking forward to it. I remember when my Mum died, there was so much that my Dad had to do. The worst thing is that I don't know whether Mary's mother is still alive. I know they parted company when her father died, and I don't think they've spoken to each other since. I guess we can try to find her. Willson, with the two ells, is not all that common.'

'I can do that for you, if you like,' Georgina said without thinking.

'Would you?' Ben replied. 'That would be one thing off my mind.'

'And I'm quite happy to stay here to look after Alex, too.'

'I should take her up on that offer, Ben. She's wonderful with Alex, and he loves her, too.'

'But what about your work?' Ben said.

'I can do a lot of it from here. I've been working from home a lot lately. I phone round my customers and take any orders. I only go to visit the ones that have problems or queries that can't be dealt with over the phone.'

'Are you sure? It would be a great help.'

'That's done, then. Would you like me to stay here overnight? It would mean you could get some rest. It's up to you, really.'

'No, I don't think that's necessary. I'll be able to take care of Alex overnight. But if you could be here during the daytime, it would mean I can go out without worrying about him. That would be very helpful.'

Later that evening, both girls left the house and Ben was left alone with Alex – and his thoughts.

His mind was full of darkness. Until a few hours ago he was the happiest man on the planet. Everything was going perfectly, and the rest of his days seemed to be laid out before him. His wife, their gorgeous little son and a life in one of the most beautiful parts of France. Now the future held none of those things.

He remembered that he had been in this situation before when Mary had left him to live with Donald. It was the same then, the feeling of despair, but on that occasion, he always knew that she was still out there. He could hope. Now there was no hope. She was gone from his life.

Whilst his sadness was all about Mary, his bitterness was focused on Donald O'Hanlon. Ben was still convinced that he had instigated the attempt on Mary's life in France. He was equally convinced that he had now completed his objective. He was deep into his feeling of hatred when his mobile buzzed. It was the officer from Thames Valley Police.

'Mr Coverdale, I thought you'd be pleased to know that we have arrested Mr O'Hanlon and he is being questioned as we speak.'

'Great news,' Ben said. 'I presume he's denying everything.'

'Oh, yes. But we have some interesting evidence. We found him at home as you said, although he didn't want us to. But the most interesting thing is what a woman constable found in the garage. His Mercedes was there, and guess what? The front offside wing was damaged and there were signs of red paint along the side of the car. Pretty convincing evidence I would think.'

'Sounds good to me.' Ben said.

'The other thing is – and this might interest you even more – is that the police in Paris want to interview him. They have a man in custody over there who is willing to testify that O'Hanlon gave him the instructions to have your girlfriend attacked in France.'

'You mean killed.'

'Yes, those were his instructions, but as you know it all went wrong for them.'

Ben was in tears. At last somebody was believing what he had said all along.

'I just hope you have enough on him to be able to put him away for a long time,' Ben said through his snuffles.

'I just thought you would like to know,' the officer said.

'Yes, thanks. Thank you very much.'

Ben shut down his mobile, but noticed that he had a number of messages. The word was getting round fast. Four messages were from people who had just heard the news and were sending condolences. An earlier one was the one that caught Ben's eye. It was from Basheer, dated Monday midday.

*Donald is working hard today. He hasn't left his computer for the last five hours. I'll try to find out what he is doing and let you know.*

Ben read the message four or five times and managed to raise a smile. The irony of it amused him. Donald had *not* been in Reading on Monday but the police had arrested him and seemingly had enough evidence to charge him with Mary's death. How beautifully bizarre.

There was no way that he would divulge what he now knew, no way he would do anything to assist Donald to claw his way out of this.

As it stood, Donald had been arrested and would probably be charged with Mary's murder. No doubt, he would appeal, and it was a fair bet that he would win his appeal, but by then he would be wanted by the French police, and almost certainly would be charged with Mary's murder again in collusion with Bear and this other man called Chas.

If that wasn't enough, an extradition order might be possible between South Africa and the UK. From what Ben knew about such things, this could take a long time to bring about, but Donald had plenty of time, didn't he.

Ben's feelings of sadness were now infused with satisfaction. His feelings of bleakness now pervaded with thoughts of justice.

Meanwhile, he had to find a way through the coming days and weeks. A way of facing up to life without Mary, a way of finding ways to take care of Alex, and a way of believing that he had a future that was worth all the effort.

# Finale

So much has happened in the last six months that I hardly know where to begin.

Ben had to stay on at Katie's house in Reading for three weeks. It was not the favourite time of his life, that was obvious, but he gave the impression that he was taking everything in his stride. That's Ben; whatever life throws at him, he seems to be able to fight his way through it. The first few days were hard for him. He was very quiet. What was going on in his mind was anybody's guess.

As the days turned into weeks, he did start to come out from his depression. He began to show more interest in Alex, taking him for walks and playing with him in the house.

During that time, he still showed little interest in me. It was as if I didn't exist but I could cope with that. I spent almost every day at the house doing all the "wifey" things. I kept the house tidy, did the washing and ironing, cooked our meals. I was sure that he appreciated what I was doing even if he never actually said so.

Much of my time was spent keeping Alex amused. Ben and Mary had only intended to stay for a few days so they hadn't brought many of Alex's toys with them. I had to conjure up new ideas to keep him occupied. The big problem was that at home in France, he had his garden to play in. He could run in and out of the cottage as he wanted. So much so, that Ben had erected a notice at the gate: "Warning- Free range child at large" in both English and French.

It was clear that Alex spent a lot of time in the sun. His skin was golden brown, and his hair was strawberry blonde. He was much too pretty to be a boy.

During those three weeks, Ben had to deal with solicitors, the registry office, funeral directors, and the police. Some days, I hardly saw him from first thing in the morning until the evening. He became very tired, but he never actually complained. He told me that he was able to tick things off as being dealt with each day, relieving him of those obligations one at a time. The more he did that, the more time he had to take notice of Alex and me.

Katie kept in touch most days. She was still living at *La Sanctuaire* and said she would do so until Ben and Alex returned. It was obvious from the tone of her emails and phone calls that she didn't want to stay there any longer than she had to.

She thought she wouldn't have to stay there very long, but she received three late bookings, which meant that she had to be there for the guests. Poor Katie.

I knew she would never let Ben down. They were long-time friends. More than that really; there was a bond between them. I don't know the full story, but it was something very special, something unique. Anyway, things were being looked after in France, and I was doing my best to help out in any way I could in Reading for as long as I was needed.

I can't say that my boss was altogether happy when I told him what I was doing, but he told me that as long as the orders kept coming in and his business did not suffer, he was happy to indulge me. Nice guy, my boss. So I spent part of my day making phone calls, taking orders where I could. In some cases, I think I got a sympathy order, and the overall outcome was that my sales rate went up rather than down. Everybody was happy.

Ben didn't tell me at the time, but has since told me that the *post mortem* showed that Mary died, not of the head injury that was at first suspected, but by a huge internal haemorrhage, which was probably related to her abdominal injury, the result of the knife attack in France. There was no way that the paramedics could have saved her. She would have died almost instantaneously.

On the day of his final meeting with the police, he actually came home with a smile on his face. He had learned that not only was Donald being held in custody, but the French police were holding a man called Chas, who they believe was Donald's middle man. Also the man that Tommy had talked about, Bear, who was also linked to Chas, was already in custody. All-in-all, the two police forces, between them, had put together each part of the jigsaw, and now the whole picture could be seen. I think that was the day when Ben came back to life. He still had to get over Mary, somehow, but he could see that justice was being done.

The large stone mantelpiece in the lounge was strewn with cards, many of them from France, of condolences, sympathy and good wishes. He read me a letter that he received from Madame Delphine. It was so full of feeling, so filled with love that it could have been from his mother. Ben's relationship with this woman is another thing that I find it hard to get to grips with. He told me that from the very first time he met her, she had taken on this mother character. She and a few of her friends had been instrumental in finding the cottages that he had bought, and he had always known that, when he needed help, she would be the one to provide it.

Ben, it seemed, was able to form these extraordinary associations with people. I guess it was true of us as well. When I first got to know him, soon after Mary had left him to live with Donald, we formed a special friendship. Neither of us wanted, or expected, a romantic attachment. We just enjoyed each other's company. We felt at ease with each other, and we had a lot of fun. I took him to some outrageous places that he would never have ventured into and showed him a different world. Mind you, at that time I was into punk - the awful fashions, the terrible hair-dos, the whole gamut. We were, I suppose a chalk-and-cheese couple, but it worked for us.

Now I'm a reformed and much more responsible person. To be honest, I sometimes wonder whether he would prefer the old me rather than the sensible person that I am now.

I only started to fall in love with him when I took Mary and Alex over to meet up again after their separation. I saw him one evening outside the cottage with his four months old son, chattering away to him about the wonderful world that we lived in, pointing out the stars and the moon. 'It's all here for you, little man,' he said. 'Just make sure you enjoy it!' It was such a moving sight; something I have never forgotten.

It was only on my last visit to *La Sanctuaire* that I managed to make a fool of myself and blurted out my true feelings for him. It was awful, and we left each other not knowing if we would ever see each other again.

Those three weeks in Reading were fraught with problems and traumas, but between us, we got through it and I suppose we became closer because of it. When I saw it drawing to a close, I so wanted to suggest that I return to France with him, but I couldn't find a way to say it. I was sure that he would say no, so I kept my mouth shut on that subject.

Mary's funeral was by far the saddest day. It was a very low-key affair. Many of the people who attended the wedding came to pay their respects, but it was a very short and basic service in the church of St. Mary's Butts. Ben told me that it held a special significance in Mary's life, but he didn't say more than that. Our old boss, Ray, came up trumps again. He said that if he wasn't able to provide a post wedding party, the least he could do was to offer a wake, and it was a beautiful, tasteful affair.

Ben coped with the stress well. I could see that he was deep in thought throughout the wake, but we didn't have the chance to talk.

Imagine, then, how overjoyed I was when we returned home after the funeral and the first words he said as we went into the house were, 'Is there any chance that you would be able to come back to France with us?' I didn't want to show him that I had been hoping for three long weeks to hear those words and replied, 'I guess it's possible'.

'What about your job?' he said.

I told him that I would much prefer to live at *La Sanctuaire* than keep a job that I didn't really like all that much. It took just an extra two days in Reading to get everything sorted. I had to give notice not only to my boss, but to my landlord as well. Neither of them was terribly pleased but to be honest, I couldn't have cared less. I was going to France to be with the man I'd fallen so desperately in love with.

It didn't matter that he probably didn't love me. I considered that I had enough love for both of us.

When we first moved back to France, there was a strange tension between me and Ben. I think we both wanted to talk in order to clear the air, as it were, but neither of us did. It wasn't that we didn't talk at all. We did, but it was all about what to eat, when to go shopping, whether Alex needed new clothes. There were, however, certain subjects that were strictly taboo. For instance, Mary was never mentioned. There had been no rules laid down. It was just understood. It was a difficult time for us both. Ben told me that he had tried to explain to Alex where his Mum had gone. He was not sure that his son had understood, and Alex was certainly not his usual ebullient little self for quite a long time.

As to anything between Ben and me, there was still nothing. I felt that I was simply there to do my job, nothing more. I know that was what I was expecting, but when it happened, I felt let down. As time went on, I started to wonder whether I had done the right thing.

My feelings for him had not diminished. When we were in close proximity, I still had this feeling like static electricity running through me. On the odd occasion when we touched, the brush of our arms as we passed each other, the accidental meeting of hands, it was like an electric current passing down my body. It was agony.

For all that, I am still able to see him every day. I am still able to watch him, still experience the static on a daily basis. And there is always hope. I once read a poem by Alexander Pope which said:

*Hope springs eternal in the human breast;*
*Man never is, but always to be blessed:*
*The soul, uneasy and confined from home,*
*Rests and expatiates in a life to come.*

So, I would wait. I would let things take their course. I hoped I wouldn't have to wait for a life to come, though.

As time went on, things did improve, the tension dissipated, and the occasional touches became more frequent. It became natural to share things like outings and shopping with each other. Slowly but surely I saw the Ben I remembered emerging like some beautiful butterfly from its chrysalis. Gradually, a genuine friendship was developing. He showed more appreciation for what I was doing, always thanking me for cooking his meals and doing a 'good job', as he put it, with Alex.

I tried to involve Alex with some part of everything we did and he responded brilliantly. He seemed quite happy for me to be there all the time and I began to love the new life I had chosen.

Ben was beginning to pick up the pieces. He started making contact with his friends again. They, like me, had been wary of making any advances but were happy when Ben made the initial moves. Madame Delphine was one such friend. On the first occasion that we visited her restaurant after returning to France, I thought she was going to burst into tears, such was her fervent welcome for Ben, Alex and me. Gradually, life was getting back to normal.

Whereas I had been waking up in the morning, somewhat pensive as to what the day might hold, now my waking moments were filled with joy, excitement and expectations. Would this be the day that we could start to really relax with each other? Could today be the beginning of something that I had hoped and dreamed of for years?

I knew, of course, that I could never replace Mary. For all the unkind things that I had thought and said about her, she had always been Ben's woman. I couldn't compete with that, and I didn't want to, but given the chance, I know that I could love him, honour and obey him just as well as anybody else. Just give me the chance.

As the weeks unfolded, Ben was beginning to think of the future. He called in the builders who had made such a brilliant job of rebuilding Dairy Cottage, the part of *La Sanctuaire* that he rented out to holidaymakers.

He wanted to discover how feasible it would be to turn the larger of the two barns behind the cottages into living accommodation. To me it looked like a mammoth task. The barn was much bigger than the cottage we lived in but it was just four stone walls and a roof. A lot of imagination and expertise would have to be invested if there was to be any chance of rebuilding it. However, Ben was convinced that there was a way, and called in the experts. For days, a group of men worked with Ben – builders, architects and surveyors - sketching ideas, measuring, excavating the site and within a week, they were back with some initial plans.

Ben couldn't help but show his excitement when he showed me the plans that evening. Once again, his builders had come up with some amazing concepts of how best to use the space. If it were to be believed, the old barn would become a state-of-the-art home, whilst keeping the old exterior intact. I became as enthusiastic as he was with the project. The thought of being able to watch our future home take shape before our eyes was awesome.

In France, it is the mayor who controls any building regulations and development in the town. Ben was certain that he would approve of what he wanted to do and apparently, it was well within his budget.

That night, we celebrated with a bottle of champagne, and I got my first big hug. How good was that?

Ben made an appointment with the mayor, and all three of us went to get his reaction to the plans.

The mayor was a nice friendly man and he welcomed Ben warmly. He remembered Ben's previous application regarding Dairy Cottage, and thoroughly approved of what Ben was planning to do this time. However, he told us that the final decision in this case was not his. He had to submit the plans to the authorities in Angers. The mayor said he had no doubts that the project would be approved, but it would take a little longer than last time. Ben said there was no immediate hurry, but was hoping the building work would be finished before the start of next year's holiday season.

Ben's most recent idea was to change the garden area. He told me that they produced too much last year, and a lot of the produce went to waste. He wanted to reduce the size of the vegetable area, and use the space for a safe play area for Alex, and any kids who came on holiday here. That was something I could help with and I have been working in the garden most days recently with Alex who loves getting his hands dirty. Ben has been busy levelling the ground and laying turf.

Three weeks ago, the building work started on the barn. This would be where we lived. There was much more space, and the facilities were going to be much better than in our present cottage. I've tried to imagine Alex in the big wet room that is planned. He'll have the time of his life.

We are all looking forward to our guests arriving in the spring and I am thoroughly enjoying my new life here. Everything as they say, is coming up roses, especially for me.

Yesterday, I had worked hard in the garden all morning and after lunch I decided to take a break. I went up to my bedroom. It used to be Katie's room, but she has moved out now, so I have taken it over. It was cool and dark in there. The French have got it right. Their windows open inwards letting in fresh air, but the exterior wooden shutters can be pulled in shutting out any mid-day heat.

I lay on my bed and before I knew it, I drifted off into a peaceful, light sleep.

I was surprised to be woken by somebody stroking my forehead. Ben was sitting on the bed beside me.

'Are you OK?' he asked. 'It's not like you to take naps.'

I had never seen Ben this close. His tanned face with its usual stubble was just inches from mine. I was looking into his warm, brown eyes. I could smell his body fragrance, see the bleached hairs on his arms and the feel of his fingers lingered on my forehead.

'I'm fine, Ben. I just needed a break.'

I expected him to move away. He didn't. His eyes were devouring me. I didn't know what to do. I almost felt embarrassed.

Then he kissed me, his lips a fairy touch on mine.

'I'm sorry,' he said as he pulled away. 'I don't know what ...'

I could not let this opportunity pass. I pulled him back and reciprocated with a much firmer kiss, holding his head with my free hand.

'Sorry for what?' I asked. I must have had the biggest, widest grin on my face. He didn't reply with words.

I had always wondered what sex felt like. Now I know. Ben was so gentle with me, stroking and caressing me until I was crying out for him to make love with me.

He did.

It was unbelievably beautiful. He knew exactly what to do, even if I didn't. He teased my body, bringing me on and then slowing down again. I thought it couldn't get any better but it did.

We came together and my scream must have been heard for miles around. I never thought, in a million years that my body could experience anything like that.

So, this sometimes stupid, often crazy, twenty-seven year old virgin is, at last, a woman.

I can't even try to tell you how much I love Ben. There are no words

The future? Who cares about the future? I'm quite happy to live in the present.

Very happy, in fact.

# ACKNOWLEDGEMENTS

Once again, I must thank everyone who has supported me through the four years that it has taken to complete the Ben Coverdale Trilogy.

Firstly, my appreciation goes to my readers and especially those that have taken the time to post a review on Amazon, Goodreads and the like. Your few minutes means so much.

Then there are the beta readers, bless them, who have to delve through many a typo to offer their opinion on the book as a whole. In the case of 'The Reckoning', several major changes were made to the story based on their conclusions.

My indebtedness also goes to my proof-reader and editors for their dedication to detail. When writing such a complex novel as this one, it needs a careful eye to be kept on chronological details and references back to previous storylines, something an author can often by-pass.

A special word of thanks goes to my cover designer, Lloyd Lelina. The delay in the publication of 'The Reckoning' was due to the fact that Lloyd and his family were hit by typhoon Haiyan in the Philippines just as he was starting work on the cover. They had to escape, firstly to Cebu city, and later to Manila to recover from their traumatic experience. Thank you Lloyd.

Finally, although this may seem to be strange, I want to acknowledge the part that my characters have played in my writing. I feel I know them almost as well as I know my own friends. Many has been the time that one or other of them would invade my sleep to point out that the words I had written that day were wrong. Katie, especially, has told me on several occasions 'I wouldn't have said that!' or 'I would never do that!' and every time I had to admit that she was right.

And, of course, thank you for reading this.

If you could spare a few moments to post a review on Amazon, Goodreads etc it would be appreciated. Thanks.